HOWEVER MANY MORE

A JAKE HOUSER MYSTERY (BOOK #2)

BO THUNBOE

WESTON PRESS, LLC

Published in 2018 by Weston Press, LLC

Cover Design by Jeroen ten Berge (jeroentenberge.com)
Interior Design by Kevin G. Summers (kevingsummers.com)

ISBN: 978-1-949632-02-6

Weston Press, LLC
Naperville, IL
www.thunboe.com

For Diane

ALSO BY BO THUNBOE

What Can't Be True
A Jake Houser Mystery (Book #1)

PROLOGUE
July, 1973

Larry was a good boy who did what his momma told him to do, even though he was twenty-three years old and any normal person would have asked some serious questions about tonight's chore.

A mosquito flew out of the thick night air and buzzed in Larry's ear. He swatted it away, then pulled another loaf from the double row he'd lined up along the back of the truck. The man who drove the truck had called the big silver bars ingots, but to Larry they looked like loaves of bread. When he dragged one off the stack it made a sound he'd never heard before. He decided to call it a *skritch* when he wrote about this in his diary.

He hooked his fingers under the ends of the heavy chunk of metal and swung it off the truck to rest against his thighs. He'd carried enough bags of sand and cement and such to know what a thing weighed, give or take. These loaves each weighed about the same as a bag and a half of gravel. Sixty-five pounds. Half his own weight. Not bad for a little guy; that's what Mr. Martin next door always said when Larry did heavy work over at his place.

Larry walked his load to the back of the barn and added it to the rest. The loaves were narrower on the top than the bottom, so he flipped over every other one to fit them together and make a solid wall. The excitement of his new experience wore off as he settled into the work, his arms and shoulders loosening up, then holding strong for a long time before starting to tire and weaken.

He took a break and walked over to the hose at the back of the house. A sudden breeze, heavy with the muddy scent of the river, pushed up over the bluff and cleared away the mosquitos. After he'd had his fill of the cold clear hose water, Larry peeked in the kitchen window. Momma was at the table playing cards with the man who drove the truck. She caught Larry looking and he dropped down. He knew the rules. Work first; play later.

Seeing Momma made Larry remember she said this chore here was a secret business. He needed to keep that in mind when doing something secret, or he sometimes forgot. That's how Momma figured out he'd been down in the caves. He was so proud of what he'd found that he forgot he wasn't supposed to go down there. When he showed her the bottles, she immediately knew where he'd been and he didn't get dessert for a week.

He got back to work, his wandering thoughts now focusing on finishing. The muscles across his shoulders and back were sore, his grip weakening. His breathing coming in grunts and gasps.

When he was done, Larry pulled the old tarp up over the loaves and stacked the firewood in a long row in front of them, the wood light and rough in his hands after the smooth weight of the metal. He piled the old newspapers on top of it all, turned off the barn light, and went out in the yard. *Secret, secret*, he reminded himself. He rang the dinner bell on the post by the back door to let them know he was done, like Momma had said.

He stretched his shoulders and flexed his hands. The weak breeze passing through the yard wicked the sweat from his shirt and cooled him. He cupped his hands to catch the moving air and whirled his arms like a windmill. He lost himself in the motion until the back door swung open and the man came out.

"All done?" The man walked over and looked into the back of the truck. "Your mom *said* you were a good worker."

"Yep," Larry said. He liked the man because *he* was different, too. He had a big brown mark on his cheek that Momma said was an angel's kiss. Larry rubbed his own jaw, wondering what that would feel like. Then a mosquito bit him and he slapped it away.

The man peered into the shadowy depth of the barn, then looked at Larry and raised his eyebrows like Momma did when she wanted his secrets. But Larry kept his mouth closed.

The man shrugged. "Your mom says those little ones are for you." He pointed at the plastic-wrapped stack of smaller bars up by the driver's seat. Each one was about the size of the buns Momma used for beef sandwiches. The man climbed up, ripped away the plastic, picked one up, and rubbed his palm down it like he was petting a dog. "Well, come on then," he said to Larry. "Haul these out of here so I can get back on the road."

Larry jumped up into the truck. A gift just for him! He knew exactly where to put them. A place no one would even *want* to look for them.

CHAPTER ONE

Detective Jake Houser didn't like working in a task force. Too much talk, not enough action, and too many pointing fingers. The only useful thing the task force did was share information, and it did that best by email. But Deputy Chief Braff said to go to the meeting, so Jake was driving north to the county building for another edition of the blame game.

As he crossed Butterfield Road, his phone vibrated with an incoming call. Braff.

"You're catching and we got a case," Braff said. "A body on Redhawk Court."

There was only one house on Redhawk Court, and Jake's lifelong friend, Henry Fox, lived there alone.

A coldness gripped Jake's chest, and he pressed the phone tighter to his ear. "Can you repeat that?"

"Body. House at the end of Redhawk Court." Braff's big voice roared from the phone. "You good to take this, Houser? You sound funny. I can make Diggs primary instead of taking the task force meeting for you."

"No-o." Jake's voice broke. He cleared his throat. "Who's on scene?"

"Grady. He went out there on a well-being check."

"Good." Grady understood the job and what doing it right meant to the community, to the force, and to himself. "Any details?"

"Said it was a BFT. That's it so far."

Blunt force trauma. Murder. *Jesus!* Jake squeezed his eyes shut. "I'm on my way, boss."

"I'll have Diggs join you when she gets out of the meeting."

Jake put his phone away. His hands slipped on the steering wheel as he pulled a U-turn on Winfield Road. He wiped them on his pants then rolled the front windows down. The cold fall air whisked away his sudden sweat.

It couldn't be Henry, Jake thought. But he knew it could. In ten years patrolling Chicago's streets and a decade back home investigating Weston's major crimes, he'd seen time and again that sudden violence could strike anywhere, and anyone. His pulse pounded against his temples and his breathing became fast and shallow. He forced himself to take long, slow breaths until his breathing smoothed out and the pounding subsided.

He turned west on Jackson and slowed the Crown Vic as he entered Henry's riverside neighborhood. Most of the original homes had been replaced during a teardown craze where giant new homes were crammed onto the small city lots. He slowed further as he turned down Redhawk Court, a narrow gravel road that threaded between two of the new mini-mansions before spreading out into an ill-defined circle of weed-choked gravel in front of Henry's single-story house. A Weston police cruiser sat with its light bar flashing red and blue against the thinning fall foliage.

Jake parked next to the cruiser, put his hand on the door handle, then released it as a memory pushed into his mind. Two years earlier, an officer had caught Henry's daughter, April, naked in the back seat of the high school quarterback's car. April dropped Jake's name to the officer, and Jake talked him out of charging her. He then brought April here to her dad's house, where they sat for a long, silent minute, both reluctant to deliver the news that would forever change the way Henry saw his daughter.

He felt a similar reluctance today. What he saw inside would be more than a new memory; it would be a filter through which he'd see all his other memories of Henry.

That's how it was with Jake's memories of his own wife. When she was murdered, he was first on the scene—and ever since then, every memory he had of her was interrupted by an image of her face going pale as blood pumped from a gash on her neck.

That image filled his mind again now.

He clenched his teeth and got moving.

Leaves carpeted the yard, and Jake waded through them toward the familiar bright-red front door. Painting that door "Redhawk Red" had been the first improvement Henry made when he inherited the place from his uncle. Jake had helped with that, and with many other projects to rehab the house. He puffed his cheeks to stretch the grief off his face.

The door opened. "I heard you coming." Officer Grady stepped onto the front stoop and pulled the door closed behind him before noting Jake's arrival on his clipboard. "Detective Houser. Three seventeen p.m."

"Hey, Grady." Jake managed a smile. He was glad protocol gave him another few minutes before he went inside. "What do you have so far?"

"When I got here I found both doors, front and back, were unlocked, and all the lights were on. I confirmed the victim was dead, cleared the building, and secured the scene." Securing the scene included ensuring no condition existed that could compromise the scene or the time of death determination: no stove on, no window open, no loose pets.

"Who called it in?"

"Mrs. Brueder." Grady jabbed a thumb over his shoulder at the house on Jackson to the west. "Said she was up several times in the night and saw all the lights on over here. When she didn't see Mr. Fox this morning—she apparently keeps a close eye on him—she got worried and finally called it in at 2:43 this afternoon." Grady wiped a hand over his forehead, and his voice dropped as if he was telling a secret. "No one answered the door, but it was unlocked, like I said, so I went in. I found him right away. It looks like he was…" Grady's voice caught, and he ended his report there with a tight shake of his head, his eyes pulling away from Jake's.

That was fine with Jake. He preferred to make his own observations and draw his own conclusions. "Have you identified the victim?"

"I didn't search the… uh, body, you know, for a wallet."

"Coroner and forensic team on the way?"

"Yes. And I set up the booties and gloves." Grady pointed at two cardboard boxes sitting on the concrete by the front door.

"Good work." Jake stepped onto the stoop and began pulling on a pair of booties. "Call out another patrol unit to guard the back yard and the barn."

"Will do." Grady smiled; it looked like his natural energy was returning. "Mrs. Brueder says she saw Mr. Fox come home around nine thirty last night."

"Good." Post-mortem analysis rarely established time of death on its own. Concurrent information like a witness seeing the victim alive was a big help. "She say anything else?"

"I didn't question her. She just came over when I pulled up. I sent her home before I went inside. Just in case."

"That was the right way to handle it." Jake pulled on a pair of latex gloves, then put his hand on the doorknob. His stomach quivered, and he rubbed it with the other hand. He reminded himself that whatever he was about to see, he'd seen worse. Lived through worse.

He eased the door open. "I'm going in."

CHAPTER TWO

It was warm and still inside the house, with the faint scent of a citrus air freshener. Jake didn't smell death—no coppery blood, no pungent stench of decomposing flesh, no evacuated bowels.

He paused in the entryway, a pulsing gloom filling him, his limbs suddenly heavy and his mouth dry. He flexed his hands and rolled his shoulders. Maybe he should let Callie Diggs take the case after all. A quick phone call and he could walk out the door and avoid the memory he was about to create.

He took a step back, but he was too close to the door and his shoulders and back hit the door with a thud.

"You okay in there, Detective?"

"Fine," Jake said, standing up straight and taking a deep breath. He could, and should, investigate Henry's murder. And the victim might not even be Henry—and it might not be a murder. A houseguest might have collapsed from a heart attack and hit his head as he fell.

Holding on to that slim possibility, Jake got to work, sweeping his gaze across the space. The front room spanned the entire width of the house, and Henry had divided it into two functional areas. To the right, bookshelves boxed in small windows bright with sunlight that lit on dust motes floating in the still air. A glass-topped coffee table sat before Henry's reading chair in the far front corner. To the left, a pair of leather couches angled around a giant television. Behind them, a low wall separated the front room from the dining room and kitchen. In the center of the back wall, a hallway led past a pair of bedrooms and a bathroom, ending at the kitchen.

Jake had spent enough time here watching games and drinking beer to immediately see that nothing was out of place.

Jake edged past the couches. A pair of feet came into view in the opening to the dining room—toes up, gray socks. A slipper on the right foot, another slipper upside down against the baseboard. Jake's pulse ticked up and he fought off a churning wave of nausea. He suppressed an urge to rush forward. If he couldn't do his job the way it deserved to be done, he needed to turn around and leave this to Callie. He took a few slow breaths, and his nerves steadied.

With another two steps, the entire body came into view. A man, on his back, sprawled among a scattering of large sheets of paper, his right arm flung above his head and his left at his side. A flannel shirt in blues and blacks under brown bib overalls. Henry's standard work outfit. A small puddle of blood spread across the worn oak floor from the victim's head. One paper sheet had touched the pool and drawn the blood up in a bright red arc.

Jake stepped through the opening and into the dining room. He made sure the floor was clear, then squatted next to the body, finally letting his eyes rise to the face and confirm what he already knew: it was Henry. His friend's always-smiling face was now frozen in a grimace, teeth clenched.

And there it was. The image that would haunt Jake whenever he thought of his old friend.

Jake's hand went to his chest. It took a moment before the sharp edges of his cross registered on his fingertips. A gift from Mary before their wedding. He'd always touched the cross when he prayed, but after Mary died, that practice had faded, along with his faith. Now he pressed the cross into his chest as memories of Henry swirled: the two of them as boys, then as young men, then as couples with their wives… then as men without women once more.

Jake's stomach twisted. As primary on the case, he was responsible for notifying Henry's next of kin. He'd known Lynn, Henry's ex-wife, for forty years. He'd known April her entire life. He was even her godfather. The notification would be… difficult.

Because you're biased, Houser. And shouldn't be on the case.

Technically. But technicalities were for bureaucrats. Jake had been close to investigations before; he knew he could handle the mental gymnastics needed to do it right. He would just lock down his emotions. He had the rest of his life to deal with Henry's murder. Right now he needed to avenge it.

Jake stepped across the body and squatted to examine Henry's left forearm. The flesh was already hardening with rigor and felt wooden. When Jake lifted the arm, it came up stiffly, and the body—*Henry*—rolled with it. Rigor had advanced from the smaller muscles all the way to the shoulders and torso, which meant Henry's death had occurred closer to the beginning of their time window—nine thirty, when the neighbor saw Henry come home—than to Grady's visit seventeen hours later.

Jake pulled up Henry's sleeve and found purple splotches and streaks of lividity displayed evenly along the length of his lower arm, where his blood had pooled after his heart stopped pumping. So—Henry hadn't been moved since death. He examined Henry's hand and arm carefully for defensive wounds and found nothing beyond the little nicks and paint flecks the handyman always carried.

He stepped back over Henry, checked the other arm, and confirmed his conclusions.

Jake then leaned in for a closer look at the wound, careful to stay out of the blood. A blunt object had hit Henry on the hairline above his left eye, cleaving both skin and skull, gray matter showing through the bone and flesh. Jake rubbed at a sudden pain in his chest. He took a couple more deep breaths, blinking away a blur in his eyes, and refocused. The wound had only one edge, which indicated a single blow. Blood had run down the side of Henry's head and pooled during the final beats of his heart. The pool hadn't been disturbed, indicating Henry hadn't moved his head after hitting the floor.

Jake stepped back near Henry's feet and took in the whole scene. The killer had stood here, near the opening between the two rooms, and hit Henry with an overhand blow. Henry had fallen back. His right hand reached out to the table for support, but succeeded only in pulling the maps to the floor with him as he fell. Once he was down, he stayed down.

No struggle.

A single blow.

No defensive wounds.

Either Henry had known his attacker or the violence was so sudden he didn't have a chance to react.

Or both.

* * *

Henry had converted the dining area into a workroom for his hobby: excavating outhouse pits in search of historic artifacts from Weston's past. He had tied the chandelier tight to the ceiling with a black zip tie and had set a banquet table against the outside wall. Maps and charts tabbed with Post-it notes covered the table's left side in a loose stack that had spilled onto the floor. The table's right side held a laptop computer and a printer/scanner combo. A mesh-backed chair was pushed under the table in front of the computer. The back wall was solid shelving crammed full of books and papers and magazines.

Jake saw nothing capable of causing the damage done to Henry's skull.

Blunt force trauma usually left blood splatter, but Jake didn't see any. With a single blow there wouldn't be a flinging trail from a back swing, but there should still be a splash from the impact. He checked the ceiling, floor, and walls, but found nothing. He'd have to wait for what the forensic team and their eagle eyes—and luminol—turned up.

From outside the house came the sound of gravel crunching under tires. Help was arriving. But Jake wanted to take a quick look through the house before the deputy coroner and the forensic team crowded in, so he moved back to the entryway.

A stack of cardboard boxes stood next to the front door. The top box had been slit open, but that had been done long ago, as the dust was undisturbed along the edge of the loose flap. Jake lifted the flap with a fingertip and found the box full of Henry's book: *Outhouse Archeology*. It was a coffee-table book of interesting antiquities Henry had found in the outhouse pits. Jake had a signed copy, of course. He thought Henry had done a great job of pulling together each artifact with a short history of the family who had lived on the property.

Henry's recliner sat in the front corner under a wall-mounted reading lamp. A double stack of books rose from the floor next to the chair. Jake shuffled through them: a mix of American histories and biographies, black-marbled composition books, and books about Weston and Paget County, including a historical novel for children by a local author.

Jake then inspected the items under the coffee table's glass top. These were the best Indian artifacts Henry had found along the river—dozens of arrowheads, a grinding stone, and worked flint chunks—each nestled in a fold of shiny black fabric. A place for everything, and everything in its place.

He continued on to the shelving. Henry had been proud of the outhouse finds he displayed on the front edge of each shelf: little glass medicine bottles, broken ceramics, a pipe, coins, a belt buckle, and on and on. But now these outhouse mementos were all jammed together at one end or the other of each shelf. The books were out of place, too: some weren't lined up evenly, and others had been pulled partly out and left that way.

Someone had searched the shelves.

Jake swept his gaze back over the other end of the room. The television and stereo and gaming system were untouched. If the killer were a druggie, those easily fenced electronics would be gone and the search for other valuables would have left everything strewn across the floor. This was something else. A careful search for something specific.

Something the killer knew about and wanted.

But what?

And had the killer found it?

CHAPTER THREE

Grady opened the front door and leaned in. "Detective? The deputy coroner and the forensic team are both out here. Let me know when you're ready."

"Let them in in ten minutes."

Jake moved on to the back hall. All three doors were open—two bedrooms and a bathroom—and all the lights were on. He went to the larger bedroom first—April's bedroom when she stayed with her dad, which was most weekends. She was a freshman at Paget Community College and lived with her mom a few blocks away. Her room smelled faintly of something flowery, perfume or a hidden air freshener. She was an avid reader, and fantasy and romance paperbacks filled the shelf above her desk. This room had been searched too: the books were jumbled, the bedding mussed, the clothes in the drawers and closet pushed to the sides.

Henry's room had received a similar going-over, and in the bathroom the cabinet door under the sink stood open and the cleaning products were shoved aside, the glass cleaner toppled.

The door at the end of the hallway opened into a small kitchen with metal cabinets and chrome-edged countertops. Two drawers were partly open and the killer had swept the packaged food in the tall pantry to the side of each shelf as he searched.

Jake stepped onto what had once been the back porch before Henry enclosed it and turned it into the office for his handyman business. This room was cooler than the rest of the house, and the gritty odors of leaves and dirt leaked through the thin walls. It was a tiny space, barely large enough for Henry's metal desk, a pair of filing cabinets, and a single bookshelf. An open file drawer and a stack of Fox Handyman marketing fliers spilled across the floor, indicating the search had continued out here.

A wall calendar above the desk listed all of Henry's appointments. Jake knew Henry as a go-getter, always hustling to pay his child support and support his hobbies, but the November schedule didn't reflect that. Some days this month had nothing scheduled at all. Jake flipped back to October, which was busier, with at least one job every day and sometimes two or three: cleaning gutters, replacing sump pumps, painting a living room. And August and September looked like the typical chaos of activity that Jake remembered—every single day crammed with jobs. Did things slow down in the fall, or did something slow Henry down?

Back in the kitchen, a narrow door opened to steep stairs dropping into gloom. Jake had never been in Henry's basement and couldn't find the light switch. He pulled his flashlight from the pocket of his blazer, adjusted the beam to a wide swath, and took the stairs sideways, aiming his flashlight ahead of him. At the bottom he swung the light in an arc and found a string hanging from the ceiling. When he pulled it, a pair of bulbs came on to light a laundry area—washer and dryer, a sink on metal legs, a long table piled with folded clothes. A dehumidifier hummed and rattled in the corner, and the dry and dusty basement air prickled Jake's nose with a faint scent of laundry detergent. He found the same signs of a search here. A cabinet door was open above the washer, and a spill of grainy detergent was scattered across the floor. A scuff in the spillage looked like a partial footprint; Jake made a mental note to have the forensic team take a sample of the detergent in case they found a suspect with some on his shoes.

The rest of the basement was blocked off by a heavy green tarp nailed to the floor joists above. Jake walked around it into a large open space, lit by a row of bare bulbs down the center. This was clearly a storage area. It held an assortment of wood furniture, three bicycles, and a long table stacked with books. Jake examined a few of the books. Book-of-the-month editions of popular fiction from the sixties and seventies: good quality for reading, but worthless as collectables.

The floor above him shook and creaked under the onslaught of incoming criminalists, and Jake ducked his head in reflex.

There wasn't much here for the killer to search through. Jake probed the dark corner behind the water heater and furnace with his flashlight's beam but found nothing. A workbench along the wall had a shelf under it holding paint cans, but everything else was out in the open.

A digital camera sat on top of a barstool. Jake turned it on and scrolled back through the stored photos. It showed individual items from the clutter posed in front of the canvas room divider. Henry must have been selling some of this junk, or trying to.

As Jake headed back upstairs, his phone vibrated in his pocket. He pulled it out and checked the screen. It was Coogan, Jake's best friend since second grade. He had been as close to Henry as Jake had been. The three of them were inseparable all the way through high school, when Jake and Coogan left town for college and Henry stayed behind, already earning a good living as a handyman.

"Hey," Jake said, sitting down on a hard plank step.

"Jake?" Coogan's voice held his usual midafternoon dark roast–infused energy. "We still on for—"

"I'm over at Henry's, Coog. He…" Jake trailed off. He was unable to get the words out.

"Jake? What is it?" Coogan's voice dropped. "What about Henry?"

"He's been murdered." Jake squeezed his eyes shut.

"Jesus." Coogan breathed the word. "What happened?"

"I… can't get into it yet." Jake straightened. "I'm heading over to tell April and Lynn in a bit. I…"

"I'll call Judy and let her know. Maybe she could go be with Lynn?"

"But have her wait outside until I leave, okay?"

"Damn it, Jake." Coogan's voice caught. "I just can't believe…"

"I know. I'll call you later, okay?"

"Okay. I'll be here."

Jake pulled out his handkerchief and wiped his eyes. He took a deep breath, flexed the grimace off his face, and got moving.

* * *

Three technicians in white Tyvek jumpsuits were already at work—one angling around Henry's body with his camera clicking, another kneeling on the floor with a tape measure and a clipboard, and a third working the front room near the bulky silhouette of Duke Fanning, the forensic investigator in charge. Jake was glad to see Fanning was on the case; he was the county's best FIC.

A small, sharply dressed man with a gleaming bald dome stood next to Fanning, his back to the body. Jansen, Paget County coroner. In Illinois, coroner was an elected position, and the coroner wasn't required to have criminal justice experience. Which Jansen didn't. The man was a buffoon who owned a clothing store and had bought his way into office through the Republican machine. Jake's temper rose, but he fought it down as he strode across the floor.

"Jansen," Jake said. "What are you doing here?"

Jansen flinched at the sound of Jake's voice. "Detective Houser." He stepped behind Fanning's bulk. "I didn't know this was your case."

"Now you do."

Jansen swallowed, his giant Adam's apple running up and down his throat like a flag on a pole. "Yes. I…" He pulled a handkerchief out and dabbed at the sweat suddenly beading on his skull. He leaned to look past Jake. "You have this, Deputy Chen." Then he spun and bolted for the front door.

Fanning cracked a half smile. "I'm not going to ask what that was about."

"Good," Jake said.

Jake filled in FIC Fanning on everything he'd observed, including the signs that the house had been searched, the detergent spill in the basement, and the possibility of a trace on a suspect.

When Jake turned back toward the dining room he spotted Deputy Coroner Liz Chen against the wall, a large plastic equipment box at her feet. Rubber bands were wrapped around her arms and legs to control the Tyvek jumpsuit's excess bulk on her slight frame.

"I'm glad to see you, DC Chen."

"Detective Houser." She nodded, then turned back to observing the techs at work around Henry's body. She stood completely still, her eyes darting around the room methodically. When she expanded her visual search to include the ceiling, she squinted. Maybe she saw something. Then she shook her head and brought her gaze back to Jake.

"Was the house closed up when he was found?"

"Yes. Are you going to take a liver temp?" It was the best estimator of time of death in closed and constant conditions like this.

"Of course."

Which meant it was time for Jake to go. He'd already made enough rough memories without seeing Chen cut Henry open to insert her giant thermometer into his torso. And he sure as hell wasn't going to attend the autopsy and see his friend's face pulled down or his chest cut open. *Christ.*

Whoever did this was going to pay.

He stopped on the front stoop to talk to Grady. "Anyone guarding the back?"

Behind the house, Henry's lot ran down toward the river; a barn huddled under the trees where the lot bordered Riverfront Park. Jake would need to look at the barn before Fanning and his team left, but not right now. The clock was ticking for him to get to Lynn and April before social media made the notification for him.

"Bantam," Grady said.

"Good. Detective Diggs is going to handle the canvas when she gets here. Probably after five." Jake stripped off the booties and gloves and tossed them in the trash bag flapping in the breeze by the front door.

"And where are you headed?" Grady asked.

Jack sighed. "I'm going to notify the next of kin."

CHAPTER FOUR

Jake maneuvered his car past the boxy forensics van and the coroner's wagon now parked in Henry's front yard, then turned east on Jackson. Henry's ex and his daughter lived less than a mile away in a small bungalow just north of downtown.

His cell phone buzzed with a call from Erin. Officially she was the department's civilian investigator. Unofficially she was a lot more, including Jake's liaison with the rest of the department. He stayed away from the station and its politics as much as possible.

He pulled to the curb by Centennial Beach. "I should have called you," he said upon answering. Erin had known Henry as long as he and Coogan had, maybe longer. She'd even dated him in high school.

"Is it really Henry?" Erin's voice was thick with emotion. "I just... I can't..."

"It is Henry."

"And it's BFT? Like the radio said? That means he..."

"Was murdered," Jake said.

"You need to take this." Erin's voice grew quiet. "I know it's probably a conflict—"

"I *am* taking it. Deputy Chief Braff doesn't need to know Henry was my friend."

"If he finds out and tries to pull you, I'll handle him."

Jake believed her. She'd handled him on many occasions. "What can I do?" she asked.

"Check for any calls in that patrol zone in the last twenty-four hours and talk to the patrol officers about any suspicious vehicles or people over the last week."

"Will do. What else?"

Henry's thin appointment calendar came to mind. If Henry's income was down, he might have had trouble paying his child support. "Call Coogan; he represents Henry. Ask him if anything was happening with Henry's child support case."

Her pencil scratched away, then: "You'll need a search warrant."

She was right. Without a warrant Coogan could get in trouble for sharing his client's information. "Can you—"

"Callie is up at the county complex for the opioid task force meeting. I'll have her visit the warrant judge before she comes back."

"Perfect," Jake said. "Let Coogan know it's coming. We also need to know whether Henry had a will."

"Got it."

Jake ended the call and pulled back onto the road. Coogan and Erin weren't the only people who would be hit hard by Henry's murder. Jake couldn't think of a person in town with a wider group of friends than Henry. At least a hundred of them had gathered around Henry's backyard fire pit just a couple weeks earlier after the Redhawks' homecoming game, drinking beer and retelling old stories. It had been a good night.

It has also been the last time Jake had seen Henry alive.

Jake pushed the pain aside to concentrate on where he was going.

And what he had to do when he got there.

Every notification had two purposes: to inform next of kin and to investigate. It was the first, and best, opportunity to observe the people closest to the victim and probe them with as many questions as their mental state would allow. Jake needed to lock down his emotions so he could be alert to every verbal and non-verbal indication of deception.

Statistics, experience, and protocol all said Lynn, as Henry's ex-wife, was a person of interest. But statistics were for politicians and actuaries. Only facts mattered. And Jake had been close enough to Henry to have a solid feel for his relationship with Lynn. The two got along well and still spent a lot of time together, supporting April in marching band and gymnastics and environmental club. Jake also doubted Lynn would benefit from Henry's death; in fact, she'd likely be hurt by it because child support payments would stop. Plus she was short and slight and not capable of the massive blow that killed Henry.

No motive. No means. These were objective facts not clouded by bias. They held more weight than any statistic.

* * *

Lynn Fox tried not to think about her problems, but raking leaves was so boring it left her entire mind free to wallow in them. Utility bills and mortgage payments and the car loan and gas and even food for Christ's sake. And now she had to pay a penalty to the government because she didn't have health insurance. If she couldn't afford health insurance, how could she afford the penalty?

She pulled the rake toward the street, the tines scratching through the thin grass, moving a fat mound of leaves. How had this happened to her? She was a good person. She didn't steal and she didn't lie. Not any more than everyone else. She kicked at the leaves, sending a wad of them against the tree trunk.

"I thought we were supposed to rake them," April said.

Lynn smiled. April was the one thing Lynn felt good about. The only person in her life who cared whether she lived or died. Or used to, anyway. Now all she cared about was Connor and college.

"Are you talking to me again?" Lynn asked, trying for a playful tone.

April had been pouting about something all morning. Most likely boyfriend trouble, which was okay with Lynn. April could do better than Conner.

April shrugged.

"Why don't you wear that Paget Community College sweatshirt I got you? With the cool bird on it?"

April had on the Northwestern hoodie Conner had given her. Lynn kept telling her purple was not her color, but April didn't listen to her mother anymore.

"I don't like green, and no one wears those things. Not even at school."

"But you go there."

"And if I wear it everyone will know that. And I'm going to transfer to Northwestern."

Lynn let that go. Henry's promise to send April there had turned out to be worthless. No surprise, really. The man could barely pay April's community college tuition, much less fifty grand for Northwestern.

Lynn's hands got back to her raking, her mind back to her bills. She needed a man with money. Money would solve every single one of her problems.

"Who's that?" April asked.

A car was coming down the street, slowing as it approached. It was big, and black, and didn't look familiar. As it turned into their driveway, she lifted a hand to block the sun shining in her eyes. It was Jake.

Lynn straightened her flannel shirt and ran a hand through her hair. She hoped she had a flush in her cheeks from the cold. Jake was single and decent-looking. Not handsome, exactly, but he was still slim and had his hair and never looked grungy. Not even when she saw him out running.

She smiled as he got out of the car.

"It's Mr. Houser," April said.

"Hey, Jake."

"Lynn," Jake said. He looked toward April. "Hey, kiddo. I'm going to borrow your mom for a minute, okay?"

"Sure." April pulled her hood up and got back to raking. She wasn't a very good worker, but every little bit helped.

As Jake walked toward Lynn, his eyes flitted over hers but didn't hold. That wasn't like him. He was an eye contact guy. Always looking deep inside of her like he could see something there. But his face was always so still, and she could never tell if he liked what he saw or not. He had on the same gray pants, white shirt, and black blazer that he'd once told April's Girl Scout troop was his "detective uniform," which got a laugh. She took another look at the car. It was his detective car.

Shit. "What is it, Jake?"

He stopped in front of her but didn't say anything. She squinted against the sun setting behind him. His eyes drifted away, then came back and settled on her forehead. Finally, he smiled, but it wasn't a real smile.

"How about we go inside for a cup of coffee?"

Lynn swallowed a lump in her throat. "April? We're going inside for a minute." She dropped her rake and wiped her hands on her shirt. "You keep at it."

"Okay, Mom."

Lynn wondered what April had done this time. Her boyfriend was away at college, so she couldn't have been caught bumping uglies again. Whatever it was, she just hoped it wasn't too serious.

Or too expensive.

She had enough problems already.

CHAPTER FIVE

Jake's heart had risen into his throat when he saw April out front, raking. She'd been a cute kid—curly blond hair and chubby cheeks and an amazing dimpled smile. Teenage angst had burned the smile away, but lately it had been coming back. He hoped Henry's death didn't kill it.

He followed Lynn around the side of the house. Jake had helped Henry remodel the little two-bedroom bungalow when he bought it fifteen years before. When Lynn divorced him, Henry insisted she get the house because he wanted April growing up there. Henry moved into a tiny apartment above the chocolate shop, where he'd lived for years until his uncle died and left him the house by the river.

As they rounded the back corner, Jake focused on Lynn. She wore a form-fitting flannel shirt over a pair of tight jeans tucked into green rubber boots. She'd married Henry when his handyman business was booming—that was back during the growing economy, when upwardly mobile junior executives were spending freely to get their old houses ready for sale and to put their own touches on their bigger and newer places. Things were so good back then, Henry even had some employees. But when the economy slowed down and the business shrank, Lynn divorced Henry because—so she'd told him—she aspired to being more than a handyman's wife. Lynn still hadn't found her Mr. Right, though the rumor mill said she tried out a lot of prospects she met while waitressing at the country club.

Jake followed Lynn inside. The back door opened into a utility room crammed with a washer and dryer. A row of coats on hooks hung above a jumble of shoes and boots. A narrow archway led into the kitchen, which smelled of coffee and popcorn.

Lynn pushed together a scatter of newspapers to clear space at the table, and pointed at a chair. Jake sat and waited while Lynn poured him a cup of coffee from her drip machine.

"I already had this going," she said. Her voice shook, and the mug rattled against the table as she set it in front of him. Apparently she'd figured out this wasn't a social call.

He took her hands and guided her into the chair next to him. Her hands were cold from being outside. "Lynn, I'm sorry to—" His phone pinged, announcing a text message.

"Do you need to check that?"

"It'll keep."

"Is April in trouble again?" Lynn pulled her hands away and clutched her thighs, rocking slightly. "She's been tricky since, I don't know, I guess when this college thing came up."

"I'm here about Henry. He's dead." Jake got it out fast, because it was easier for him—and, he hoped, easier for her.

She paled. Her eyes squeezed shut and she covered her face with her hands. Genuine emotion, he was almost sure.

"What… how did it happen?" She pulled her hands down and fought off a sob.

"He was murdered last night. That's all I can tell you right now."

Lynn gasped. "Nobody would—that can't be. That just can't be." Her head shook gently back and forth.

Jake fought the urge to offer an empty platitude. He'd assembled an arsenal of them over the years, but after his wife's murder he'd stopped using them. Because then he got it. The idea that someone had deliberately killed a loved one was too sickening for a worn-out cliché to provide any comfort. It was better to simply deliver the news and then wait, giving the person some time to absorb the shock before asking questions.

He picked up the coffee mug and took a sip. The bitter brew was too hot to drink, so he blew on it, the long deep breaths also helping settle his own nerves.

"People *loved* that man." Lynn covered her face again and turned away, her shoulders shaking with sobs.

That man. Her phrasing implied disapproval—like she didn't understand the love or thought Henry didn't deserve it. Or maybe that was just her way of subconsciously putting some emotional distance between her and Henry, to lessen her pain.

Jake kept quiet and got up to get Lynn a glass of water. He opened cabinets until he found a glass, then ran water in the sink, hand under the stream, waiting for it to get cold. He took the opportunity to look around. A stack of bills on the counter; several of them showing the red of a late payment notice. A calendar on the fridge noting her work schedule, with a penciled-in dollar amount for every day already passed. Tips, maybe. Not big amounts. And on the fifth of the month, "CS—Pay Bills" with a red *X* through it.

Jake knew from his days serving warrants on deadbeat dads that child support collected through the court system was paid out on the fifth. The "CS" and "Pay Bills" paired together implied Lynn used the money to pay her bills. The red X could mean Henry missed the payment.

But April was eighteen and out of high school, so Henry's child support obligation might be over. Which would explain the past due notices if Lynn needed Henry's payments to cover her bills. Of course, none of that was motive: Henry's death wouldn't start the payments again.

He filled the glass, shut off the water, then paused before rejoining Lynn at the table. The first wave of grief had passed through her, and she was wiping her face with a sleeve. But it would hit her again. Soon, and then later, and years from now when a sight or sound or smell pulled up a memory.

He checked the message on his phone. It was from Deputy Coroner Chen: *BFT. 1. TOD 12+-2*

Henry died from blunt force trauma. The killing blow had been delivered at midnight, plus or minus two hours. Jake forwarded the text to Diggs with a request that she begin canvassing the neighbors as soon as she got back to town from the task force meeting. He got an immediate response that she had obtained the warrant for Coogan's records and was now on her way. Jake adjusted his settings so the phone would vibrate with future messages and put it back in his pocket.

As he set the water down next to Lynn, she turned and reached for him. He knelt, wrapped an arm around her, and stroked her shoulder. Heat poured from her. She shuddered and buried her face in his shoulder, and her sobs started again, her body trembling with each new onslaught. Her emotion strummed Jake's heartstrings, and he had to fight a swell of sentiment. He chewed his lips and blinked back a tear and held her until the sobbing wore her out. Then she pulled back and said she was okay, patting him on the shoulder.

"I need to tell April." She grabbed a paper napkin from a basket on the table and wiped her eyes. She grabbed another and blew her nose. "Someone will tweet it or instant message it. I…"

"I'll do it," Jake said. April was an adult, and protocol required he personally notify all adult family members when possible.

"No." Lynn barked the word, then her voice softened. "I'll tell her. I'm her mother. And we only have each other, now."

Jake opened his mouth to insist, but then closed it. He owed his goddaughter that much sensitivity. "I will need to talk with April," he said. "When she's ready."

"Okay."

Jake stood to go. He was through the utility room and had his hand on the doorknob before he realized his bias was getting in the way. He turned back. "Can I ask you a few questions before I leave? About Henry and who might have done this?"

"Who might have *done* this?" She had followed him into the laundry room and stood with her fists clenched, the napkin between them, twisting it. Her voice high and shaky. "*No one.* Henry is the nicest man in town. Undercharges all his clients. Doesn't even charge some of them. Even ones that can pay. Some of those ladies take complete advantage. He—" She stopped and twisted the napkin, bits of paper falling to the floor.

"Did he mention a recent problem with anyone?"

Lynn shook her head.

"Lynn, please consider this carefully. *Would* Henry have told you if he had a problem with anyone?"

"I don't know. At one time… probably. But now, I just don't know."

"What's different now?"

She shifted her feet and her eyes cut away. "We are divorced, you know. We argue about money and about what's best for April."

"Okay." She was leaving something out. He would talk to her again when he knew more about the child support situation. He pulled the door open. "The killer searched Henry's house. Any idea what he might have been looking for?"

She shook her head. "I really have to talk to April. She's always on that damn phone. I can't let her find out about her dad from the damn Twitter."

He put a hand on her shoulder. "Call me if you need anything or remember someone giving Henry trouble."

Lynn nodded and wiped her eyes with the crushed napkin. "April's going to be so…" She choked back a sob. "They were so close."

Jake nodded but could think of nothing else to say, so he left her there, twisting her napkin.

As he stepped out from between the houses the cold wind whipped against him. April had given up on raking and sat on the front stoop holding her phone. He worried she might have already heard about her dad through social media, but when she looked up her eyes were dry. He gave her a wave, and her face pulled into a grimace. The kid was smart and knew something was off. But Lynn was probably right—it was best for her to get this news from her mom.

Or was he just being a coward?

CHAPTER SIX

Conner Bowen couldn't stop looking at the photo April had sent him. It showed her wearing the Northwestern hoodie he'd bought her, and her hair was messy and her smile was a little crooked. She had a million different smiles, and he wanted to spend the rest of his life getting to know every one of them. God, he missed her. If she transferred to Northwestern everything would be perfect. She would so love the total spectacle around the football games. Conner even went to them, though he had no idea what was going on. Football was his dad's obsession, and at home Conner stayed as far away from it as he did from the old man himself.

He stuck the phone back in his pocket and stretched out on his bed with his laptop on his stomach. One of his courses, The Journalism of Empathy, was taking up a lot of his time, but he loved it. They were writing nonfiction narratives about marginalized people. He'd barely known what that meant when he started the semester, and now he was writing stories about these interesting communities. He was constantly blown away by how poorly his white-bread suburban upbringing had prepared him for this. Professor K told them to imagine the ideal reader as they wrote. Conner imagined himself a year ago. The only child of a perfect suburban family attending one of the best public high schools in the state, with an acceptance letter from Northwestern tacked to his bulletin board. Completely ignorant of things outside his easy, sheltered existence.

Some of that was a lie, of course. His family only looked perfect from the outside. In reality his dad was an asshole and his parents didn't talk to each other. But Conner didn't write to the real him. He wrote to the other guy; the one other people saw.

His cell phone vibrated. A text from April. *Conner!*

He smiled. She liked to grab his attention then send a fast string of short texts. People he'd met at school didn't think their long-distance romance would survive, but they didn't know April—or him, really. They were perfectly and exactly right for each other.

The little bubble popped up with the dots. She was texting him right now. He felt the connection opening between them as a bloom of heat in his heart.

* * *

Lynn stood in the kitchen, arms wrapped tight around herself, eyes tearing. Henry was the only good man she'd ever loved. She'd *tried* to love other men since their divorce, but none of them was as good as Henry. He was the one who'd gotten away even though she knew that was all her fault; she'd pushed him away, then got so angry with herself for doing it she pushed even harder to prove she'd been right.

She wiped her eyes, then walked through the house and cracked open the front door. April sat on the front stoop staring at her phone. The girl had so many friends she was always texting. And why shouldn't she? Lynn had had a lot of friends when she was younger, too. Back before everyone got married or obsessed with their careers or moved away. She had friends now, but they were mostly men she met at the club. And they didn't text. Which was a blessing really. Who wants to be bothered every minute?

She pushed the storm door open, wincing at the long squeak. Now Henry wasn't going to be around to fix such things. Who would do it? April's boyfriend was useless. The least manly man Lynn had ever met.

"Honey?"

April pulled her eyes from her phone and turned. "Yeah?"

"Come inside for a minute. I need to tell you something." Lynn pushed the door farther open.

"I just need to finish this text to Conner, okay?"

"But just that one, okay?" April's texting sessions could go on forever.

Lynn waited with the door open, the breeze catching it and almost pulling it out of her hand. A rattling swirl of leaves jumped the stoop, and Lynn kicked at them, the cold wind that carried them slapping against her face.

A last furious stab of April's thumbs was followed by a *whoosh* as the text shot off. She stuffed the phone in the pocket of her hoodie and stood. Lynn tried to smile, but whatever made it to her face caused April to flinch as she slipped inside.

"Let's talk in the kitchen," Lynn said. She followed April down the hall and through the swinging door. Lynn wiped her eyes and pulled her shoulders back.

April stopped at the table with a hand on the back of a chair. "What is it, Mom?"

Lynn turned two chairs to face each other, sat down in one, and patted the other. "Sit."

April plopped into the chair. "Mom… you're scaring me. Why was Mr. Houser here?"

"It's your dad, honey. He's…" Lynn bit back a sob and squeezed her hands into fists, nails digging into her palms. "He's dead."

"What?" April pushed back in her chair, the legs squeaking against the floor. "What happened to him? Mom? What happened?"

Lynn grabbed her daughter's hands and held tight. "It doesn't matter, honey. He's dead. That's all."

"Of course it matters! I'm not a little kid anymore. Tell me what happened. He's my dad!" Her beautiful face twisted with grief, and her eyes welled with tears.

Lynn squeezed her eyes shut. April was right. She deserved to know, and no matter how much Lynn wanted to protect her, the truth would be out there somewhere. She needed to hear it now, from her mom. "Someone killed him."

April broke into sobs.

Lynn knelt in front of her chair and held her, stroking her hair, repeating over and over that it would be all right. Hoping the words didn't sound as empty as they felt.

A knock sounded on the back door. April pulled away and wiped her sleeve across her face. "I don't want to get it."

"I know, honey." Lynn grabbed a paper napkin from the table and wiped her eyes as she went to the back door. She stood on her tiptoes and looked through the little window. It was Judy, Coogan's wife. One of the few who had never taken sides in the divorce.

Lynn opened the door, and without a word Judy stepped forward, wrapped her arms around Lynn, and squeezed her tight.

"Lynn, I'm so sorry about Henry. He was such a good man." Judy stepped back, spotted April, and walked over and gave her an equally big hug.

Lynn bit her lip, wanting to scream, *Get out!* She wanted to be alone with April to... what, she didn't know. To cry. And to get mad. And to cry some more. This wasn't about Judy. Or Jake. Or Coogan. Or any of the rest of them.

Shit. Everybody was going to know. Jake had told Coogan, who had told Judy, and the news would go around until everyone knew what had happened to Lynn.

CHAPTER SEVEN

Jake drove back toward Henry's house, the streetlights flicking on as the first day of his investigation bled away.

He'd made some progress.

He'd found a possible motive: the killer had been looking for something in Henry's house. Something small enough to fit on a bookshelf or in a cabinet.

He'd notified Henry's next of kin, though not directly. April was Henry's only blood relation, but letting her mom give her the news had been the right thing to do. Jake would talk with April in the morning.

He'd also ruled out a person of obvious, statistical interest. Lynn's emotional response to Henry's death had confirmed what Jake had already thought. Clearly she hadn't been involved in killing Henry.

Jake cut through the Centennial Beach parking lot, past the baseball field where his team had won the city championship when he was nine, then down the long narrow lot that fronted the length of Riverside Park. When he was a kid this had been the city's yard waste dump. Now it was a beautiful park with picnic pavilions and brick walkways and an elaborate playground. All empty in the fall chill, with night dropping fast. Here in the flats along the river it was already almost full dark, other than the luminous blobs of the widely spaced light poles in the parking lot.

Jake slowed at a gap in the row of bushes separating the parking lot from the houses along Jackson. That gap led to the barn on the back of Henry's property. A uniformed officer stood there now, talking with an old man in a thick wool coat with a watch cap pushed up his forehead. The old man had bushy gray eyebrows and a dark birthmark along his jaw. Binoculars hung on a strap around his neck.

Jake angled his car toward them, and the officer waved him forward. As he pulled the car up to the gap, the officer finished with the old man, who ambled off.

Jake rolled down his window and held up his badge.

"Good evening, Detective Houser." The officer pointed across the patchy back lawn to Henry's house. "Officer Grady has the crime scene log at the front door."

"I'm headed that way." Jake looked at the old man, now walking down the parking lot, then back to the officer. "You're Bantam, right?"

"Yes, sir."

"Please—Detective or Houser. I'm not a boss."

Bantam nodded.

"Any problems down here?" Jake asked.

"A reporter tried to sneak in, but I caught him and sent him away." He checked his watch. "That was forty-three minutes ago. And some kids on bikes."

Jake didn't like the press and was glad Bantam had run the reporter off. "Anyone go in the barn?"

"No, s—Detective."

"Did you write up the reporter and that old man? I need them for the murder book." As lead investigator, Jake documented the entire investigation in the murder book. "Names and addresses and phone numbers and the what and why and when. You know the drill."

Bantam nodded, and his gaze stabbed toward the parking lot. He licked his lips and pulled out his notebook. "The old guy's name was Titus Cole."

"Get it all, Officer."

"I will, Detective."

Jake pulled his car through the gap and parked on the gravel area in front of the barn. The back yard was secluded, the bushes along the back and thick pine trees along both lot lines shielding it from view. The yard light was on, a large dim bulb on a high pole. Jake got out of the car and started toward the house. The air was thick with the muddy scent off the river. He stopped for a moment by the fire pit ringed with wood benches. This was where he'd last seen Henry alive. Standing on top of that log, leading a crowd of Weston Central alumni through the school's fight song. Henry was the only one who ever remembered all the words.

Behind him, Bantam yelled for the old man to "Hang on a sec!"

Jake pulled his blazer tight against the creeping cold. Someone upwind was burning leaves, the smoke invisible in the dark but dense enough to tickle the back of his throat with its ashy taste. He climbed the low hill toward the front of the house, the effort pushing his heart rate up more than it should. He found two vehicles parked in the front yard—Callie Diggs's cruiser and Fanning's forensics van. The coroner's van was gone, and with it Henry. *Thank God*, he thought and let out a big breath. He wouldn't have to see his dead friend again.

Until the funeral.

He pulled in a couple of long breaths, slowing his pulse down, and took a long look around. The mini-mansion to the west loomed over the yard behind a lattice of bare branches that clattered together in the wind. Brueder, the woman who had called 911, lived there. Two mini-mansions to the east had only small windows facing this way, so they probably hadn't seen anything. Callie would pull it out of them if they had.

Jake joined Grady on the front stoop. "Is Detective Diggs still on the canvass?"

"Yes, Detective."

"Fanning still inside?"

"Yes." Grady checked the log, then his watch. "But Deputy Coroner Chen left twenty-six minutes ago with Mr. Fox's remains."

Jake put on a fresh set of booties and a pair of gloves, then shoved extra pair of gloves in his pocket in case the first pair filled with sweat.

Inside, Fanning stood from where he'd been crouching by the bookshelves displaying the outhouse souvenirs. He waved a hand over the room. "I agree with you that someone searched the place."

"Prints?"

"Yes and no."

"Meaning?" Jake appreciated Fanning's terse style, but wished he would save it for the courtroom.

"No prints where there are signs of a search, but plenty of them elsewhere."

"Because the killer wore gloves," Jake suggested.

"Or wiped down what he touched."

Which meant print analysis would be a bust. But it still had to be done, every print collected and compared to the prints expected to be here—Henry's and April's and even Jake's.

"I'm going to look through the dining room and back office if you guys are done with them," Jake said.

"We are. Go ahead."

Though Henry was gone, his blood was still on the dining room floor: a half-moon where his head had lain and a long streak where the map had been pulled away, probably when they removed Henry's body. Jake avoided the blood as he examined the things on the table.

The maps were early plats of Weston, with Henry's penciled notations where he had located outhouse pits. Jake was familiar with the maps from Henry's book and found nothing unusual among them. As he pulled the chair out to sit down, he noticed it was an Aeron, a high-end office chair that probably cost around a thousand dollars. Spending that kind of money on a chair wasn't Henry's style. Maybe it had been a gift from a satisfied customer who didn't need it anymore.

Jake sat down on the springy mesh fabric, and his knee bumped something under the table. A wastebasket. He pulled it into the open and examined the contents. He found pages from a manuscript marked up with heavy edits. The header listed the title as *Privy to History*; it looked to be a sequel to Henry's outhouse book. Nothing else caught Jake's eye, and he pushed the can back under the table.

The laptop had been processed for fingerprints and was coated in a dusting of print powder. Jake jiggled his finger on the track pad, and the screen lit up to show Henry's desktop. No password protection. A whir as the internal fan kicked on.

He opened the word processing program and clicked the file tab to bring up the last few documents Henry had opened. They were all revised drafts of his new book, each labeled as PTH with the date.

Jake opened the web browser next. Henry's bookmarks were organized into folders, each labeled with some area of Henry's interests in local history and writing. Nothing jumped out as unusual. Henry's browser history showed no activity before the first of the month—apparently Henry cleared the history every month—and none of the activity that was still there raised any flags.

Jake went to the office at the back of the house. Cold air moved across the floor at ankle level, stirring a flier lying on the worn wood. Jake spotted a space heater in the corner and flipped the switch. It wound itself up to a soft purr, and soon warm air smelling of burnt dust wafted from the machine.

Henry conducted his handyman business from an old metal desk crammed with a desktop computer, monitor, and printer. The chair in front of it had several duct tape patches on the seat and felt lumpy when Jake sat down. He swiveled around to size the job ahead of him. A pair of three-drawer lateral file cabinets spanned the inside wall, with a long row of manuals for household appliances across their tops. The left cabinet was marked *Personal*, the right one *Business*.

He started on the left.

The top drawer was nearly empty, the few files inside holding bills and credit card statements. The other two drawers contained nearly six feet of paper on Henry's divorce and resulting child support saga. Jake read enough to confirm Coogan handled everything, and decided to save time and wait for Coogan's report.

The business files proved more interesting, starting with a stack of old appointment calendars for the handyman business. Jake flipped through them and found that a decline in business in November was typical, although none of the old calendars contained as much blank space as this year's did.

Jake also found files covering the business side of Henry's outhouse book. Henry had even saved a thick file of rejection letters from when he shopped the book around before landing a publisher almost two years after he started. It was another year after that before the book came out, and it looked like Henry had made almost thirty thousand dollars since then. A thin file contained the contract on Henry's new book. Jake glanced through it, then looked closer. There were several deadlines for different stages in the book's production, and it looked like Henry had missed the final delivery date. Henry had never mentioned missing a deadline.

In the bottom drawer Jake found manila folders bunched at either end. Every file had a number penciled on its tab, but the folders to the left were also marked Closed and had a dollar amount in red or black on the tab.

Jake flipped through a few of the folders. Henry had apparently started a new business buying the contents of abandoned storage units. Each file covered the purchase of a single unit. When Henry bought a unit he received a bill of sale from the storage facility, granting him title to the locker's contents and showing what he'd paid for it. Henry then went through the contents, making notes on a yellow legal pad about what the unit contained and what he planned to do with each item: sell, dump, or recondition. Many files had printouts of Craigslist ads Henry had posted to sell "classic" and "antique" furniture and "collectable toys." The stuff in the basement.

Henry had kept precise figures on each unit, including reconditioning expenses, disposal fees, and sales revenue. He had hit a couple of lockers full of office furniture that made good money: probably the source of the Aeron chair. He'd sold any soft goods—clothes, bedding, drapes—to a resale shop in Kirwin. Most files contained a receipt from the Paget County Dump.

The dollar figures on the closed tabs appeared to show the final net result of each unit purchase—black for profit and red for a loss—but as Jake flipped through a few more files, it looked like the figures on the tabs were only about half of what the accounting inside the folders would indicate. Was Henry cooking his books? If so, he had saved the records that proved it. Henry wasn't that dumb—or dishonest—so the math meant something else.

As Jake returned the files to the drawer, he noticed that the last file in the closed group didn't have a dollar figure on the tab. He pulled it out. Something else *had* been written on the tab but was later erased. He turned the folder in the light and found indentations in the shape of two stars. He rubbed his thumb over them and wondered what the stars meant and why they were erased. Was the file reused? None of the others had been.

He opened the file and found the expected bill of sale from the storage facility, with two extra copies clipped to it.

Why would Henry need more than one copy of the bill of sale? Jake fanned through them and found a pink page interleaved.

It was a receipt from Paget County Coins for $2,312 for something described as "Ag 100 OZ 999 GWU."

CHAPTER EIGHT

Jake stared at the receipt for a full minute. None of the other files he looked at had a receipt like this one. Maybe Henry had misfiled it. It was dated June ninth; the bill of sale for the storage unit said May eighth. Behind the clipped papers he found the usual yellow sheet in Henry's scrawl. The only items described were "27 boxes of books" and "soft goods."

But there was no accounting.

Everything about the file was a bit off: filed with the closed files but not marked closed, no dollar amount on the tab, two stars erased from the tab, no accounting, and multiple copies of the bill of sale from the storage facility.

And the odd receipt.

Something about it tugged on the thread of a memory, but Jake couldn't quite pull it up.

He woke up Henry's business computer and confirmed it wasn't protected by a password either, then called Erin. When she didn't answer, he left a message asking her to have the department's forensic accountant come out ASAP and have him pay particular attention to the storage unit business. He explained where the files were and that the computer was not protected by a password.

He turned off the space heater, took the coin shop receipt into the dining room, and made a copy of it using Henry's scanner.

As he left Henry's house he thrummed with energy. The receipt meant something, and the answer it held was just a few minutes away.

* * *

Conner moved with the flood of commuters out of the train car and onto the platform. He hitched up his jeans, settled his backpack on his shoulders, and joined the throng heading west. Night had fallen and bugs sputtered about in the bright glare of the overhead lights. The platform crossed above Washington Street before ending at the parking lot for the Paget County Children's Museum, where dozens of cars waited for the train's passengers.

Conner threaded his way through the jumbled minivans and SUVs, then headed south along Washington Street. As he walked, he pulled out his phone and looked at April's text message again. He still couldn't believe it: *Cop is here and I overheard him tell my mom—NOT ME—that my dad's been MURDERED! He's my dad. She divorced him!!!*

The text had literarily knocked the breath out of him. He couldn't imagine someone killing Mr. Fox. He was one of the nicest guys Conner had ever met. Always happy. Always interested. Always doing something.

Conner had googled "Weston murder" several times during the train ride, but nothing came up. He reopened the Google app now, renewed the search, and got a single hit. A brief article from the *Chicago Tribune*, but it didn't have the victim's name and said nothing about how he was killed. But still, seeing it right there on his phone… *Damn!*

He leaned into the cold wind blowing down Washington Street, then cut down Franklin, the ache he felt for April growing as he got closer. He stopped on the sidewalk in front of her house, the wind whipping against him and lifting a swirl of leaves to clatter against the storm door. Mrs. Fox was not going to be happy to see him. She never was.

He texted April that he was out front, then waited on the stoop. He heard pounding feet, then the front door burst inward and there she was.

"Hi!" Her voice was high, and the word left a fog on the glass of the storm door.

He pulled it open and stepped into her hug. Her hair smelled like strawberries.

"Who is it?" Mrs. Fox yelled. The kitchen door swung open. "Is it—oh."

"It's Conner, Mom. Isn't it great that he came home from Northwestern to be here for me?" April pulled him into the house.

Mrs. Fox shook her head, then caught herself. "Yes," she said. "Hi, Conner."

"I'm so sorry about Mr. Fox…" Conner turned to April. "About your dad. I just can't—"

"I'm so glad you're here. Mom, we're just going to go into my room—"

"Not in your room." Mrs. Fox crossed her arms, staring lasers at Conner. "You know the rule."

"But Mom. We just—"

"Of course, Mrs. Fox."

Mrs. Fox dropped her arms, then crossed them again. Her eyes were red and her hair was pulled back from her face in uneven clumps. She turned around and went back through the kitchen door.

April sighed, then led him to the couch.

"How are you?" he asked.

"Better now that you're here." She put her head on his shoulder, then broke into sobs.

He held her.

* * *

Conner zipped up his coat and slung the backpack over his shoulder. Mrs. Fox had kicked him out after only twenty minutes, telling him she needed her daughter and April needed her mom, and to call before he came over again. April had been furious, but Conner had figured Mrs. Fox was at least half right: she sure did need April. The woman was a bottomless pit of need.

He walked back up to the tracks and then west along the right-of-way. The moon was bright and glinted off the rails stretching ahead of him. He stepped into the weeds as an empty commuter train roared past on its way back to the city, then continued on. A breeze kicked up as the tracks passed the Burlington Woods Forest Preserve, and the bare branches knocking together made him walk a little faster. He moved between the rails to cross the bridge over the Paget River, then scuttled down the embankment, surfing the last few feet on the loose stone. From there it was a short walk across the park and down a few blocks to his own house.

His dad would be home, as always. Sitting down there in his office with his door closed doing whatever the hell he did while Mom was out supporting the family. Conner checked his phone. 8:24 p.m. She wouldn't be home from her work trip for a couple of hours.

Which meant he and Dad would be home alone.

With any luck, the old man would stay in his office and never even know Conner was there.

CHAPTER NINE

As Jake stepped out the front door, he spotted Detective Callie Diggs walking toward him down Redhawk Court, passing in and out of the shadows in the moonlight cast by the trees bordering Henry's property. Up until a few months before, he and Callie had had a casual thing going—friends with benefits—but that dissolved when he tried to turn it into something more. Now they were working to turn what was left between them into a true friendship. It wasn't easy. Callie wore tight black pants over low-heeled boots with a trench coat cinched tight around her waist. It accentuated her figure and grabbed his attention. She noticed, and smiled.

"Learn anything new from the canvass?" Jake asked while he stripped off his gloves and booties.

"The neighbor," Callie pointed over her shoulder, "the one who called it in? She keeps a very close eye on Mr. Fox. I think she has a bit of a thing for him." The wind flapped the tails of her coat but couldn't move her hair, tight black curls she kept trimmed close to her scalp. Her dark skin glowed in the moonlight. "She says she noticed his lights still on at around eleven thirty and several more times during the night when insomnia had her wandering her house. None of his other neighbors saw anything."

"Was that normal?"

"She says it wasn't. He sometimes came home in the middle of the night—thinks he has a lady friend somewhere—a bit jealous, I think—but it's always lights out within a few minutes of getting home. And get this. She walks her dog a lot and has seen the same guy, a stranger, lurking around the neighborhood twice. Most recently last Saturday night."

"Description?"

"White. Tall. Big. Cowboy. Long coat."

"Cowboy because he wore a hat?"

"Boots. He did have a hat on, but it was a baseball hat with a logo of a Van Halen album cover on it." Callie shrugged. "That's what she said, anyway. Red and white triangles?"

Jake remembered that cover. "Can she describe him to the sketch artist?"

"She says no. She could only say he was white."

"What about his age?"

"Said he moved like a young man but she got the impression he was closer to fifty. I couldn't get her to articulate what gave her that impression."

She had pushed Mrs. Brueder to the limit of her conscious observations, like a good cop should. "Where'd she get such a good look at him?"

"Down there." Callie pointed down the hill toward the barn. "She was walking the dog along the parking lot and he was under the yard light and coming toward her through the gap in the bushes."

"When was the other time she saw him?"

"Last Thursday. Why? What are you thinking?"

"That I need to take a look at the barn."

"Want help?"

"I'm good. Thanks, Callie."

"What else do you want me to do?"

"Tell Erin what you learned. She's looking at the patrol reports. And call Henry's customers over the last two months to see if they noticed a change."

"Got it," she said, but didn't move toward her car. "You okay, Jake? You seem a little... unfocused."

"I'm good. Let me know what you find out."

Callie nodded and stepped away, the night swallowing her up as a cloud passed over the moon.

Jake headed for the barn. He needed to decide whether to spend the city's money on forensic work there before Fanning and his crew called it a night. Any evidence found after Jake released the crime scene was close to worthless in court.

Jake knew the barn well. As teens, the three of them—Henry, Jake, and Coog—had launched a lot of adventures from it. They'd even built a fort in the rafters and had sleepovers there, cooking their dinner outside in the firepit. Since Henry took over the place, he'd replaced the barn's original side roller with a roll-up door and added large lean-tos off each side, each with a pair of steel doors of its own.

As he approached, Jake realized one of those lean-to doors was cracked a few inches. It shouldn't be; Henry always kept it locked up tight. Jake pulled on the extra pair of latex gloves from his pocket and examined the slightly open door under the yard light. It was buckled where the latch met the strike plate.

He went inside, the whistle of the cold breeze dropping away. The air here smelled of sawdust and motor oil. He pulled out his pocket flashlight and shined it through the gloom until he found the light switch and flicked it on.

This lean-to was Henry's woodworking studio. He reconditioned furniture and built simple tables of maple and oak. Aged lumber Henry had acquired from who knew where rose in a teetering stack along one wall, and woodworking machines stood in a row down the center—a planer, a band saw, a table saw, several types of sanders, and a lathe. Wood furniture in every state of disrepair was scattered across the back.

Jake stepped through a narrow opening into the original barn space, which housed Henry's prized 1970 Chevy C-10 pickup, the only vehicle he ever drove. It was a rust-free import from Arizona, where Henry went to buy a replacement whenever his current ride rusted through. This one was a dusty dark red and had Fox HANDYMAN SERVICES painted on the door.

In front of the truck, two tall wood cabinets held Henry's hand tools. Normally these were secured by padlocks, but the locks now lay on the floor, and the wood was splintered where the hasps had been pried off.

Jake opened the doors and found tools hung on pegs and laid out on shelves with screws and nails and bolts and such in jars and little drawers. Jake wasn't familiar enough with the contents to know for sure, but nothing appeared to be missing.

The opposite wall held a row of yard equipment: a rototiller, a commercial-grade mower, a snow blower, and some other things Jake wasn't familiar with. Probably valuable, but bulky.

Jake continued into the other lean-to addition. Running his hand along the rough wood of the door jamb, he found the light switch and flipped it on to reveal Henry's utility vehicle and its little trailer. Gas-powered and about the size of a golf cart, it had fat knobby tires and four-wheel drive. Henry drove it on his local jobs. The trailer held shovels, a pickaxe, and a stack of buckets for hauling dirt. Henry had probably been excavating another outhouse pit.

Jake turned off all the lights as he left the barn. It had clearly been searched, but not last Saturday when Brueder saw Cowboy. Henry would have fixed the door as soon as he saw it, so it must have happened sometime after Henry had parked the truck. Last night. Perhaps the killer started his search out here, and when he failed to find what he was looking for, he went into the house, ran into Henry, and killed him with a single blow.

Jake called FIC Fanning and asked him to come down and print the doors and the broken cabinets. Maybe the killer got sloppy out here and made a mistake.

You never knew.

CHAPTER TEN

Jake's stomach grumbled as he got in the car. He needed to eat something or he'd get short-tempered. Mary had called it getting *hangry*. Although anger could be an effective tool to crack open a reluctant interview subject, he needed his brain to be in control of it, not his stomach. He shuffled through the energy bars he kept in the glove compartment and picked the biggest one. He chewed through its gritty protein as he drove, the flavor so bland he couldn't decide if it was supposed to be peanut butter or blueberry. Not that it mattered.

As he headed west on Jefferson, his phone buzzed.

"This is Houser."

"Still can't believe it." Coogan's voice was soft. "Better man didn't exist."

Coogan's sorrow amplified Jake's own, and he had to suppress a sudden sob. "What can you tell me?"

"I got the warrant by fax. I've gone through everything I've done for Henry, and I have copies of the documents ready for you."

"Can you brief me now? Starting with the will?"

"Sure." Paper rustled in the background. "We redid Henry's will and estate plan after the divorce. Henry created a trust that holds legal title to his house and truck and financial accounts. The will just pours his personal property over to the trust upon death. The trust will continue to hold the assets until whatever age Henry picked—I think it was twenty-five—then April gets it."

"All of it? Nothing to Lynn?"

"Not a dime."

"Does Lynn know?"

"Well…"

"What is it?"

"She called me on my cell a few minutes ago asking about it. I told her I couldn't tell her anything about Henry's estate. She kept at me, and I finally told her I could only talk to the trust beneficiary about it."

"And since you wouldn't talk to her, she's obviously not the trust beneficiary."

"Yeah, she picked up on that."

"Was she surprised?"

"She said, 'It figures,' and that she would have April call me."

"With a trust, the trustee handles the money until April gets it, right?" Jake's memory of his trusts and estates course in law school was thin. "Is Lynn the trustee?"

"No, I am." Coogan flipped through some pages. "Oh, and it's thirty, not twenty-five. April gets the entire corpus of the trust when she turns thirty. Until then, the trustee—me—must use it for her health, education, and general welfare. Standard stuff."

"Tell me about the child support."

Coogan started with the divorce and worked his way forward to the present. Jake pulled out his notebook and scribbled down the important facts. Henry didn't fight the divorce. They'd only been married for a couple years, so Henry didn't have to pay alimony. And there'd been no assets to divide, only debts, which Henry had agreed to pay off. Henry was fine with all of that as long as he got joint custody of April.

"Three years later Henry inherited the house down by the river and Lynn tried to grab a piece of it," Coog continued. "She alleged that the marital settlement agreement was fraudulent because Henry never disclosed the expected inheritance. But it wasn't expected—Henry's uncle never gave him a clue—so we won that. Then she went after the inheritance as income. We won that one too."

"But the child support payments caused some problems, judging by Henry's files," Jake said.

"Child support is basically set by state law as a percentage of income. But Lynn claimed Henry was hiding income."

"Was he?" Henry wasn't a liar, but divorces could get bitter, and there *was* something funky about the math in those storage unit files.

"Absolutely not. But Lynn brought up the hidden income issue every few years. Henry settled most of those battles—against my advice—and his monthly child support payment worked its way up to thirteen hundred even. Way too much, and still never enough for Lynn." Coogan's voice went gravelly with suppressed anger. "Hell, she even came after him after his payments ended."

"How?"

"Henry's child support obligation ended when April graduated from high school. His last payment was June fifth. Within a month, Lynn's lawyer filed a two-count complaint. First they claimed he lied when he said the storage unit business hadn't yet made a profit. They claimed to have proof that it had, but they never sent it to me. Then they went after Henry for April's college tuition, which is a kind of child support under Illinois law."

"I thought Henry was already paying her tuition."

"He was. To Paget Community College, where April goes now. But the petition asked for tuition to Northwestern, which no court would force him to pay. Not at his income level."

"So what happened?"

"They failed to show for a preliminary hearing and the judge dismissed it. This was in, let me see… late July."

"So it was dead?"

"Yep."

"What do you know about the storage unit business?"

"You know Henry. It was a hobby he hoped to turn into something more. Like the outhouse excavations that he turned into books."

"Well, let me know if you think of anything else," Jake said.

"Will do."

Jake's phone had vibrated with an incoming text while he was talking with Coogan, and he checked it now. It was from Erin: *Doc Franklin is working on Henry right now.*

Jake fought to keep his mind off what Franklin was doing to his friend's body, but he was glad the doc was moving quickly. The sooner Jake got the autopsy results, the faster he could use anything that turned up.

* * *

Conner's dad had been surprised to see him. Apparently he thought his son was an emotionless robot—like him—who wouldn't even come home to support his girlfriend when her dad had been murdered. After a brief and awkward conversation about school and the book his dad claimed to be writing, the old man went back into his office and closed his door.

So. Nothing had changed.

Conner nuked a couple of frozen burritos and took them up to his room. They weren't as good as the food at the dorm, but with some hot sauce they were edible. He sat at his desk and ate while he surfed the Internet. This time he found a news article with Mr. Fox's name in it. He emailed it to his professors, explaining that the murder victim was his girlfriend's father and asking to make up his assignments next week. Their responses trickled back to him over the next hour, every one of them agreeing to his request.

He got back to work on his current Empathy paper. It was about the Romani people—gypsies—living in Chicago. They'd come to Chicago in two separate groups in the 1800s, with a third group arriving in the 1970s. Conner had interviewed seven of them at their church and now had so much information he was having trouble focusing on one emotional hook to pull it all together.

His phone buzzed with an incoming call. April.

"Hey," he said. He spun his chair to face away from his computer.

"I'm *so* glad you came here even though Mom kicked you out. It feels good just knowing you're here. Even though you're not *right* here, it almost feels like you are."

"I can't believe anyone would hurt your dad. Even your mom still loved him."

"I can't either. I know it's stupid, but I always thought they'd get back together."

Conner thought Mr. Fox could have done a lot better, but he kept that opinion to himself. "How's your mom doing?"

"She's a disaster." April barked out a laugh that turned into a sob. "You know how dramatic she is. I finally put on one of those stupid movies she loves on Netflix. She fell asleep watching it."

"How about you?"

"I'm… I mean…." April sobbed and sniffled. "The cops think my mom did it."

"But only because she's the ex-wife, right?" Conner had watched enough *Law & Order* reruns to know cops always looked at the spouse. "They don't, like, seriously think she did it."

"I know, you're right. But remember Mr. Houser? My dad's friend? He's the one who told us about… Dad. He sent over this woman who's, like, the only person my mom still talks to from high school. She asked a lot of questions."

"Like she was undercover? Trying to get secrets from your mom? I thought that Houser guy was your mom's friend, too."

"Everybody picked sides when they got divorced. According to Mom, anyways." April sighed. "Mr. Houser will be chasing your dad next."

"My dad?"

"Because of their argument a—"

"But they straightened that all out months ago."

Her voice dropped almost to a whisper. "But then he got that email last week about the big bars."

Shit.

Conner occasionally read some of his dad's emails. A while back, after his dad lost his job and started acting weird, Conner snuck monitoring software on his dad's computer and captured his passwords. He wished he hadn't; as a result of it, he'd learned some things about his dad he'd rather not have known. But it didn't stop him from checking his dad's email from time to time.

"That email was just a hypothetical," he said.

"But what did your dad think when he read it? I mean—" April stopped, then whispered, "I think Mom's awake. I gotta go." She hung up.

Conner swiveled the chair back to face his laptop. But he couldn't refocus. April's question had struck a nerve. What would his dad have made of that email? Conner was sure he would have read the email the same way April had.

And he would have been just as pissed.

CHAPTER ELEVEN

Paget County Coins was on North Kirwin Road, occupying the end unit in an old strip mall behind a corner gas station. Jake remembered when the strip was first built out in the empty lands between Weston and Kirwin. Now bigger and shinier strip malls surrounded it, and the parking lot was cracked and potholed.

Jake parked the Crown Vic in a dark spot between the glow of two overhead lights, and checked his latest text from Erin: *Cowboy not in patrol logs but maybe his truck. A big white pickup with Texas plate TH TEX noted twice in logs over the last week. In the lot behind Henry's and once on West Douglas near Jefferson. Truck owned by Texas Corporation TH Inc.*

A truck from Texas. Texas was full of cowboys. It was a small leap to assume, for now, that the truck belonged to Cowboy.

Jake forwarded the text to Callie and asked her to re-canvass for any sightings on the truck.

He put his phone away and observed the coin shop. Its name was painted in green Gallic script on the middle pane of a wall of windows, and beneath it was a pot of gold under a rainbow. Beyond the glass was a vast space filled with antique furniture and bordered by display cabinets.

Jake folded the receipt from Henry's file, slid it into his pocket, and got out of the car. His holster dug into his side, and he adjusted it without finding a more comfortable spot. That was okay. Carrying a gun shouldn't be comfortable. A cop should feel it, to remind him why it's there and what it can do.

A bell jangled above Jake's head as he opened the door. A heavyset man on a high stool behind the back counter shot a glance his way, then turned back to watch three customers who ranged along the display cabinets, hunched over and peering down at whatever was below the glass. Jake wandered the floor to get a feel for the place. The store was stuffy and too warm, the air scented with the sharp tang of a lemony wood polish. No piped-in music, no conversations. Just an uneasy silence.

The furniture was of a hodgepodge of styles and qualities. To Jake's untrained eye, it didn't look any nicer than the junky stuff jumbled in Henry's basement, but everything was priced like a prized antique. He crossed the floor and looked into the glass-topped display cabinets. The cabinets themselves were real antiques—solid oak with carved detail and thick glass tops scratched over decades of use—but Jake was less impressed by the items for sale under the glass: watches, pens, jewelry, political buttons. Maybe to the right buyer it was valuable, but to him much of it would look at home in a junk drawer.

Jake felt eyes on him and lifted his gaze to find the big man watching him. Flipping open his badge open, he held it up. The man's eyebrows rose, and he dropped from the stool and waved for Jake to follow him through a doorway in the back wall.

A black curtain hung behind the opening, and when Jake pushed through it he found himself in a large windowless room. Narrow tables were spread with trays of coins and jewelry, lit by cheap shop lights hanging from the ceiling. A safe the size of a minivan sat in one corner, with a wheel on its door like the helm of a sailing schooner. Two women worked the tables, the light of a camera's flash pulsing from where one bent over an array of shiny objects.

"Sheila?" the big man said.

The older woman looked up.

"Cover the front for me."

Sheila took off without a word. The other woman went back to what she was doing.

The big man faced Jake. "So, what now?" He leaned against a scarred wood table stacked with coin catalogues. He wore smooth black slacks and a dress shirt pinstriped in faint yellow. He crossed thick arms over a hard round belly and gave Jake a don't-mess-with-me look.

Jake put his badge back on his belt. "I have some questions for the owner. Is that you?"

"Yes. Mark Griffin. My records are perfect and I don't appreciate you coming in here and implying otherwise. Who are you, anyway?"

"Detective Houser. Tell me about your business. Where do you get all this old stuff?"

"This is not *old stuff*," Griffin said. "These are personal treasures of people now deceased." He picked up a brooch from the table beside him. "This came from an estate sale over in Plano. Bought a box of jewelry for $96.50. This piece alone is worth somewhere in the five- to seven-hundred-dollar range." A small tag hung from the brooch by a white string. "See this code? With it I can tell you when and where and from whom I bought this piece and for how much. When I sell it, I plug all the sale information into the computer. The entire record is supported by scans of the bills of sale and proof of ownership, and it's all backed up to the cloud continuously. So ask your questions and I'll show you what I have."

"Why did the box of jewelry go so cheap?"

"It's a knowledge business." Griffin stuck out his chest. "You have to know what things are worth and where to find the right buyers. That auction did a bad job finding buyers."

"How are *you* with finding buyers?"

"I'm still in business." Griffin put the brooch back. "And I don't buy stolen goods, so just show me the photos already and we can be done."

"Let's sit down."

Griffin frowned, but he led Jake to a glassed-in office in the back corner where a giant oak desk held a pair of flat-screen monitors. Griffin closed the door behind them, then circled around the desk and settled into a high-backed leather chair. He gestured for Jake to sit in the leather couch in front of the desk. The couch was low and too soft, and Jake felt like a little boy sitting in front of his principal. The air in the closed space became dense with Griffin's cologne, a sweet balsam scent.

"Henry Fox," Jake said.

Griffin rubbed his hands over the desk, then pulled them back to rest on the edge. "Henry refinished this desk for me a few years ago." He shook his head. "What's going on here? I don't deal in stolen goods and I can't believe Henry does either. No way."

The clustered deception indicators—hand motion, body motion, answer avoidance, preaching his own honesty—meant Griffin was holding something back, if not lying outright.

"Did you do other business together?"

"A few years ago I sold him some old plat maps." Griffin slapped the desk with both hands. "He used them for that out-house project."

Jake pulled the receipt from his pocket, unfolded it, and laid it on the desk. "What's this?" He pushed the paper across the desk. Griffin's eyes followed it the entire way.

"It's a receipt. Part of the documentation I told you about before."

"For what?"

Griffin leaned forward. "I buy and sell precious metals. When prices are dropping or rising fast I do well. But it's usually gold." He spun the paper around, a thick finger with a glossy nail tracking the line identifying the object. "We use the metal's abbreviation from the periodic table—you know, like from chemistry class. So silver is Ag, like here. This was a one-hundred-ounce bar of silver of 99.9 percent purity with the mint mark GWU."

"You bought a silver bar from Henry?"

Griffin pulled the receipt back and looked across the top before jabbing it with his finger again. "Henry Fox. Paid him $2,312."

"What else can you tell me about this transaction?"

Griffin spun toward the monitors and pulled a wireless keyboard from the back table. "Read off the invoice number and I'll pull it up."

Jake read it out and Griffin typed it into his system. He hit enter with a hard jab, and several windows popped up on the right-hand screen. He manipulated them with the mouse then spun the monitor in Jake's direction. "He got the silver bar from a storage unit. He's one of those guys who bids on abandoned units."

Jake leaned forward to see the screen. It showed the bill of sale from the storage facility. "That only says 'Contents of storage locker 103e.'" Jake gestured toward the screen. "It doesn't say anything about a silver bar."

"I also have a signed affidavit." Griffin worked the mouse. Images popped and faded, then one froze on the screen. It was a form document, its blanks filled in by hand with a blue pen. On it Henry Fox swore he owned the "item(s) sold to Paget County Coins." The affidavit didn't mention the silver bar, but it did reference the invoice number, tying it all together.

"Can you print me out a copy?"

"I'll give you my entire record." More sliding and clicking of the mouse. The printer on Griffin's credenza bucked to life and started spitting out paper. When it was done, Griffin snatched the pages off the tray and slapped them down in front of Jake. "There you go." He settled back with his arms crossed.

Jake shuffled through the documents: the invoice, the storage facility bill of sale, the affidavit, a check made out to Henry, and a printout that appeared to be the shop's internal accounting of the transaction.

"What's this?" Jake held up the last page.

"Shows what I paid and when, and my sale of it. When it comes to commodities, I sell whenever the market spikes even a bit—especially silver, because the price bounces around like a pogo stick."

"What do you mean by commodity?"

"Meaning it's all the same. Gold is gold, silver is silver. Doesn't matter what form it's in, bars or ingots, as long as they're all basically the same purity, the price is determined solely by what they weigh. Not like jewelry, or even a quality coin, which sells for three or four bucks more per ounce."

"I see," Jake said.

Griffin's sudden cooperation after the initial bluster and denial raised a flag. Jake needed to absorb the information these printouts contained, as well as Griffin's narrative about the metals market. When he understood them better, he was sure he'd have more questions.

But Griffin still had more to tell him. Jake settled back onto the couch and spread his arms along its back. Relaxed—signaling to Griffin that he was here for as long as it took. "What did Henry say about the silver bar?" Jake deliberately worded his question with the implicit assumption that Henry had said *something* about the bar.

Griffin's chair squeaked as he turned toward the computer and fidgeted with the mouse. "I, uh… remember him saying they finally made a profit on the storage unit business."

Here we go. "They?"

"What?"

"You said Henry told you 'they' finally made a profit on the business. Was someone with him on it?"

"His daughter was with him." Griffin swiveled his chair and rubbed his face.

Two indicators of deception—the anchor point movement and touching his face. Griffin was leaving something out or lying. Not about April being involved, because that was too easy to verify, but something.

Jake needed more information before pushing harder. He would talk to the property crime division detectives about Griffin—and he would talk with April about the sale. Then he'd take another run at Griffin.

He collected the printouts off the desk and stood. "That's all for now."

Jake returned to his car, feeling confident his investigation now had the focus it needed. When something new and unusual entered a victim's life, it needed a hard look.

A silver bar was unusual.

And Henry always talked up his unusual outhouse finds. But he had kept *this* find a secret.

CHAPTER TWELVE

Lynn woke to a silent television, the Netflix logo bouncing across the screen. Her eyes felt crusty, and she wiped away the coarse lumps stuck in the corners of her eyes before realizing they were dried tears.

Henry was dead.

The tears came again. Then the sobs. She grabbed a tissue and pressed it to her eyes. She and Henry would never be together again. She needed to accept that she would be broke for the rest of her life. She needed to—

"Mom?"

Lynn choked back a sob and found a smile for her baby girl. "Come here, honey." She patted the couch next to her. "How are you doing?"

"Fine. I mean… I don't know." April sat down so heavily it was like her legs had failed.

"We're going to miss him, aren't we?"

"Yeah, but…" April bit her lip. "I'm worried too."

"There's no need to be scared, honey. Whatever your dad was into that got him killed, he—"

"He didn't do anything to get killed, Mom. That makes it sound like it was his fault."

"What I mean is, he lived his own life and nothing he was into—*if* he was into something—can hurt us." Lynn's legs started to shake as her mind flooded with doubts. What if that was wrong? She pressed her feet to the floor to still them.

"That's not…" April rubbed her face, then shook her head. "I'm not worried about that, Mom. I'm worried about you."

"I'm just—I'll be fine. It's *my* job to worry about *you*."

"But the cops think you did it."

"What?" Lynn's mouth dropped open and her heart skipped a beat. "What are you talking about?"

"You're the ex-wife. And you sued Dad all the time."

"That was for child support. For *you*." Lynn's chest was hammering now, blood rushing to her face. "But I don't get anything from—"

"Calling Mr. Coogan about the money right away made you look desperate."

"You heard that?" But of course she had. April was a champion snoop. She'd always known what was in her presents before she opened them Christmas morning.

"You didn't know that some trust gets Dad's money until you talked to Mr. Coogan. So before then… maybe… maybe you thought whatever Dad had came to you."

"But it doesn't."

"But you *thought* it might. Mom, didn't you notice that Judy Coogan came in right after Mr. Houser left? He must have sent her in. She was probably waiting outside."

Judy *had* shown up real quickly. Lynn had barely had time to tell April about her dad before Judy knocked. *Damn it.* "What do I do?"

"Well…"

"You have an idea. Don't worry about making me feel dumb, just tell me."

"Mr. Bowen."

"Conner's dad? But—didn't they work that all out months ago?"

"That was all before Mr. Bowen found out about the bigger silver bars."

"What bigger bars?"

* * *

While Jake was inside the coin shop, the other stores in the strip mall had closed and the parking lot lights had gone dark. Now only the light spilling from the coin shop windows showed the way to his car. He hustled across the potholed asphalt, ducking his chin and holding his blazer closed against the flapping breeze. He cranked the heater as soon as he got in the car.

As he pulled out of the lot, his intent was to go talk with April about her dad selling the silver bar. But he had second thoughts. It was now after nine, and he remembered how exhausting grief could be.

He gritted his teeth. He was thinking like a friend and not a cop. The silver bar was important, and April knew something about it. He should head straight there.

But those poor women.

His grip tightened on the steering wheel, his hands wringing it like it was the killer's neck.

Tomorrow.

They deserved a night to their grief.

Traffic was thin, and it took him less than twenty minutes to wind through town to his house on south Webster. He'd bought the two-bedroom ranch from the estate of the original owner because of its amazing location—a half block from Redhawk Field and two blocks south of downtown. He was in the process of remodeling the house, replacing its warren of tiny rooms with a single master suite on one side and a great room/kitchen combo on the other. It would kill resale, but reselling it wasn't his plan. This house was for him. It was his second attempt to move out of the apartment he'd created in the old commercial building on Spring Street, and he planned to make this one stick.

He parked in the driveway next to the empty dumpster, then walked through the garage and the big screened-in porch into the house. The smell of freshly sawed wood always made him feel like he was making progress with the remodel. He had completely gutted the main rooms, the walls were drywalled and primed, and the floors covered in plywood underlayment. The whole space was a giant blank slate waiting for him to unleash its possibilities.

For now, he'd furnished the big room with two card tables—one by the fridge to hold the microwave and coffee-maker, the other in the corner for eating and working—and a low table under the front window for his old college stereo. He took off his blazer and hung it over a chair at the work table, then grabbed a beer from the fridge and stood by the front window, staring out at his new neighborhood but seeing none of it. His thoughts were on Henry. He'd been a great friend, always—

A knock on the front door. He flipped on the outside light. A petite blond stood there, holding a foil-wrapped plate. Erin. He opened the door.

She stepped inside, holding up the plate. "I managed to save a slab of lasagna from the twins. Thought you could use it."

The tangy tomato aroma made Jake's mouth water. "Were they okay with that?" The twins were in tenth grade and famous, even among their peers, for their eating abilities.

She shrugged, her green eyes twinkling. "They can stand to miss a third helping once in a while." She looked around for a place to put the plate down, and settled on the work table.

"Can I get you a beer?" Jake asked.

"Sure."

He got her the beer, and they sat together at the table. Jake's gun dug into his gut, so he pulled the holster off his belt and set it on the table.

Erin's gaze dropped to the gun, then came back up to his face. She smiled softly. "I know you… aren't a talker, Jake. But if you want to…"

"How are *you*?" Jake asked.

"I'm… shocked, like everyone I guess. Even working in law enforcement and knowing how random crime can be, I just can't believe it happened to someone like Henry. He was so…" Erin balled her hands into fists and pounded them gently on the table. "I just want to *do* something. You know?"

"There are a couple things you can do for me."

"Name them," she said.

"How about the forensic accountant?"

"He'll be at Henry's first thing."

"I'd like you to take a hard look at the guy who owns Paget County Coins, Mark Griffin. And at his business. Has property crimes busted him for anything? Does he get sued a lot? Like that."

"How's he connected?"

Jake explained the receipt he'd found and the conversation he'd had with Griffin. The two of them then fell quiet, each lost in their own thoughts. Erin nursed her beer. Then suddenly Jake remembered something he'd known since high school. Erin hated beer.

"Sorry about the beer. I don't have any Pinot Grigio on hand."

Erin shrugged, then stood. "I should get home. Be sure to eat that lasagna."

"You know I will."

They hugged, a long tight embrace of old friends. Then she was gone.

And Jake was alone.

Again.

CHAPTER THIRTEEN

Jake leaned back in his chair and sipped his beer. An image flashed through his mind: the bright red arc of Henry's blood drawn into the paper next to his head.

He squeezed his eyes shut and focused his thoughts on the case.

Henry's murder had to be about the silver bar. The child support saga and Lynn's money troubles were ordinary by comparison. Most murder was ordinary, but most murder victims hadn't sold a silver bar they'd kept secret from their closest friends.

He finished the beer and considered having another two or twelve of them. But tomorrow was going to be a big day. He'd get Dr. Franklin's autopsy report and the forensic accountant's report on Henry's records, and he'd find out what April knew about the silver. He'd get the results of Callie's follow-up canvass on the truck, dig into the Cowboy, and talk to Lynn about the most recent child support petition she'd filed.

He stared at his beer bottle, picking at the label. He and Henry had enjoyed a lot of beer together over the years, starting with a stash they found hidden in Burlington Woods when they were in junior high. The three of them—Coogan was there too—made the most of their find.

Before he knew it, Jake had his phone out and was calling Coog. He felt like he had to share this memory with someone. And he couldn't share it with Henry—never again.

Coogan laughed when Jake explained why he'd called. "It was Lowenbrau!" he said.

"You sure?"

"Would I forget my first beer?"

The two men reminisced for a while about those days—Coogan remembered a lot more details than Jake did—before going silent.

"I still can't believe it," Coogan said quietly.

"Yeah."

"You'll find the guy."

"I will." Jake was sure of that. What he wasn't sure of was what would happen when the justice system took over. It was a garble of politics and prejudice all the way from the politically sensitive state's attorney and his rubber-stamp grand jury to the elected judge and the everyman jury. Anything could happen in that miasma.

"Hang on," Coogan said. "Judy wants to talk to you."

A shuffling sound, then Judy's voice came on the line. "Hey, Jake."

"Hey, Judy. How was Lynn?"

"Really torn up." Judy's tone was heavy. Somber. "And I feel bad, because I found myself judging her for it. She divorced Henry *so* long ago. And last time I saw her she was so mad at him. All worked up about college tuition."

"Northwestern?"

"I think so." Judy sighed. "But don't try to interrogate me."

"Judy…" Jake struggled for a softer explanation, but she beat him to it.

"I watch enough cop shows to know the ex is always a suspect." Judy exhaled loudly through her nose like she did when she was mad at him for keeping Coogan out late. "But I'm not your informant."

"She's not a suspect, just a person of interest."

"Just!"

He'd made it worse. "Your cop shows are right," he said. "Statistics and procedure require me to look at her. But it's a formality. The more I know, the faster I can strike her from my list."

Judy was silent for a few seconds. Then: "Well, you know how Lynn can get going worrying about herself. She was wondering about insurance and Henry's will. April cut her off—several times. But you know, Lynn never let go of April's hand. I went there to comfort her, but she had April and... it's their grief. I guess it's normal to want to hold on to it before sharing it."

Jake had seen it many times during his career. He'd even experienced it himself when Mary was killed. It had taken him a while before he could let other people in. "Well, I'm glad you went over there. Now she knows she has someone to talk to when she's ready."

After talking with Coogan and Judy—sharing grief with them—Jake's mood was lighter, but he was still too wired to sleep, and despite the aroma of that lasagna, he wasn't ready to eat either. So he changed into jeans and a T-shirt, put on his work boots, and went down to the basement. When you lived in a house during a remodel, there was always something to do. And the basement alone had provided far more work than Jake had anticipated.

The original owner had finished half the basement off as a rec room, complete with a fireplace, walnut paneling, and Berber carpet. But after the man died the place had deteriorated badly. His wife had lived into her nineties and apparently never went into the basement. Water had seeped in, and mold and rot had ravaged the carpet and paneling. Jake had had no choice but to gut it.

Before he was halfway done with that, a freak storm flooded the basement while he was in Arizona visiting his dad.

Jake heard about the storm and called Henry to check on the house. Sure enough, thanks to a failed sump pump, the entire basement level was knee-deep in water. Henry drained it and replaced the sump pump before Jack even got home. That was the kind of friend Henry was.

Since then, Jake had been busy pulling out everything that wasn't structural or part of a house system. All he had left to remove now was the fireplace: a giant, fieldstone-faced, concrete block structure set right in the middle of the basement. Now felt like the perfect time to pull out the sledgehammer and burn off some energy.

He pulled on a pair of leather gloves and safety glasses, swung his arms a few times to loosen up, then got to work. It took a few blows to find a rhythm, but soon pieces of stone and concrete block were shooting off in all directions. The impacts from the eight-pound sledge vibrated up his arms and into his shoulders. He changed his point of attack every few strokes and rested every twenty, counting them out with grunted breath. His ears rang with the loud strikes, and soon his hearing dulled so he could no longer hear the continuous hum of the dehumidifier. Even his own gasps faded. Masonry dust hung in the air and stuck to his sweaty skin and to his teeth. But he kept at it, resting when he needed to, spitting out the grit, shoveling the rubble to the side, until every stone and block was separated from the others. It was a substantial pile. Tons—literally.

Sometimes it just felt good to destroy something.

And now he was ready for that lasagna.

He showered, put on some sweats, then cut a big square from Erin's lasagna and stuck it in the microwave. While it heated, he checked his phone. He had a missed call from Doc Franklin. He called him back.

"Jake, I found something." The doc's voice was quick and breathy.

"Tell me."

"I agree with DC Chen that a single blow killed Mr. Fox. I believe it came from a heavy piece of silver. Probably five pounds or more. I found a piece of it embedded in his skull."

Silver. "How do you know it was heavy?" Jake trapped the phone against his shoulder with his cheek, pulled his notebook out of his blazer pocket, and did some quick math. A hundred-ounce silver bar weighed about six pounds.

"By the damage. The dynamic energy needed to do the damage we see to Mr. Fox's skull would take a light object moving impossibly fast, or a slower object of more mass."

"Doc, I'm not following."

"Dynamic energy is a formula: one-half mass times velocity squared. I can calculate the dynamic energy needed to do this damage based on the characteristics of Mr. Fox's skull. Then it's simply a matter of playing with some numbers to see what the possibilities are to achieve that energy. Either a super-fast object or a slower object of large mass. Also, the angle of the wound tells us it was an overhead blow. I understand the ceiling there is normal height, so the blow was probably delivered by a person swinging the object in an arc. Fast-moving objects travel in straight lines."

Jake still didn't entirely follow all of that, but he cut to the chase. "Could a six-pound silver bar do this damage?"

"Yeah, that's heavy enough, and yes, I do believe the weapon was an ingot of some kind. Most 'silver' objects—candlesticks, jewelry—are actually sterling silver, which is about eight percent copper. Pure silver is too soft for most functional uses. But this silver in Mr. Fox's scalp is ninety-nine point nine percent pure, and was poured into a form as a lump. I can see the folds under the microscope. That strongly suggests an ingot."

"Doc, thanks for working late to help me out."

"Erin told me he was a friend of yours. Let me know what else I can do."

After the call Jake sat down at the table with the lasagna. Talking about what had killed Henry had destroyed his appetite but he shoveled it in anyway; he would need the fuel for tomorrow. If the murder weapon was a silver bar, then Henry had found more than just the one he'd sold to Griffin. But how many more? At over two thousand dollars each, a pile of them would add up to real money very quickly. Did Griffin know about the other bars? He hadn't volunteered anything, and Jake hadn't known to ask him. Maybe he'd decided he could make more money by stealing the bars rather than buying them.

The owner of Paget County Coins would definitely get some hard questions tomorrow.

CHAPTER FOURTEEN

Jake woke suddenly, his eyes snapping open to find the room bathed in the soft light of approaching dawn. The distant hum of traffic along Washington Street was the only sound. He threw off the sheet and sat up, the draft from the ceiling fan chilling his sweat-drenched body. He knew from the sweat and the fog in his brain that what had woken him wasn't outside, or even in the room. It was in his head.

Royce Fletcher. The name burned him with shame.

He swung his feet off the bed, then bent over with his elbows on his knees, his back and shoulders protesting after the work he'd done in the basement last night. He plodded into the bathroom, sweaty feet sticking to the floor, flicked on the light, splashed cold water on his face, then stared at himself in the mirror, water dripping off his nose.

His thoughts went back to that night twelve years before.

Everyone had agreed it was a good shooting.

It was his second case as lead detective, and he was convinced the burglary of an electronics warehouse had required inside information. He and his partner, Lee Hilleman, were working their way through finding and interviewing the warehouse's former employees. Royce Fletcher was one of those former employees, and when Jake showed his badge in the man's apartment doorway, Fletcher bolted, pushing past Jake and knocking Hilleman down.

Jake gave chase. Hilleman screamed behind him that he was okay and to get the bastard.

Jake burst out the building's front door in time to see Fletcher duck down the opposite alley. Jake followed, dodging garbage cans and pallets until he cornered Fletcher behind a string of retail stores off Halsted. He pulled his gun, and Fletcher turned to face him with a revolver in his hand.

Jake's memory was clear up to this point. After that, it got fuzzy. But a surveillance camera had recorded the encounter, and Jake watched that recording at least a hundred times with his union rep before the mandatory Officer Involved Shooting hearing. The rep pulled apart every frame to explore what could have been happening—not an easy task, given the lousy camera angle and the lack of sound. By the time Jake testified, he honestly wasn't sure what he actually remembered and what was merely one of the possibilities the rep had planted in his head. Had Fletcher pointed his gun at Jake or just held it out? Had Fletcher emitted an unintelligible scream when cornered, as Hilleman had testified, or had he yelled that he surrendered? Had Jake shot the man because he feared for his own life, or because of the anger burning inside him since his wife's death?

Jake hadn't found answers to those questions in twelve years, and he certainly wouldn't find them today.

He splashed more cold water on his face, then toweled off. He felt a hard knot of pain in his lower back, and arched to try and release it, but instead his deltoids joined in. Maybe he was getting too old to swing a sledgehammer.

As he worked through a series of stretches on the bedroom rug, thoughts of Henry's murder flooded him with fresh sadness. Lynn and April would be yearning for even one moment of normalcy this morning. Jake had been in the same dark place in the days and weeks after his wife's murder. But eventually their grief would settle—as his had—to a kind of dullness that allowed a return to almost-normal life.

Until something triggered a memory and it all flooded back in.

For now, all he could do for Henry's family was to find the person who had taken Henry from them.

Over a bowl of cereal, Jake entered his notes into the murder book, an online tool where all relevant information was entered and available to other contributors and department decision-makers. Erin had already started a book on Henry's murder with the basics, and Jake added what he had learned. Building the book was a great opportunity to give everything a fresh look. He liked working on it in the morning to let whatever wiggled through his subconscious during the night come to the surface. This morning he didn't have any great insights, but the work organized his thoughts.

He got dressed, grabbed his equipment, and headed out.

* * *

At this early hour the VFW's bar wasn't open yet, so there was little traffic on Jackson. Jake maneuvered the tight left into Redhawk Court and rolled slowly toward Henry's house, gravel crunching under his tires. A hard wind swirled leaves around a tired minivan parked in front of the house. A patrol car guarded the front door, and Officer Grady popped out of it as Jake parked.

"Accountant's the only one inside," Grady said, noting Jake's arrival in his book. "FIC Fanning and his team left last night at 8:46 p.m. They finished everything except the barn, which is sealed. Coming back for that today. So long as you don't go in the barn, you don't need gloves or booties."

"Thanks, Grady. I'll stick with the accountant."

Inside, the house was so still it felt like it had already forgotten Henry. Even the citrus air freshener had faded so much it barely scented the air. Jake kept his eyes off the blood on the dining room floor, his pulse fluttering as he stepped over the spot. He found the department's forensic accountant, Ryan Beck, hunched at the computer in the back office, his jacket wrapped tight against the chill coming through the thin walls.

"Anything yet?"

Beck jerked in his chair, then held out his hands. "Frostbite."

Jake turned on the space heater, stretched its cord across the floor, and set the unit a few feet behind Beck's chair.

"Thanks. Didn't notice that."

"What've you turned up?" Jake bent to look at what Beck had on Henry's computer. Spreadsheets were windowed across it.

"Well, nothing funky. That's for sure." Ryan stroked his goatee, then gestured to the filing cabinets and computer. "Mr. Fox's records are really well organized and detailed. Even without the tax returns I can see in his divorce files where he made his money and where he spent it. The mandatory financial disclosures are super comprehensive."

"And they jibe with the real numbers from the books?" Jake asked.

"To the penny." Ryan worked the cursor down the spreadsheet. "He pieced together a decent living with the odd jobs and the outhouse book. The one thing I find curious is he doesn't show any income from excavating the pits themselves. Wasn't some of the stuff he found worth money?"

"It goes to the landowner. Henry's deal is he gets to write about what he finds and keep one souvenir of his choice."

"Then so far everything does jibe."

"What about the storage unit business? Do you have that figured out?"

Beck nodded. "Erin told me to start there. Each time Mr. Fox bought the contents of a storage unit, he assigned it a number and made a new manila folder with the number on the tab. There's a spreadsheet of expenses and revenues for each unit organized by that assigned number." Beck rolled his chair to the filing cabinet, the wheels making a hollow rumble across the wood floor. He pulled a file from the drawer for the storage business. "If I enter this file number…" He entered the digits penciled on the tab into the computer, then clicked through a couple screens of data. "You get this spreadsheet." He pointed to the file and back to the screen. "This unit netted $340.57, represented by these two entries, one for $170.39 and the other $170.38. While the other guy was involved, Mr. Fox always gave him the extra penny."

"What other guy?"

"His partner." Ryan clicked the mouse a few times, then pointed to the monitor, which displayed a check from Fox Handyman Service, LLC, to Jim Bowen. "Bowen also provided the start-up capital: five thousand dollars." Ryan clicked the mouse and typed in a few characters to reveal the check from Bowen.

Jake wrote down Bowen's name, address, and phone number from the check, his energy surging. This guy was his next visit.

"You said *while* he was involved."

"Yeah, it looks like sometime in June Mr. Fox went solo. No more splitting the profits."

"Had he paid the front money back to Bowen?"

"Not yet."

Jake pulled out the file with the receipt for the silver bar. "Tell me about this one," he said. "File thirty-seven."

Beck pulled up a spreadsheet. "Let's see. He bought the contents of that unit from Weston Self Storage on May eighth for $115, and sold it in different lots for a total of $300. Profit of $92.50 each." He scrolled down. "Wait a minute. Then on

June fourteenth he entered another $2,312 coming in from 'PVC,' then issued a pair of checks for $1,156 each."

The proceeds from selling the silver bar. "Why separate checks?"

Beck shrugged. "Mr. Fox always waited until he'd liquidated everything before issuing the checks. This is the only time he issued two checks on a storage unit. That I've seen, anyway. And look here. The $2,312 came into the account as cash, not as a check from PVC. Hang on a minute." He typed and clicked. "Yeah. Mr. Fox has sold a few other items to PVC—furniture and some jewelry—and always got a check. Never cash, except here." He sat back. "Do you want me to go deeper into this one?"

"Do it. And take a close look at these while you're at it." Jake pulled out the documents Griffin had given him about the transaction.

* * *

Grady signed Jake out of the crime scene, and Jake's tires threw gravel as he goosed it down the narrow driveway. Bowen only lived a couple miles to the west, and an early-morning visit from a homicide detective might shake him enough to spill everything he knew.

As Jake drove, his conversation with Griffin came back to him. Griffin had said *they* finally made a profit on the storage unit business. Jake had assumed he was referring to Henry and April, but maybe he'd meant Henry and Bowen. Jake played the conversation back from memory but wasn't sure if Griffin had sidestepped the question or if Jake had led the man away from the truth with his follow-up questions. Griffin would get another visit.

But first, Bowen.

CHAPTER FIFTEEN

Jake climbed the concrete steps to Bowen's front door, his left hand pressing the gun to his side to stop it from bouncing. Touching it called up an image of Royce Fletcher, blood bubbling on his lips as he died from a sucking chest wound. A nauseating reminder of what a gun could do.

As he hit the top step he pulled his hand off the gun and refocused. Bowen was involved in the silver, and the silver had killed Henry. Literally. It was time to find out what Bowen knew.

He rang the bell, stepped back, and worked up the right amount of smile.

The door cracked open and stopped with a clank against the security chain. A woman, presumably Bowen's wife, appeared in the crack, then the door closed while she unlatched the chain before opening wide. She was within a few years of Jake's age, maybe forty-five, and wore a thick white robe held tight to her chest with a hand near her throat.

"Yes?" She smiled and tilted her head, straight brown hair draping across her shoulders.

"Good morning," Jake said. "I'm Homicide Detective Jake Houser with the Weston Police Department. I'm looking for Jim Bowen."

The woman's face drooped on the word "homicide."

"Henry Fox," she said. "We heard about it on the radio this morning." She stepped away from the door, slippers scratching on the slate floor, and waved for him to come in. "I'm Susan. Jim's wife. I'll get him for you."

Jake stepped inside and closed the door behind him. The sugary scent of cinnamon buns wafted in from the kitchen straight ahead, and he spotted a monstrous pan of them on the stove. A wheeled suitcase with a laptop bag propped against it stood against the wall next to the kitchen entry.

His pulse ticked faster.

"Someone traveling?" he asked. He kept his tone conversational, polite curiosity.

Susan tracked his gaze to the luggage. "Oh, those are mine. I got back from a trade show in Cincy late last night. Haven't unpacked yet."

"How long were you gone?"

She scratched her jaw, then took a half step back. "Three nights."

Bowen didn't have his wife for an alibi.

She leaned down a stairway to the left and called out, "Jim, can you come up? There's a police officer here to see you about Henry."

After a short silence, a door squeaked.

"Here?" a man's voice called. It was deep and scratchy.

"Yes."

"Send him down."

"Why don't you come up? I'll make more coffee."

"No." Bowen's voice was suddenly sharp. "I'll talk to him in my office."

Mrs. Bowen shrugged apologetically to Jake. "First door on the left."

Jake thanked her and took the stairs down, wondering why Bowen wanted to talk there. Given the choice, most people wanted a family member with them when talking with the police.

But not people with secrets.

The door Mrs. Bowen had indicated stood open. Jake stepped through and found Jim Bowen sitting behind his paper-choked desk. He was dressed in khakis and a soft green sweater—cashmere, maybe—over a blue button-down. He looked like a former high school offensive lineman gone soft. He was closely shaven, and with the door closed, the woodsy scent of his aftershave filled the room. Why did all men's colognes smell the same?

Jake extended his hand across the mess. "I'm Detective Jake Houser, Homicide. It's okay if you want your wife to sit in with us."

"We're fine." Bowen grabbed Jake's hand and gave it a quick squeeze and release. His hand was soft and slippery with lotion or sweat. Jake fought the urge to wipe his own hand on his pants.

"Sorry for the mess." Bowen waved his big soft hands across the desk. "Battling a deadline."

"No problem. I appreciate you taking the time to talk with me." Jake spotted a folding chair pushed into the narrow space between a bookshelf and a stack of boxes. He pulled it out, unfolded it, and sat down.

Bowen frowned, then came around the desk and closed the door, separating him even further from his wife's support. He definitely had a secret. The wife seemed to already know about Bowen's relationship with Henry, so that wasn't it.

"That's a nice chair," Jake said, nodding at the Aeron behind the desk. It was a twin to Henry's. They must have found them in a storage unit during the partnership.

"It's okay."

"Mr. Fox has one exactly like it," Jake said, offering Bowen an easy way into the storage unit business.

Bowen didn't take it.

Instead, he sat down and swiveled to face the computer on the return between the desk and a credenza clustered with equipment and reference books.

Jake pulled out his notebook, opened it to a blank page, and tapped his pen against the paper. The strategy often led to subjects giving him something worth writing down.

But Bowen didn't bite, and the silence lengthened.

Jake waited.

Finally, Bowen spoke. "We heard about Henry. Couldn't believe it."

"Why not?"

"I mean, it's hard to believe anyone I know might be murdered. But Henry... he's about the nicest guy I know. Always helping people out."

Bowen still hadn't mentioned the storage unit business.

"How did you know Mr. Fox?"

"Well, I'm trying to be a writer—no, I *am* a writer. I've got to own that. And he got his book published, so I thought he could help me."

"Was he able to?"

"Not yet. He writes—wrote—non-fiction. I write fiction. This is a thriller." He pointed at the screen.

"Is that what you do for a living, Mr. Bowen? Write novels?"

Bowen grunted a laugh. "Not for a living. I'm retired from sales. Not by choice. I picked up writing to fill the time." He shrugged. "But you never know."

"So what's the deadline?"

"One thousand six hundred and sixty-seven words a day, every day, all month." He scratched his chin. "Sounds silly, I suppose, but that's the goal for Na-No."

Jake was familiar with the term. National Novel Writing Month. The local newspaper wrote it up every November. Thousands of people across the country trying to write a novel in one month.

"How're you doing so far?"

"I'm hitting my numbers."

"So your connection to Henry was the writing?" Jake tapped his notebook, warning Bowen any lies would be written down.

Bowen nodded. "I think he could have helped when I'm ready to publish." He shrugged, then swiveled toward his computer, his fingers finding the keyboard, his eyes wandering to the screen, where a cursor blinked at him from the end of a short paragraph of text. Antsy to get at it—like his daily word count goal was a real-world deadline.

Jake sat quietly, waiting. It had to be obvious to Bowen that the writing connection was news to Jake, and that something else had brought him here. As the silence lengthened Jake almost smiled. Bowen had a secret weighty enough to risk this deception when the connection was so easy to find.

Bowen typed a few letters into his document, then stopped. His eyes shifted to Jake, then toward the door. "If there's nothing else, Detective?"

Nothing else? They hadn't exchanged fifty words.

Jake put an angry edge into his words. "You can't really think I came here to talk about your book. I'm here about the storage unit business."

CHAPTER SIXTEEN

Jake got the result he expected. Bowen snapped to attention. He swallowed and spun his chair to face Jake.

"I, uh..." Bowen shut his mouth and gathered himself, then pushed his chest and chin out and got loud. "What about it?"

Confront. Defeat. Bowen had definitely played football.

"Tell me how you came to be Mr. Fox's business partner."

"Well, I thought his book, *Outhouse Archaeology*, was fascinating. I like old stuff like what he found in those pits. So when I heard he was doing a second book I asked if I could partner with him—but he wanted to keep that for himself." Bowen settled into his chair, as if calmed by having told some truth. It must have felt good, because he continued.

"But then he asked me if I'd ever seen the reality show where people bought the contents of abandoned storage units. He wanted to get into that but didn't have the start-up money, so he invited me in. It sounded like fun, so I gave him the start-up money and off we went."

"Other than the money, what was your part in it?"

"I was going to help with all of it. Go to the auctions, move the stuff out of the units, go through it and sell it. But I have a bad back, so I stopped helping with the heavy lifting after a few units. And Henry was better at the bidding—he knew what the stuff was worth—so then I mainly helped with selling the stuff. Taking it around to the places Henry said would buy whatever the thing was. But Henry didn't really need me for that either, so we ended the business."

"But he kept going on his own."

"So I heard," said Bowen, a blush of anger reddening his face.

"How much did you front him for the business?"

"Five thousand. Way back in February."

"Did you get it back?" Jake asked, knowing he hadn't.

Bowen licked his lips and turned toward the blinking cursor on his computer screen. "We're okay."

That was a lie. And the man had still not mentioned the silver.

"It seems like an interesting business." Jake scribbled in his notebook as he floated his next line. "I bet there's some unusual stuff in those storage units."

"That's why I got into it. But we never found anything really cool. We did okay, money-wise, with the furniture and old toys and books. Henry knows that stuff. But we also got burned a few times. Twice, boxes were filled with old patient records, which cost us because Henry insisted on shredding them. Forty bucks a box."

"What's the most interesting thing you guys found?"

Bowen's gaze wandered away, and he rubbed his face while he set the chair twisting again. Three indicators of deception. Lies were coming.

"Henry got excited about old books a couple times, but none of those were worth real money."

Bowen turned back to the blinking cursor.

So much deception here. Maybe Jake had already found Henry's killer.

Jake leaned back, his hand falling to his waist and hitting the hard lump of his gun. He snatched his hand back. He wasn't going to need the gun with a faded athlete like Bowen. Then again, maybe that's what Henry had thought.

The silence lengthened, and Jake waited for Bowen to fill it. But Bowen must have convinced himself the silver was still a secret. He slapped his hands down on his desk and started to stand. "Well, if that's everything..."

"Tell me about the hundred-ounce silver bars."

Bowen flopped back down in the chair. His face flushed. Then he shook his head and pulled himself up to the desk, his expression suddenly hard. "What about them?"

"Were you unhappy with your cut?"

Bowen raised his voice. "I didn't do anything wrong!" His words, his tone, his behavior screamed deception. "Henry's the one who—"

The door burst open. Bowen's wife. She looked at her husband, then at Jake, then back. Both of them silent now.

"What's going on in here?"

"I asked your husband about the silver."

Mrs. Bowen opened her mouth, then closed it. Her face darkened and she shot a long look at her husband before turning back to Jake. "You need to leave."

"I'm trying to understand the relationship between your husband and Mr. Fox."

"Relationship!" She stiffened, straightening to her full height. "They were business partners. Nothing more!"

"Mrs. Bowen, if your husband answers a few questions I can strike him from my list." No one wanted to be on a cop's list. "If I leave now it'll be with the suspicion that Mr. Bowen murdered Henry Fox in a dispute over the silver bars they found in a storage unit."

"Out!"

Jake stood and faced Bowen. "We can clear this up right here if you tell me where you were night before last."

Bowen's eyes went to his wife, then back to Houser. "I need an alibi?"

Mrs. Bowen glared. "Tell the detective where you were."

"I don't have to tell him anything." Bowen's face bloomed red and sweat trickled from his temples.

"Then I'll note you don't have an alibi for the murder of Henry Fox, your business partner in the discovery and sale of the silver bars." Jake turned and left the room.

Susan Bowen followed him as he returned to the main level. A young man sat on the stairs leading up to the next floor. He was skinny and pale, with thick dark hair that swirled around his head like a mop. He gripped a smartphone in both hands, thumbs flying, and looked up from it with hooded eyes.

"Get out!" Mrs. Bowen yelled as Jake reached the top of the stairs.

He left.

* * *

Lynn woke to thoughts of Henry—and immediately started crying. But then she remembered the big silver bars. Henry had made April keep them a secret. He was always making her keep little secrets, undermining Lynn's relationship with April and making *him* the fun parent.

A sob broke through her anger. "He *was* the fun one."

Still, that silver…

It would solve all of Lynn's problems, and more. Five hundred giant silver bars! Each one ten times as big as the little bars Henry had found, which meant they were worth ten times as much. Twenty thousand dollars each. *Ten million* dollars. Lynn had had trouble even imagining it at first, but after a night dreaming about it she had their future all laid out. A big house in the Weston Historic District, a nice little shop downtown, a pair of fancy cars.

All they needed to do was *find* the silver. April didn't know where it was, but Lynn was certain she would figure it out. No one knew Henry better than April did.

She got out of bed and made a pot of coffee and some buttered toast. But she lost interest after the second bite.

"Mom?"

April's voice came through the wall from her bedroom, and the sound of her fatherless daughter's voice broke another sob loose from deep inside Lynn. Her baby was going to miss her dad. They'd always been so close, even when April entered her teens and things had gotten pretty ugly here.

"Mom? Come here! You gotta read these texts from Conner."

Lynn rose and walked to her daughter's bedroom. But as she reached for the knob, the door popped open so fast the air swept Lynn's hair into her face. April grabbed her arm and pulled her inside, then held out her phone.

"Start here."

Lynn took the phone, warm from April's hands. It was the first time she'd been allowed to touch it since she'd given it to April the previous Christmas. The thought her daughter trusted her enough to read a text from her boyfriend brought a small smile to her face.

By the time she'd finished reading Conner's string of texts her smile had faded.

That detective is here. Houser. Talking to my dad in his office.

Dads blabbing about his writing crap.

Cop led him into a trap about buying the storage junk.

Now the cop brought up the little bars and my dad lost it. Mom saved his ass as usual. Kicked Houser out of the house!!!

"Jake knows about the little bars," Lynn said, her stomach twisting. "He'll find out your dad gave me some of that money. He'll be mad I didn't tell him when he asked if I knew about anything new in your dad's life."

"Just say that it wasn't new—it was over the summer."

Lynn nodded, but she'd rather lie. She didn't want to get into anything about the silver. "Maybe he won't ask me. Maybe he won't ever figure out I know about the silver. Right?"

April took her phone back. "He's pretty smart, Mom."

"Maybe he won't talk to me again." Lynn sure as hell hoped not. "When he was here yesterday he said he wanted to talk to you next."

"I'll call him. Maybe I can figure out what he's thinking."

"Good idea." April was a lot better under pressure.

"But I think you're going to be okay, Mom. It sounds like Mr. Houser thinks it was Conner's dad. And it could have been. His mom was on a work trip that night, so Mr. Bowen was home alone. And he knew about the big bars."

"Jesus," Lynn said. Conner's dad. The idea that she might *know* Henry's killer sent a flutter through her stomach. "I'm sorry, April."

"Don't be sorry. I'd rather have Mr. Houser chasing after Mr. Bowen than chasing after you."

CHAPTER SEVENTEEN

Jake started the car and ran the heater. What had Bowen wanted to keep from his wife? She'd known about both the storage unit business and the silver, so Bowen had been worried about something else.

Jake took a minute to write down Bowen's exact words while they were fresh in his mind. When Jake brought up the silver, Bowen immediately denied doing anything wrong and said "Henry's the one who—" Then the wife barged in and saved him.

What had Henry done?

Something with the silver, clearly. When Jake raised the possibility of a dispute about it being a motive for the husband to kill Henry, neither Bowen denied it. And why the odd tension between them when he asked for an alibi?

Jake would come back at Bowen when he knew more. He would shake the truth out of the man.

He dropped the car in gear and headed back toward Redhawk Court. As he turned the corner he spotted a white crew cab pickup parked at the curb up the block. Fog covered its windshield except for a circular patch on the driver's side where it had been wiped away. Someone was sitting in the truck. Jake kept it in the corner of his eye as he finished the turn, and he caught the silhouette of a large man sitting inside, wearing a baseball hat.

Cowboy. And he'd been watching Bowen.

Jake slowed, checked his side mirror, and saw the truck cross the intersection behind him, a cloud of diesel exhaust swirling in its wake. Jake swerved into a driveway to turn around and follow, but got stuck there while a short bus passed.

"Come on!" He banged the wheel until the bus cleared his bumper, then backed out with a squelch of rubber, shot back the way he'd come, and turned up Bowen's street.

The truck was gone.

He sped down the block, stopped in the next intersection, and looked down each street. Nothing. He spent a few minutes cutting back and forth across the neighborhood, but there was no sign of the truck.

He pulled to the curb, called Erin, and asked her to put out a citywide BOLO on the truck. It was a big vehicle, and he had no doubt a patrol officer would spot it. Cowboy would be stopped and identified and questioned about what he was doing and where he was staying. Then Jake could have a nice chat with him.

"And I need you to dig up whatever you can on James Bowen and his wife, Susan." Jake explained who they were and their odd reactions to his questions.

"I'll get right on both," she said. "One other thing. About the dinner we had scheduled for tonight."

"What din—" But then he remembered. Erin had been pushing him to "get back out there" ever since he'd moved home to Weston. Once or twice a year he agreed to meet one of her friends over dinner. He always insisted Erin and her husband come along to keep it casual. Jake had no interest in a relationship and zero interest in "hooking up" with one of Erin's friends. "Oh–yeah. Can we cancel it?"

"Don't worry. I already rescheduled it. You have two weeks to come up with a new excuse."

"Thank you," Jake said. "I don't think either of us would be good company right now."

"No, we wouldn't."

They sat silently with the line open between them, Jake drawing comfort from the connection. But he had work to do. "I have to go."

He ended the call, but the phone vibrated before he could get it back in his pocket. He answered it.

"Hi, Mr. Houser."

It was April, her voice low and soft like he remembered it when he used to take her to church. They would always go out for a treat afterward, and she would ask for extra marshmallows in her hot chocolate.

"How are you, April? I'm so sorry about your dad."

"Thanks. Mom said you wanted to talk to me about Dad? Can we just do it by phone?"

"I… okay. I assume your mom told you your dad was… killed?"

"Yes." A sob burst from her. "She told me."

A phone call wasn't going to cut it. She needed him to be there. As her dad's friend and as her godfather. "You know what? I'm coming over right now."

He hung up and was dropping the car into gear when his phone buzzed with a text from Beck: *Call me.*

He hesitated, thinking about April, but then made the call. Beck might have found something to unlock this thing.

Beck answered with a sleepy "hello" that ended in a stretched-out yawn.

"What do you have for me?"

"You know the printout you gave me from the coin shop? The guy told you it was for a hundred-ounce silver bar, right?" Beck's voice gained energy as he talked. "I checked, and the spot buy price for silver that day was $23.12 an ounce. That's what he paid Mr. Fox for it. By check, made out to Mr. Fox, not to the LLC, by the way. Even though Mr. Fox deposited cash into his business account. But according to the paperwork he gave you, the coin shop guy sold the bar for $3,312, which was ten dollars an ounce higher than its value. An even thousand dollars over what he paid for it. And on his printout the sale amount was underlined, which probably means it's clickable on his system to information about his sale of the bar. He didn't give you any information on that sale."

"Did the spot price go up before he sold it?"

"Nope. It was flat."

Jake mulled that for a minute. "He said the bar was a commodity worth only what it weighed in silver, not like a coin, which is a collectable and sells at a premium."

"Maybe there was something special about this bar that made it collectible."

"What could make a silver bar collectible?" Jake wondered. "They're all the same."

"Provenance, maybe. Those picker guys on TV are always willing to pay up for stuff if there's proof it once belonged to someone famous. Cars. Clothes. Sunglasses, even."

Jake thanked Beck for the update, then headed for April's house. But his mind was once again on silver. Why had someone paid Griffin a thousand-dollar premium for the bar? And why did Griffin make his check for the silver bar payable to Henry rather than to the business, like he did for everything else he bought from Henry?

The answer to that second question seemed obvious: Henry had decided to keep the money for the silver separate from the business, so he could keep it all to himself. But then something must have changed his mind, because he deposited the cash into his business account and split it with Bowen.

What changed his mind? Bowen must have discovered Henry's deception and forced the split.

Henry's attempt to cheat Bowen out of his half of the proceeds was the thing Henry had done wrong that Bowen had started to explain before his wife burst into the room and shut him up. Or maybe... maybe she had shut him up to keep him from talking about what happened *next*. When Bowen found out there had been more than that one bar, killed Henry, and took them.

Plausible.

Bowen was quick to anger and didn't have an alibi.

And the silver was a great motive, especially if there were a lot more bars.

None of this put Henry in a great light. Cheating a business partner—or trying to, anyway? It didn't seem like the Henry Jake knew.

But everyone had secrets.

CHAPTER EIGHTEEN

Jake parked the car short of the leaf pile the Fox women had built at the curb. He sat for a minute, trying to focus on what April needed from him—as her dad's friend and her godfather—instead of what he needed from her. When she was growing up there'd been a lot to his role as her godfather—religion classes, first communion, confirmation—but nothing since then. Yet now…

If she wanted to talk about God and death and the hereafter, he owed her his best effort.

As he walked up the driveway, the cold wind whipped through his pant legs. More leaves had fallen and a wind-blown berm blocked the front door, so he headed around back. The twang of an old Garth Brooks song came from the house and faded as he rounded the back corner.

He gave the door a hard rap to pierce through the country music. A half minute later the door swung inward—Lynn, wearing baggy gray sweatpants and a Redhawks hoodie, her hair flat on one side, a pillow crease on her cheek, her eyes red.

She was grieving; that was clear. Jake could only imagine how much worse April would be taking Henry's death. She still loved her dad and had spent as much time with him as any teenage girl Jake knew. Lynn, on the other hand, had divorced Henry because she thought he was a failure.

This was not going to be easy.

* * *

Lynn wished Jake had just talked to April on the phone. But April thought this visit gave them a good chance to point him at Bowen. Lynn just hoped she could pull it off without spilling about the big bars.

She pointed Jake to a chair, then went to the counter and poured him a cup of coffee. Her hand shook, and she grabbed the cup with both hands to steady it. She took a breath, pulled her shoulders back, and turned back around to give him the coffee, only to find him still standing in the doorway, looking at her with flat pity in his eyes. She knew she looked like hell.

"Sit," she said, her voice louder than she intended.

Jake sat and took the cup from her. "How are you doing, Lynn?"

"Fine." Lynn sat down across the corner of the table from him. April had told her to hide her lies behind as many truths as she could—especially truths that looked bad. "No, not fine. I can't decide what to do." Truth. She laughed softly. "Shower? Get dressed? Cry some more?" She shook her head, then tried to smile. "How are you doing?"

"Well, I'm..." Jake stopped. "I'm more concerned with you, and with April. She called me to talk. That's why I'm here. How is she?"

Lynn pulled her mug to her chest. "She's strong. Stronger than me. She's going with me to Everson's this afternoon."

"They'll take good care of you."

"You know... I..." Lynn shook her head. "April said I came off kind of desperate yesterday."

"I don't think—"

"Let me get this out." Tears welled and spilled onto her cheeks. She hadn't planned that, but it would help sell what she had to say. Honest emotion. "I'd been living on those child support payments, and I wasn't ready when they stopped." She wiped her eyes with her sleeve. "But I get nothing from his death." Truth.

"What can you tell me about the silver Henry found?"

Lynn looked down at her cup and took a long breath. "He gave me half of his share. That money kept me out of bankruptcy."

"Half of how many?"

"Ten bars. He gave me half of what he got for them. A little over ten thousand dollars."

Jake nodded like he was adding the information to a list. "Why did Henry give you half? His child support obligation had ended, right?"

"You know why." Her tears started up again. "Because he's so damn good." She sniffled and grabbed a tissue from a box on the table and dabbed at her eyes. "*Was* so good."

"You'd filed another child support petition that claimed he lied about his income and asked for tuition to Northwestern?"

"Henry basically *told* April he'd pay for her to go to Northwestern. Why would he do that to her? Pure nonsense. So I threw it back in his face. I dropped it when he shared the silver money with me." More truth. "Do you think he was killed because of those bars? That was months ago, and he sold them all to that coin dealer on fifty-nine. The leprechaun guy with the TV commercials."

"Not all."

Shit. Did he know about the big bars? Lynn took a long breath to calm herself. "What do you mean?"

"He had a partner. A guy named Jim Bowen."

Perfect. "Bowen got half because he was Henry's partner in the storage unit business. When Henry started that up I thought, 'Here we go! Another Fox classic!' But then he made money on it." Everything Henry touched since their divorce had turned to gold.

"Fox classic?"

"Like the shit-shoveling thing he did. That book was my idea, you know. I told him if he was such an expert he should write a book about it. God, that book was embarrassing. Everyone knowing he liked to dig through other people's shit. Like it was okay because the shit was old. It was still shit."

"The book turned out pretty well."

She shook her head. "I deserved a piece—"

"Mom?"

April stood in the doorway leading into the hall. Lynn set down her coffee mug, sprang up, and held her daughter tight. "Good timing," she whispered.

"Good morning, April."

"Thanks for coming over, Mr. Houser."

"I'm glad you feel up to talking to me."

"I hope I can help."

"I'll be in the living room," Lynn said. She pushed through the door into the hall, but stayed there after it swung shut. She needed to hear this.

* * *

Jake's mind thrummed with Lynn's disclosure that there'd been twenty bars and Henry had given half to Bowen. If that was true—and he no reason to doubt it—Bowen had no motive to kill Henry and was an unlikely suspect, despite his bizarre behavior.

"Mr. Houser?"

Jake yanked his attention away from Bowen to April. "Yes?"

"Can I ask you a question?" April slid into the chair her mom had used. She looked tired, her cheeks pale, her eyes dull and sunken.

"Of course."

"I've been trying to, you know, pray. For my dad? And I don't remember—not exactly, anyway—how to do it."

Jake smiled; he could handle that question. "Do you remember the prayer we did in church? All together holding hands?"

"Our Father who art in heaven? That one?"

"Exactly. All you have to do is recite that prayer, and God will look into your heart and know what you're asking of Him."

"He looks inside me and knows?" She licked her lips and her shoulders curled forward.

"That does sound too simple, doesn't it?" Jake said. "If you want to, you can talk to Him like He's a friend."

She sat up straighter. A small smile. "I'll try it."

"Good."

"I overheard you talking to Mom about Mr. Bowen."

"His name came up. He was a business partner of your dad's."

She nodded. "For a while. Then they quit it."

Jake kept his expression neutral. "Do you know why?"

"That silver you asked Mom about? My dad found twenty silver bars and didn't share them with Mr. Bowen. Not at first."

"Do you know why that was?"

"Dad said he found them in a pit, you know, an outhouse hole. But Mr. Bowen said Dad found them in a storage unit." She shrugged.

"And because they were partners, Mr. Bowen thought he was entitled to half."

April nodded. "But Dad found them in an outhouse pit, so they all belonged to him."

"Or the landowner."

She shrugged again. "I guess."

"Do you know where the pit was?"

"I don't remember if he ever said."

"You were with your dad when he sold one of the bars to the coin shop."

"I remember that." She wiped her eyes.

He needed to wrap this up. "Your dad told the coin shop guy he got the bar from a storage unit."

April frowned and shook her head. "I'm *sure* Dad told me he found the bars in an outhouse pit."

"What do you think?"

"Are you asking me if I think my dad lied about it?" Her voice spiked. "Lied to *me* about it?"

"No, I…" Jake grimaced. But that was *exactly* what he'd just asked the grieving daughter of his murdered friend. "I'm sorry, April. Thanks for talking with me. I'll be… ah, I'll be going now."

CHAPTER NINETEEN

Lynn stepped away from the swinging door when she heard Jake get up from the kitchen table. April had handled that perfectly. Jake definitely thought Jim Bowen killed Henry. The man had been so mad about the smaller bars, he must have freaked when he found out about the big ones. He must have thought he should own half of those, too.

But only half. The rest belonged to her and April. Five million dollars' worth.

A dark thought occurred to her. What if Bowen already had the silver? Jake had said the killer searched Henry's house—maybe Bowen had found the bars, or had found something telling him where they were. Which meant if Jake arrested Bowen, then she and April would lose their chance at the silver.

Lynn had to do something. Right now.

She ran to the front door and stood on tiptoe to look out the little window. She had to *do* something to stop Jake, or at least slow him down.

Think, you stupid woman!

* * *

Jake shook his head as he walked back to his car. Telling his grieving goddaughter her dad might have lied to her… that was an asshole move. But the questions had to be asked. Those and a lot more. Hell, if anything, he'd stopped short. Maybe he *shouldn't* be handling this case.

And it looked like Henry *had* lied: his business records reflected only one of the twenty bars he'd found, and he'd told two different stories about where he'd found the silver. Which raised the question of just how many lies Henry had told, and to whom.

"Jake! Hang on a minute."

Lynn came out the front door waving, leaves flying into the air from her thrusting feet. He stopped in the driveway and braced himself. He deserved whatever she was going to say to him.

"You're barking up the wrong tree with Jim." She stopped close to him, hugging herself against the cold. "He was here with me the night Henry was killed. We've been seeing each other for a couple months."

"What?" He was so startled that was the only question he could find to ask.

"James was here that night."

"Bowen was here? Because you and he…?"

"Like I said. We're seeing each other—"

"Where did you meet him?"

"Where I work. He started coming in a lot after he lost his job. We got talk—"

"He's married."

Lynn looked away. "I know that, Jake. Any man worth spending time with is married."

"And you're what… in love?"

She shook her head and her gaze came back to meet his. "It's just a… he would never leave his wife. Can't afford to."

"Does April know about—"

"No!" She hugged herself tighter, against the cold, or against his gaze, he couldn't tell. "No one knows. No one."

"Why didn't you tell me this before?"

"You never said anything about him."

She was right. "You and Bowen were together here that night? Tuesday night?"

"His wife was out of town for work." The cold was reddening her pale cheeks. Her gaze kept skittering away from his. Embarrassed. "We take time when we can find it."

"Wasn't April home?"

"She doesn't have classes on Wednesdays, and she stayed overnight at her friend Lucia's house."

Jake gritted his teeth. Back to square one. "Thanks for telling me, Lynn."

Behind her, April appeared in the doorway, still looking shell-shocked by Jake's insensitivity. He raised a hand in apology, but she looked down and stepped out of sight.

"Jake, I'm not proud of this," Lynn said, "so if you can keep it quiet, I'd appreciate it."

"I can't promise that."

He left her standing in her yard, arms wrapped around herself.

Lynn's story explained why Bowen had wanted to meet in his office with the door closed: he'd been worried Jake would bring up the affair. Or maybe Bowen had been prepared to disclose it if pressed but then his wife came into the room.

But Lynn's news did more than explain Bowen's behavior. It knocked both Bowen and Lynn both out of the suspect pool.

* * *

Lynn pulled the storm door open and stepped inside, a sharp gust of wind pushed a scatter of leaves inside with her. "Damn it." She kicked at them.

"Mom!"

She flinched away from April, who stood against the wall just inside the door. "April! You scared me."

"Mom!" April's voice was so loud the storm door vibrated. She gave Lynn her *I can't believe you're so dumb* look. Lynn had seen it a thousand times during April's teens.

"I had to do something," Lynn explained. "We can't let Jake arrest Mr. Bowen because he might already have the big bars. I'm sorry I didn't talk it through with you first, but there was no time. And now Mr. Bowen will owe us, see? For giving him the alibi. So if he already has it all, he'll give us our share."

"But—

"And after we get what's ours, then I'll tell Jake I wasn't with Mr. Bowen. I'll say he forced me to say that. He's a big man. Jake will believe me."

"Mom! I didn't sleep over at Lucia's Tuesday night. I got tired of her and came home around midnight. All Mr. Houser has to do is call her and he'll know."

"Then you can tell Jake you were here and saw Mr. Bowen."

"You want me to lie to my godfather?" April went into her room and slammed her door.

If April didn't back up Lynn's story, Jake would assume she'd been working with Bowen. And then he'd come for her.

The two bites of toast Lynn had eaten burped into her mouth. She ran into the bathroom and retched into the toilet. The retching went on and on, nothing but thin strings of gastric fluids after the first heave. When her stomach finally quit contracting she wiped down the toilet and flushed it, then washed her face with cold water.

She had to stop thinking about the silver, and *start* thinking about saving herself. At the rate she was going, she would talk herself straight into jail.

* * *

After Mr. Houser left, Conner had gone to his room to review his notes from his Romani interviews, which wasn't easy with his parents downstairs shouting at each other. Mom pushing Dad to *just go and talk*—where and about what, Conner didn't catch. Dad insisting he could handle it. Maybe this was about marriage counseling again.

When the shouting stopped and the house went quiet, Conner tiptoed downstairs, looked around, checked the garage. His mom's car was gone. He called April, but she didn't answer. Probably all tied up taking care of her mom. Mrs. Fox was a real piece of work. Immature, needy, and dumb as a rock. April definitely got her brains from her dad.

He went back to his room and returned to his notes. The stories the Romani had told him had been so interesting he'd ended up with more material than he could ever use. But somewhere in here were the exact right details to create the empathy he was shooting for.

His phone vibrated against his desk. April.

"Hey, baby." He used the rumbly sex voice that made her laugh.

"Hey." No laugh.

"How are you and your mom doing?"

"She's so damn dumb!"

Conner laughed softly, but cut it off. Now wasn't the time. "Sorry, baby."

"She told Detective Houser she was with your dad all that night."

"What?"

"She told him they were having an affair."

"Oh, shit," he said, then realized what April was saying. "She gave him an alibi!"

"I'm sorry—"

"Because she thinks he did it! Your mom thinks my dad killed your dad and has the silver."

"Yeah. I think so."

"Cops *always* verify alibis." More *Law & Order* knowledge. Which meant Houser would talk to people who knew April's mom and his dad. He'd poke away until he found the truth.

"I want to see you," April said.

"Will your mom let me come over?"

"What do you think?" Of course not. But *his* parents weren't home...

"Let me check something," he said.

He opened the find-my-phone app from their cell phone provider. He and his mom were on the same plan, and both showed on the map. His dad's didn't, of course; that would have made it harder for him to keep his secrets. Conner's mom was at a building out on Bond Street. He opened Google Maps and zoomed in on that location. The Law Offices of Donald Hallagan. He clicked the link. The guy was a big-shot criminal defense attorney. *Shit.*

"My parents went to see a lawyer."

"Guilty people get lawyers."

"My dad didn't do it, April. I know he's an asshole, but... he can't have done this. No way."

"Then who did?"

"I don't know." He sighed. "I just..."

"I'm coming over." She hung up.

Was she right?

Had his dad killed Mr. Fox?

CHAPTER TWENTY

Jake parked in the middle of the lot at Paget Valley Coins. The sun shone bright but didn't generate enough heat to beat the chill from a stiff breeze coming from the west. He hustled across the cracked pavement and inside.

Griffin stood behind the counter talking to a customer, so Jake waited while Griffin explained the "risk" the customer had assumed when he bought a used "timepiece." It sounded like a speech he'd given to other unhappy customers. This one, a cantankerous old coot with stiff gray bristles sprouting from his nostrils, had apparently bought a used Omega from Griffin and was mad about what it had cost him to get it running. Griffin pointed out the disclaimer on the man's receipt, reading out loud that "PVC makes no warranty about the condition of any timepiece. Timepieces are bought at the buyer's risk." The same message was posted on the wall behind Griffin in red and orange.

Jake's distant law school memory said a "conspicuous" disclaimer meant buyer beware. This sign was extremely conspicuous.

After the old man repeated his argument for a third time, Griffin coldly asked him if there was anything else he could do for him—as if this matter had been settled. The guy cussed his way out of the store.

Jake took the old guy's spot at the counter.

"You're back," Griffin observed without enthusiasm.

"I have more questions."

Griffin gave Jake a hard-guy stare, but Jake waited him out.

"My office." Griffin headed for the back room. "Jason, you have the floor."

A twenty-something in khakis and a red polo shirt hopped down from a tall stool in the corner and started pacing behind the counter.

Jake followed Griffin through the curtain. The same two women worked the cluttered tables in the back, hard at it with tablet computers, taking photos and tapping information into the screens.

"Is it always like this back here?" Jake asked.

"We're doing an internet auction," Griffin said.

Neither woman looked up as Jake and Griffin weaved through the maze of tables to the glass cube in the back, where Griffin plopped into his executive chair. Jake closed the door, then stood at the end of the desk. Griffin pushed his chair back and stared up at Jake. The miasma from the man's cologne was thicker today.

"Why the auction? You said you were great at finding buyers."

Griffin sneered. "That's for special pieces. I use the internet to sell the rest of it." He waved his hand at the tables where the women worked. "In just a few hours I can unload stuff that would otherwise sit around for years."

"What about the commodities like we talked about yesterday?"

"The silver?" Griffin glanced at the closed door, then turned the big monitor to face Jake. "Silver—and gold and platinum and palladium, the precious metals—are all sold in the market." He pointed at a flashing number. "The spot price for silver is $20.47 an ounce right now."

"What was it on June tenth?"

Griffin licked his lips then worked the computer, his cheeks reddening. "Spot price was $23.33."

"So you would have sold the hundred-ounce bar you bought from Henry for a hundred times that, give or take a buck or two. So about $2,333?"

Griffin squirmed in his chair.

"You sold it for a thousand more than that," Jake said. "What made the bar a *special piece*?"

Griffin's face flushed a deeper red, and his gaze flitted once more to the closed door. He opened his mouth, then went still and sucked air through his teeth. "I can't say anymore. People who hold precious metals don't want anyone to know who they are or what they have, or even why they collect it." He shook his head. "Not without a subpoena."

Jake sat on the couch. "You mean a search warrant." Griffin needed a reality check.

"Whatever."

"The two are very different," Jake said. "A subpoena is a gentlemanly discovery tool where one party in a lawsuit politely asks the other party for a certain type of document. If this were a contract dispute, for example, I would go back to my office and type up a subpoena for any and all documents and/or computer records related to the sale and purchase of the silver bar identified in the invoice." Jake smiled. "But this is a murder case, and we use search warrants. A search warrant is a court order giving me access into every nook and cranny of this store, including that vault and every drawer inside it, and every byte within your computer system. If you insist on me getting one, I'll seal this place up tight—with you outside—to protect the contents until the warrant gets here."

Jake leaned back, throwing an arm up on the back of the couch. "Your call."

Griffin reached for his phone. "I should call my lawyer."

"A guilty person would." A lawyer would tell Griffin to call Jake's bluff and demand a warrant. That tactic would fail, of course; Jake had never been refused a search warrant on a murder case in Paget County. But it would slow him down by an hour—maybe longer if the duty judge was at lunch.

"I didn't kill Henry." Griffin pulled his hand slowly back from the phone, adjusted himself in the chair, then rubbed his face. "I'm an honest businessman. When I buy something I make the seller swear he owns it, and I take down his information. If it turns out he didn't own it, then you got him dead to rights. And I don't cheat people. I paid Henry a fair price for that bar. Market price."

Deception. Selling his honesty, touching his face, and the anchor point movement. Did he kill Henry, or was he just a cheat?

Jake leaned forward. "Mr. Griffin, tell me—"

"I sold that bar to a collector."

Now we're getting somewhere. "Who?"

Griffin wouldn't meet Jake's eyes as he answered the question. "Guy named Titus Cole. I'll print out his information and then you can leave me alone."

The name tickled Jake's brain as he waited for the printout. He'd heard it recently, but couldn't place it.

Griffin pulled the sheet off the printer and slid it across the big desk.

"Tell me about Titus Cole," Jake said.

"It's all there." Griffin pointed at the printout. "That's what your search warrant would find about that silver bar."

The printout had Cole's name and address—an apartment on Jefferson out near the cookie factory. He had bought the bar with cash.

"How did you find this buyer?" Jake asked. "A guy willing to pay a thousand-dollar premium for a silver bar?"

"He found me."

Jake waited, relaxing into the couch. Griffin eyed him, then shook his head and started talking.

"He came in here maybe eight or ten years ago. Said he collected silver bars. The bars are finished to different qualities and come from different mints, so they have different mint marks. He asked me to let him look at everything that came in. I'd call him and he'd come in and take a look, but he didn't buy much. And I see some weird stuff. Whenever the price spikes up a bit—like in April of '11 when the price was double what it is today—sellers pop out of the woodwork with all kinds of stuff. So I told him he should tell me what he was looking for and I'd keep my eye out. Save himself the trips up here."

"Trips up here?" Jake rattled the page in his hand. "This says he lives here in town."

"Now he does. But back then he lived in Texas."

CHAPTER TWENTY-ONE

"A tall stocky guy in his fifties?" Jake asked. "A cowboy type?"

"No." Griffin looked down at the desk, his face shading red. "Older. Probably seventy. But solid, in good shape." He motioned with his hand along his jaw. "A strawberry on his face along here."

The old man with the binoculars talking with Bantam down by the barn.

"And did he tell you what he was looking for?"

"Said his collection needed a bar with the GWU mint mark. So we agreed I'd let him know if I bought one, and he would pay me a premium for any bar I found." Griffin leaned back in his chair. "Fox came in with the bar. I saw it had that mark, and I bought it for a fair price. There was no other collector market for the bar, so I sold it to Cole."

"How do you know there was no collector market for it?"

"I posted the question in a precious metals forum." Griffin shrugged. "I got no responses."

"Did you tell Cole where you bought the bar?"

Griffin looked away, rubbing his big hands across the desktop.

Jake waited.

"He said he needed provenance. You know, proof of where the bar came from. So I gave him a copy of the receipt."

"With Henry's name on it."

"Yes."

"How many of these bars did you buy?"

"From Henry?"

From Henry? Griffin was not a good liar. Jake stood up and came around the side of the desk. "From Henry and whoever else."

Griffin spun his chair to face Jake, sweat beading on his upper lip and along his hairline. "Nineteen. From Henry and his partner."

"Name?"

"What's he got to do with anything?"

Jake waited.

Griffin looked down. "James Bowen."

"How many bars were there in total?"

"I think there were twenty. Henry kept one."

"Did Cole buy all of them from you at a premium?"

"He only wanted the one. He's a collector. One was enough."

"Who bought the rest?"

"I sent the other eighteen through the exchange. That's all my records will show."

"When did all this happen?"

"I bought all nineteen of them within a couple weeks of that first sale."

"Why did Cole come to you? There are a lot of coin shops." It seemed like too much of a coincidence that Cole was looking for a certain mint mark and put out a feeler at the exact coin shop where the bar eventually appeared.

"Why not me?" Griffin was suddenly angry, like the question challenged him.

"Seems like Cole would have had to make a deal like yours with every coin shop around if he wanted to stop coming up here."

"Well, there's really just me. No one else—not in the western suburbs, anyway—deals in bulk silver. There's not enough money in it for as heavy as it is, but I've always liked it."

Jake peppered Griffin with more questions, but learned nothing else. He got the name of the precious metals forum, and permission to use Griffin's password to look at its archives. He told Griffin to print out his complete records for all the bars and courier them to his attention at the station.

Back in the car, he spent a few minutes making notes of his conversation with Griffin. Then he sent Erin a text to have her run Titus Cole from Texas, and now of Weston, through the system. And while he tapped the text into his phone, one thought kept bouncing around his skull.

A second man from Texas.

* * *

Jake pulled onto North Kirwin Road. Traffic was light as he headed for another strip mall, this one on Route 59 just south of Diehl Road.

Jake had met Levi a few months earlier while investigating skeletal remains found in a car pulled off the bottom of Radar Grove Lagoon. They'd become friends since then, and their talks had even led Levi to pursue an associate's degree in criminal justice at Paget Community College, with an eye toward becoming a private investigator. His keen observational skills, appetite for minutiae, and facility for online research made him a natural for modern PI work. So Jake used him for background research when a case entered a world he wasn't familiar with.

Like the markets for buying and selling silver.

Levi worked at Paget County Cleaners, one of three tenants left in a long strip mall south of the tollway. Jake sat in his car watching through the store's front window as Levi waited on a customer. When the woman left, Jake went in, enjoying the sudden warm humidity and the clean scent of starch.

Levi greeted Jake with his wide smile. "How are you doing on this day of the feast of..." His fingers flew across his keyboard. "St. Delmatius of Rodez?"

Levi had recently found a website listing Catholic feast days and thought the idea of feasting every day was hilarious. The truth was, Levi could use some feasting. He was skinny as a rail, probably weighed less than one-thirty.

He waved for Jake to come around the counter and sit on the extra stool. "Look. We have a dozen reasons to feast today." He pointed to his computer screen, where an open window showed a long list of saints.

"Actually, I'm working a case and need some help." Jake settled on the stool and pulled his feet up onto the rests.

"The Fox murder?" Levi kept up with local police activity. "I read he was a lifelong resident. Did you know him?"

"Yeah. I knew him well." Jake told Levi a little about Henry and their friendship, but he brushed off Levi's attempts at sympathy. "Levi, this case is moving fast and I need some help. I'd like you to search the archives of a precious metals forum for me." He explained what he knew about the silver, and gave Levi the web address and Griffin's password. "But if you can get into it without using his password, that would be better. Then we can re-create the search if we need to."

Levi's eyes lit up at the opportunity to learn something new. He rubbed his hands together and grinned. "I'm on it!"

CHAPTER TWENTY-TWO

Jake parked in front of Titus Cole's apartment building and left the car running and the heat on. Before going in, he called Erin to see what she'd learned. Cole was clean in Illinois but had a record in Texas, where he'd lived for forty-two years before coming to Weston.

"Looks like he was questioned seven times. Five times for assault and twice for battery. He was charged for one of each. Both dismissed. Hang on."

Multiple assaults and batteries. Cole was a violent man, and Henry had been killed by sudden violence. Jake's pulse ratcheted up. If Cole was Henry's killer, Jake would make sure he paid for it.

As he waited for Erin to continue, he looked at Cole's building. The bright clear day didn't do it any favors. It probably looked better in the dark. It had to.

"Yeah," Erin said, "that's over a couple decades, ending eleven years ago. Nothing since.

"The incidents have anything in common, other than the lack of convictions?"

"That's all I have so far."

Cole had been the subject of seven police investigations without being convicted of a single crime. That took more than luck. That took power. Connections. Or money.

"Did you hear me?" Erin said.

"What?"

"I said I talked to Beyoncé and fixed things."

Jake could only think of the one Beyoncé. "What are you talking about?"

"Are you listening now?" Erin said. "I said I rescheduled the dinner. Her name is Janet."

"Not Beyoncé?"

"Right." Erin hung up.

The dinner date fix-up. He'd forgotten all about it.

He headed up the walk toward Cole's apartment, his right hand moving under his blazer and onto the butt of his Glock. Simply checking his equipment, he told himself. The gun was one tool of many, his last resort when all else failed. If he had left it in its holster twelve years ago when he went into the alley with Royce Fletcher, maybe he could have talked the man down.

Or maybe he'd be dead instead of Fletcher.

A fold of carpet runner held the building's door open. Jake stepped over it into a hallway that smelled so strongly of garlic he could taste it. He ignored the buzzers and mailboxes and found Cole's apartment, the first unit on the right. He paused before knocking; the over-excited voice of a television sports commentator came through the door. That level of enthusiasm could only be about football.

He knocked. The television muted, and the door swung open.

"Yes?"

Titus Cole was about Jake's height and stood very straight for an older guy—shoulders back, chest forward. His gray hair was trimmed short, with a silvery stubble on his face. The left side of his jaw held the blotchy discoloration Jake had seen when the man was talking to Bantam.

"I'm Detective Houser, Weston PD."

"Yes?"

"You were outside the crime scene on West Jackson on Wednesday afternoon. I'm following up."

"I guess I should have expected a visit."

"May I come in and ask you a few questions?"

Cole's lips pulled into a hard line, and he shook his head slightly before stepping back and waving Jake across the threshold. The man had a lot of experience with police; no doubt he'd learned it was best to cooperate and get it over with.

Jake sat on the couch, a worn plaid that didn't match anything in the room. He gave the space a once-over. It looked like it was furnished with junk left behind by other tenants—except for the TV, of course. It was huge, and the complex graphics of a sports program pulsed across it.

Cole sat down in a wood chair across from the couch. "Fire away, Detective."

"What were you doing in the park that afternoon?"

Cole put his hands on his knees, then licked his lips. The chair creaked under his shifting weight. Deception was coming. "I'm a birder. My focus is the birds of the Paget River Valley. The stretch from Riverfront Park there all the way north through Blackwell Forest Preserve."

"Why the Paget River Valley?"

"It has strong year-round populations and gets high-volume migrations in both the spring and fall. The fall migration is just finishing up. With all the wetlands along the river there's also an amazing amount of waterfowl. I identified a barnacle goose two weeks ago. A wild one, not a domestic escapee. Created a buzz in birder circles."

Too much detail; the explanation sounded prepared.

"Did you meet Henry through your birding?"

Cole nodded. "Barn swallows. I was along the river and spotted some bombing in and out of the park. They're fast little buggers, but I was able to follow them to the barn. Henry was working in it and we got to talking." He shrugged.

"When was that?" Jake asked.

Cole's eyes jittered as he tried to figure out the safe answer; he didn't trust the truth. "Midsummer. The week after the Fourth."

A lie; Cole got Henry's name from Griffin in June. "How often did you talk?"

"If I saw him out in the barn, I'd stop for a chat." Cole leaned back in the chair, comfortable with how he was doing. "He was a nice guy. Always willing to give an old-timer a few minutes."

"Have you seen anyone else acting suspicious around the Fox place?"

"No."

"What's wrong with the birding in Texas?"

Cole nodded with a little smile. "After living there for forty years I'd covered it. Plus, the migration isn't as intense. When I retired, I decided to relocate for a new birding challenge."

"And Paget County is a well-known birder paradise?"

"I don't know about that, but Weston is a nice town. Good people. The birding. And lots of quality football." He gestured at the TV. "Some great high school teams, college has North Central in D3 and Northern Illinois in D1. And of course the Bears are only an hour away."

Jake didn't buy it—there were plenty of towns with good football and birding. But he wanted to know more about the man's arrest record and about the other Texan before he started hitting Cole on his lies. For now, it was enough to know Cole had lied about his relationship with Henry. There was nothing casual or accidental about how Cole had met Henry; he had sought him out to get his hands on the silver.

"Thank you for your time, Mr. Cole." Jake stood and headed for the door. "I'll let you know if I have any more questions."

Cole said nothing as Jake opened the door, but as soon as it was closed the TV volume came back on. Something about the Bears.

As Jake walked back to his car, his phone vibrated with an incoming call. Callie Diggs.

"What do you have?" he asked her.

"A man down and across the street from Fox's driveway saw that big white truck—he noticed it because of the Texas plate. It was parked on Jackson a few days ago—couldn't remember which day—in the afternoon, with a man sitting in it. And the morning bartender at the VFW comes in through the park and saw a big white crew cab down there about ten one morning. Thinks it was this last Monday."

"Either of them add anything to what we know about Cowboy?"

"The neighbor said the symbol on the hat was the flag that boats use to indicate a scuba diver is in the water."

"Diver down," Jake said. Which explained Mrs. Brueder's reference to Van Halen. The band used that flag on an album cover way back in the eighties. "What did Henry's customers have to say?"

"I've gotten through to enough of them to get a picture," Callie said. "Fox had been a bit off the last few weeks. Quiet. Distracted. Rescheduled a bunch of jobs from early November to later in the month."

"Any sense of why?"

"Two of the women said they asked him... they've known him their whole lives. He told them he was just tired."

Henry had been into something. Something that brought trouble to town that he had not seen coming. Something bigger than the twenty bars. Those had all been wrapped up in June. "Thanks, Callie."

"I've got a task force thing today, all hush-hush, but call me if you need me to chase down something else, and I'll jump on it as soon as that's done."

As Jake got back in the car, Cole's violence-filled criminal record thrummed away in his head. He pulled up his contacts and scrolled until he found the number he wanted. Grady answered on the first ring.

"Grady here."

"I'd like you to help me with something else today."

"I'm off now so I'm wide open."

"Perfect. I can get you overtime. I just questioned a guy who lives out on West Jefferson. I need you to sit on him, watch what he does and where he goes. Make sure he doesn't dump anything." Jake explained who Cole was and how he was connected to the case.

"Is this the guy?"

"Maybe, maybe not. I need to develop more information before I push him. But I want to see if my visit spooks him at all."

"I can be there in ten."

Grady's academy training had covered surveillance, but Jake explained how he wanted him to handle the loose plain-clothes tail. When he hung up he settled back to wait. He wanted to make sure Cole didn't leave before Grady arrived.

CHAPTER TWENTY-THREE

Jake's phone vibrated with another call. He kept his eyes on Cole's apartment as he answered.

"Houser."

"Good afternoon, Detective Houser!" The caller sounded delighted to be talking to Jake. "This is Donald Hallagan. I have some help for your murder case."

Jake sat up straighter. Hallagan was Paget County's best criminal defense attorney. A call from him told Jake two things: One, his investigation had struck a raw nerve. And two, he would never get to talk to that raw nerve again without Hallagan present.

"What can I do for you, counselor?"

"James Bowen has retained me to help him explain himself in the unfortunate matter of Mr. Fox."

Hallagan's careful wording implied that a simple explanation would exonerate Mr. Bowen without the need for a pesky criminal charge or trial. But the explanation wouldn't be an alibi. An alibi didn't need to be delivered by a high-priced mouthpiece.

"I talked with Mr. Bowen just this morning," Jake said. "He must have run straight to your office." Guilty people ran—away, or to their lawyers. "How did you find time for him? Is he an old friend?"

"He and his wife are here with me, and I suggest we come down to the station right now and put your mind at ease so you can concentrate on finding the killer running loose in our community."

Mrs. Bowen's presence explained why Bowen still wasn't using his alibi. "That's very thoughtful, counselor. Conditions?" Hallagan always had a few.

"Nothing to the press, of course. And Mr. Bowen will be disclosing facts that suggest behaviors that might be against other laws, ones you don't enforce, and you must agree not to refer him for prosecution to the relevant authorities."

Hallagan was referring to the same things all his white-collar clients worried about—tax laws and the IRS. Jake didn't care about tax laws or how Bowen might have screwed the IRS. He only cared about catching, and punishing, Henry's killer.

The problem was, he knew Hallagan would only let him talk with Bowen once. Jake needed to know more before he took that shot.

"I'm happy to hear Mr. Bowen is willing to talk to me. His behavior this morning left his name on my suspect list." Jake tapped his pen against his notebook. "But I'm chasing a few other leads today. How about telling me what Mr. Bowen has to say? Off the record, of course, until we get together to finish the formalities."

"One moment, Detective."

By suggesting that he was prioritizing other leads over talking to Bowen, Jake hoped to lure Hallagan into sharing Bowen's story now. It worked nearly every time.

Grady's white Jetta pulled to the curb twenty yards down the street. Grady looked in Jake's direction and held up his phone. Jake raised his free hand in a "wait a minute" gesture.

Hallagan came back on the line. "Agreed. My client met Mr. Fox through—"

"I have the background, counselor." Lawyers loved to hear themselves talk, and most would start a story with the Big Bang if you let them.

"Of course, Detective."

Hallagan started off by explaining how storage unit auctions worked. The storage facility operator would cut the lock off the unit, open the door, and allow any prospective buyers to look at the contents from outside—no picking through it. Most stuff was generally in boxes, and the boxes were rarely labeled, so the only things clearly visible were the pieces of furniture. Henry was the expert on that stuff, so Bowen added little value to the bidding. As a result, he stopped going to the auctions, leaving that part of the business to Henry. If Henry bought a unit, he'd secure the contents inside the unit with a new lock, then bring Bowen in later to help move the contents to Henry's barn. There they would sort it together, deciding what to toss, what to sell, and where. That was the process, at least, until Bowen's back started bothering him and he couldn't help move the contents anymore.

"Which meant Bowen's involvement in the business was over," Jake said. He realized he was defending Henry, but it needed to be said.

"They were *partners*, Detective. Illinois law is very clear on their legal duties to one another. And Mr. Bowen still sorted the finds and helped sell them."

"Tell me about the silver."

"With Mr. Fox buying the units and moving the contents on his own, he had first look at everything in the unit, which made it easy for him to cheat my client."

Jake's patience was growing thin. "The silver, Don."

"When Mr. Fox found the silver, his good judgment left him, and he decided to keep this find from his partner. When my client found out about the silver, he confronted Mr. Fox—"

"And killed him," Jake said, to interrupt Hallagan's flow and let him know he'd given his client a motive.

"And they worked it out. This was months ago, Detective. Houser. The two men split the find—after reimbursing my client his start-up money—and then terminated the partnership."

The front door to Cole's apartment building swung shut. Jake looked toward Grady's car and found him watching the door. They exchanged a look. Jake shrugged.

"Why had Mr. Fox kept it from Bowen?" Jake asked. Henry had never been motivated by money.

"Money poisons some men, Detective."

"What did he *tell* your client to explain not sharing the silver?"

"One minute, Detective." Hallagan was back on the phone in thirty seconds. "Mr. Fox told my client he didn't find the silver in a storage unit. He claimed he found it in an old outhouse pit."

"And why couldn't that be the truth?"

"My client has proof that it is not. And when we paper up a deal as we discussed, I'll provide it to you."

"How did your client find out about the silver?"

"Not until we have the written deal, Detective."

Bowen had probably learned it from Lynn—pillow talk—but he couldn't have told his wife that. "How about something more concrete than this circumstantial information, like an alibi for Tuesday night?"

"Characterizing our offer of proof as merely 'circumstantial' is not accurate. The matter between the men that you *thought* created a motive was settled months ago." Hallagan's voice oozed confidence.

Jake's phone vibrated. A text from Erin. "Hang on for just a minute, counselor."

Erin had forwarded a patrol report. The BOLO had worked. Officer Costello had found the crew cab truck with the Texas plate parked in front of Lanigan House Bed & Breakfast in downtown Weston. Mr. Lanigan had identified the truck's driver as Gus Trane, a fifty-seven-year-old man from Corpus

Christi, Texas, who had checked in last Thursday night. No priors. No warrants.

Jake got back to his call with Hallagan. "Counselor, tell your client I appreciate his cooperation. I'll get back to you in the next few days." Jake paused, then tried one more time. "But I have to tell you that without an alibi, Mr. Bowen will stay on my list."

"We look forward to hearing from you."

Hallagan ended the call.

Bowen would stay on Jake's list, but he was nowhere near the top. The man had an alibi, even if he was reluctant to use it. Not in front of his wife, not unless forced to. And Hallagan was right that if Henry and Bowen had worked out their differences and terminated the partnership months ago, then Bowen lacked motive. He wasn't a strong suspect.

But Titus Cole was. He'd moved here specifically to chase the silver. And that seemed like far too much effort for twenty bars worth less than fifty thousand dollars. He'd also stuck around even after the bars had been sold to Griffin.

There was something else keeping him in town.

* * *

While Conner was waiting for April, he received a text from his mom explaining they'd be gone for at least a couple hours. She apologized for not spending time with him while he was home, but said she had to "take care of this thing with your father." Of course, she didn't mention that the *thing* was getting his dad a criminal defense attorney to protect him from the cops.

When April finally got to his house, they headed straight to his room and made love. The first time was fast and urgent, her lithe athletic body a blur of motion above him. The second time, slow and soft.

Then he must have dozed off. When he woke, she was gone.

He pulled on his clothes and looked out the front window. Her little car was still parked at the curb. He found her in his dad's study, standing in the middle of the room, her big bag over her shoulder. Looking at the private space of the man who might have killed her dad.

"Hey."

She startled, her head whipping around. "Conner. I just—"

"It's okay." He leaned on the doorjamb. "You know, I haven't been in here since I put the monitoring software on his computer."

"It's just… so hard to believe."

"I know. I'm glad you came over."

She stepped toward him, and he pulled her close and held her tight.

"I'm so sorry," he said. "I can't believe my dad could have…"

"I know." She pulled her head back and looked deep into his eyes the way no one else could. "If he *did* do it, it wasn't because he was bad, or hated my dad. It was because of the silver."

"That's not an excuse."

"What I mean is, your dad isn't a monster. He just did something monstrous because of the silver. It corrupts. Like the One Ring that Sauron the Dark Lord made."

"Nerd," he said, then laughed. But the comparison did make him feel better.

She put her head on his shoulder. "The silver is still out there."

"I guess."

"My dad found it. *We* can find it." She put her lips on his ear. "And get out of this town forever."

The idea of getting away together felt like a balloon lifting him by his heart.

His phone buzzed with a text.

"It's Mom," he said. "They're headed home. You should go."

She kissed him—long and lingering. "I love you."

Then she ran up the stairs and out the front door.

CHAPTER TWENTY-FOUR

Jake drove straight to the B&B to talk to Gus Trane, the Texas cowboy in the big white pickup. On the way his phone buzzed with another message. He parked down the block from Lanigan House and read the message. Levi asking for a callback.

Jake called immediately, eager for whatever information he could get before talking to Trane.

"Did you find something?"

"Boy, did I." Levi's voice rang with delight.

"On GWU?"

"That's next, but I wanted to tell you about the forum right away."

"Go ahead."

"I found the posting the coin dealer told you about, and he represented it accurately. He asked whether anyone knew of a market for bars with the GWU mark. Only two people responded. Both said they weren't aware of any market for that mint mark."

"And when was this? June, like he said?"

"Yes. But he posted a follow-up question on November first that's attached to the earlier question. It uses the same subject line, 'Collectability of Silver Bars with GWU Mint Mark,' except he added the words '1,000-ounce bars' to the end of the subject line. Then he asked: 'Do thousand-ounce bars with the GWU mint mark have any value to a collector?'"

"*Thousand*-ounce bars?" Ten times bigger than the bars Henry had sold to Griffin. "Did anyone respond to the email?"

"A list member identified as 'TH Tex' responded that same day. He asked, quote, 'How many are you talking about?' End quote."

"TH Tex?" Jake wrote it down. "Trane's pickup has those plates." The man must have jumped in his pickup and driven north the instant he read the post.

"Gus Trane?"

"Did you come across that name?"

"I did. After finding that post in the forum, I searched 'TH Tex,' and found TH, Inc., which is the official corporate name for Treasure Hunters International. It's a company that searches for lost treasure around the world—mostly shipwrecks, some ancient and some from as recent as WWII. It's pretty cool, actually, and they claim they've found more shipwrecks than any other outfit in the last thirty years. But apparently spending millions of dollars every year digging up shipwrecks that often contain nothing valuable isn't the best business plan. They filed for bankruptcy three years ago after they lost possession of a half-billion dollar haul to Spain—apparently because the loot was being transported to Spain from Peru on a warship sunk in battle, or something. Some maritime law that basically robbed them of their find. Anyway, the company still exists—the bankruptcy case is still in the courts. And Gus Trane is the name of TH, Inc.'s majority owner."

Interesting. "Did Griffin respond to Trane's forum question?"

"Nope."

"Did you see anything else from TH Tex in the forums?"

"Nothing. I went back a year into the archive."

"Would TH Tex have been able to figure out who Griffin is?"

"Oh, sure. Griffin's posts weren't anonymous. He has own name and the coin shop's name and address in his signature line."

"Levi, this is great. Thanks for your help."

"Any time."

Jake ended the call. So, Griffin was shopping for a buyer for one or more thousand-ounce bars. It was fair to assume these bigger bars had also come from Henry.

But why assume it when the answer was only a phone call away?

He flipped through his notebook and found Griffin's number.

"Paget Valley Coins." Griffin's deep voice.

"Tell me about the big bars, the thousand-ouncers."

"I... you asked about the hundred-ounce bars and I gave you everything you asked for on them. More than you asked for."

Deception. "Get to it." Jake's car sat in the sun and was starting to get warm. He twisted the key for accessory power and lowered the front windows, and cold fresh air swirled through the car.

"Henry called me and asked if selling thousand-ounce bars is any different. I told him it isn't. Just bring me proof of ownership like before."

"When was this?"

"A week or two ago."

Jake needed a tighter timeline. "You posted the question on the forum on November first."

"He called me that same day."

"Jake?" said a voice outside the car.

Jake jumped. A gray-haired woman was leaning in the passenger window. It was Mrs. King. His third-grade teacher.

"I thought that was you," she said. "How are you?"

"Hang on, Griffin." Jake pressed the phone to his thigh. "Uh, I'm good, Mrs. King. You look well."

"Ha," she said. "I know how I look."

"I'm sorry, but I can't talk right now. I'm on a work call."

"Well, I just wanted to say hello. I'm glad you're back in town." She straightened and walked off.

Jake had been "back in town" for ten years. Apparently time moved differently for elementary school teachers.

"I'm back," Jake said into the phone. "Mr. Fox told you the big bar had the same mint mark?"

"Not until I asked, but yeah, he did."

"Did you ever tell him the bar might be worth more as a collectible?"

"Of course not."

"Did Henry have one bar or multiple bars?"

"He said bars, plural."

"Did you call Cole?"

"Of course. I thought he might want a big one. And at first it seemed he did, but then he said the little one was enough."

"At first?"

"He sounded excited to hear about them, but then cooled off."

"Did he ask you who had the big one?"

"Yes. I stretched things and said I had it."

"Did he ask where it came from?"

"No."

"So then you posted the question on the forum?"

"Well, actually, I posted the question before I called Cole."

"Why?"

"I thought Cole would be a buyer, but having two buyers is always better. A bidding war can make me real money."

"And what did the other guy say? The one who responded to your forum post."

"I didn't follow up with him because I didn't know how many there are. And because if something is collectable, the fewer there are, the higher the price per unit."

"What else haven't you told me?"

"That's all of it."

Jake didn't believe him—leaving things out seemed to be Griffin's default mode—but he ended the call. He had one other call to make before he talked to Trane. He needed to talk to Coogan.

If Trane's company was in bankruptcy, that was worth looking at. But he didn't know enough about the process to know how to get access. Coogan would. He rolled up the windows, got out of the stuffy car, and leaned against it to make the call. He quickly explained the situation.

"I guess you skipped that elective in law school," Coogan said. The two of them had taken all the core classes together, but after that they'd followed different paths: Coogan mostly business and family law, Jake criminal and constitutional law. "What you want is Pacer. It's the bankruptcy courts' online system for filing documents and keeping the docket. Everything's on there."

"Can I get access?" Jake closed his eyes and faced the sun. The breeze had died down and the warmth felt great. Like it was recharging him to face the man who might be Henry's killer.

"I can do it. I've spent plenty of time over the years deciphering the docket entries. Henry deserves our best efforts."

Yes he does. "Thanks, Coog."

CHAPTER TWENTY-FIVE

Jake climbed the wide stairs of Lanigan House, a huge Victorian two blocks north of downtown. Walt and Missy Lanigan had converted the house into a bed and breakfast way back when they were the "in" thing, and the place was so comfortable and its location so perfect it was hanging on long after the trend had died out elsewhere. The front door opened to a large relaxed room sprinkled with people reading and playing cards, their conversations a low background burble, and the air was rich with the scent of chocolate chip cookies.

Jake found Walt behind a tall counter that looked more like a bar than a front desk.

"Jake." He cast a quick look around. "Officer Costello said you might stop by. Here's Mr. Trane's registration card. He's in his room now."

"Thanks, Walt." Jake glanced at the card, but it held no information he didn't already have. "How's he been as a guest?"

"No problems." Lanigan looked around again. "Keeps odd hours. I leave the front door unlocked until nine, and after that the room keys will open it. He's used his key a time or two that I've noticed. Our apartment is by the front door so I hear everyone come and go. Always take a peek." He smiled.

"How about Tuesday night?"

"Night before last?"

Jake nodded.

"Well… I can't say about a specific night." He looked off as he tried to stretch his memory. "No, can't say one way or the other."

"Thanks, Walt. Okay if I head up?"

"Sure thing. He's in the Sunrise Room. Third floor, in the back."

* * *

Jake climbed the stairs, the oak treads solid and quiet under his feet. Both suspects—Cole and Trane—being from Texas didn't feel like a coincidence. He was glad the case was heading toward two out-of-towners chasing treasure, and away from the ex-wife with money troubles and the local business partner who thought he'd been cheated.

And away from any possibility Jake's relationship with Lynn would get in the way of his investigation.

He found the Sunrise Room at the end of the hall. He put his ear to the door before knocking. An old country song about being a drinking man droned through the wood, and a deep uneven voice sang along. When the song ended and a commercial for a body shop broke out, the voice swore and the radio went silent.

Jake stepped back and rapped his knuckles hard on the door. He waited a long second, then gave a hard triple rap.

The door cracked open, a large form blocking the gap, the face in shadow.

"Who're you?" The Texan's voice was gravelly. He looked Jake up and down.

"Jake Houser with the Weston PD." Jake pulled his jacket back to reveal the badge on his belt.

"What do you want?"

"I'd like to come in and talk with you for a few minutes." Jake stepped forward and put a hand against the door, pushing gently.

"Hold on, now." Trane stopped the door with a massive hand. "I'm a private person."

Jake stepped back, wondering what Trane was hiding in his room. Maybe he was just messy. "We can use one of the rooms downstairs if you like. Just a few questions."

Trane gave Jake another hard stare. Evaluating. Measuring. Then he slipped through the door and past Jake so smoothly Jake didn't even have a chance to step back. The man was massive, at least six-four, and thick through the chest and shoulders. Easily capable of delivering the blow that had killed Henry.

Trane led Jake to a small room set up as a parlor. A pair of wingbacks framed a front window. Trane sat in one and rested his big hands on his knees. "Well?"

Jake perched on the edge of the matching chair, keeping some weight on his feet in case he needed to move. He took a moment to look Trane over, letting the silence work on the man. In the strong sunlight coming through the west-facing window, Trane's face looked lined and rough. The sleeves of his flannel shirt were rolled up, revealing thick forearms, the skin a dark scaly red. The man spent too much time in the sun. His jeans looked new and flared over a pair of well-worn boots with low heels.

"Why were you watching Henry Fox?"

"Who says I was?"

Failing to answer a question was a clear deception marker. But Trane displayed no other markers, physical or verbal.

"But you know Mr. Fox?"

"It's a hot topic downstairs, so I know who he is. The beloved handyman killed in his home. It even made the Chicago news."

"A neighbor saw you down by the barn on Mr. Fox's property a few days before."

"I'm looking to buy some real estate here in town, and I like that area."

"I didn't say where he lived."

Trane sighed. "Everyone in town knows where the murder happened. I've been all through that neighborhood looking at land. There aren't many underdeveloped properties left down there."

If there's a hoard of thousand-ounce silver bars in Weston, that area is where Trane thinks he'll find it.

"You're not here for real estate," Jake said. "You're here for silver."

Trane's brow furrowed, then smoothed. Surprised that Jake knew about the silver, but under control. Jake waited for the big man to speak, but he didn't. A smart move when you don't know how much the other guy knows.

"You're familiar with silver bars?" Jake asked.

Trane was quiet and completely still. Waiting. Thinking.

"Hundred-ounce bars?"

Nothing.

"Thousand-ounce bars?"

Trane flinched, but caught himself and recovered. "I've handled silver as bars, rods, ingots, coins, and jewelry. Gold, too. I'm a treasure hunter."

"You *were* a treasure hunter."

"What do you mean by that crack?"

"Your company went under, didn't it?"

Trane shrugged. "The company, not me. And that doesn't change what I am."

Rich guys always wanted it to be clear they hadn't file bankruptcy *personally*; it had just been their company. "Why were you out at Jim Bowen's house this morning?"

Trane shifted in his chair. "Who's that?" He rubbed his face with a big hand.

Anchor point movement. Answering with a question. Touching his face. The trio of indicators said Trane was lying. "Bowen owns half the silver Mr. Fox found," Jake said.

Trane's mouth squeezed shut and he shook his head tightly, his eyes boring into Jake's. "Ownership isn't always so cut and dried."

"What do you mean?"

"You did your homework on me before coming here, right, Houser?" Trane's voice rose. "So you know my company filed bankruptcy after a dispute over a treasure I found."

"Is that what you're after, Mr. Trane? You're here chasing a lost treasure?"

Trane chewed his lip and pushed back into his chair. "I'm trying to educate you that finding and owning are two different things."

"An expensive lesson you learned a few years ago?"

"That's right."

"You're not the only Texan in town chasing the silver."

Trane's eyes popped wide, and he leaned forward. He opened his mouth, desperate to ask who, the first syllable forming on his lips before he caught himself. His mouth closed but his eyes had narrowed and they stayed that way.

So. The Texans weren't working together.

"Anything else, Detective?"

Jake considered. He hadn't hit Trane with the mint mark, or the forum, or the timing of his arrival in Weston, but he'd hold those back until he knew more. About this man and about the silver. "No, Mr. Trane. Thank you for your cooperation."

The big Texan sprang from the chair, and the sudden movement made Jake shoot to his feet, his adrenaline flowing. But Trane simply looked him up and down before striding away, the heels of his boots pounding against the floor.

CHAPTER TWENTY-SIX

The adrenaline hadn't yet faded when Jake got to his car, and his handwriting was a little shaky as he took notes about his conversation with Trane. Then he called Erin to see if she had anything more on Cole.

"About the arrests," she said. "He worked personal security for some billionaire, and sometimes things got physical and people complained."

"Were all the incidents related to his job? No bar fights or domestics?"

"Still getting through them, but it looks that way."

"And no convictions?" Jake asked.

"None."

That didn't surprise him. The justice system was easy on billionaires and those they protected. But more importantly, if all the charges were from more than eleven years ago and were all work-related, then Cole might not be violent at all.

"Who was the rich guy?" Jake asked.

"His name isn't in any of the reports I've seen so far. Like they're protecting him."

"Texans like their rich."

"I'm still digging."

"Good. We have two guys up here from Texas. Something down there will help unravel this."

"And I've looked at the coin dealer. He's the only guy outside of Chicago who buys and sells silver in bulk."

"And is he dirty?"

"We don't have a problem with him. Always cooperates. He's bought a few things that turned out to be stolen, but always turns his records over immediately. But he's been sued over a dozen times. Fraud, breach of contract. Civil stuff. Always settles."

"Thanks, Erin."

* * *

Conner googled the price of silver. A single thousand-ounce bar was worth over twenty-two thousand dollars. No wonder his dad had been so pissed off. That number was so big it even got Conner daydreaming. If they had even a few of the bars, maybe ten, April could join him at Northwestern—where she belonged—and he'd never have to talk to his dad again. Twenty bars would be even better.

He clicked through to Google Maps and zoomed in on the bluff along the river. April was positive her dad had found the silver there. But it was a much bigger area than he had thought: a thick forest as big as two or three city blocks, with the Bristol Yard—a group of metal buildings around a gravel parking area—in the middle of it. It would take a long time to search all that.

Worse, they wouldn't be the only ones looking. They'd be competing with the killer, who was also after the silver.

Conner pulled his feet up onto the chair and hugged his knees, his heart beating hard against his chest. He knew his strengths, and bravery wasn't one of them.

A flash of shame heated his face with the sudden hope that his dad *had* killed Mr. Fox.

His dad wouldn't hurt them even if he caught them searching for the silver.

He closed his laptop, put on his coat, and left the house. He cut through the neighborhood to the asphalt path running along the river, taking it north until he got to the Burlington railroad bridge. It had been rebuilt sometime in the far distant past, and a heap of giant concrete chunks from the original bridge were still piled up on the other side of the river. He scrambled over the bridge and down to his favorite slab, sat, and lit a joint. Smoking always helped him think.

He lay back, the rays of the falling sun pinning him in place and warming him. He tilted his face up and closed his eyes. He took a big hit and held it in, the herb pumping smoothly through his body. He didn't exhale until his pulse pounded in his temples.

Had his dad killed Mr. Fox?

He didn't want to believe it, but… it was possible. People did crazy shit all the time. And his dad had been so mad when Mr. Fox kept the little bars for himself. That email about the bigger bars would surely have set him off again. He had a scary temper, he was way bigger and stronger than Mr. Fox, and he had been home alone that night. *And* Mr. Fox's house was less than two miles away—a short walk on the paved riverside trails that were empty and unlit at night.

Yeah, it was absolutely possible. Conner's dad was both physically and psychologically capable of doing it.

He called April.

"How are you?" he said. "Can you talk?"

"Yeah, Mom's sleeping again. Fast-timing it, she calls it. Sleeping through the pain hoping she'll wake up and it'll be gone."

"I've been thinking and…" Conner stopped, realizing suddenly how cold-hearted his suggestion was in light of Mr. Fox's murder.

"You think we should look for the silver," April said. "For ourselves."

It was like they shared one mind. "I know we should be thinking about your dad and praying for him, and I *am* doing those things. But right now my dad is busy with my mom and with worrying about that cop. And if there's enough silver, it's our chance to get out of here. Together. We should try and find it."

"We can't do anything for my dad. We *can* do something for ourselves."

He took another hit and savored the clarity pumping through him.

"Are you smoking?"

"Yep." His voice was high and tight as he tried to hold on to the smoke. He failed, and it came out in a long whoosh. "But only if my dad did do it. If someone else did it, then it's too dangerous."

"I…"

"What?" he asked her.

"I think the risk is worth it."

He'd hoped she would go for it, but now he wasn't sure. His body shook with fear.

"Do you think your dad did it?" she asked him.

"I…don't know."

"You have to decide," she said. "He's your dad."

That was fair. He took another hit, and the quaking in his legs subsided. "Can you call that detective? He's your god-father, right? Maybe he's already figured it out but can't prove it yet. Invite him over to talk about god stuff and find a way to bring it up. Or maybe just come out and ask him if he knows who killed your dad. It's a natural question, right?"

"I can ask him to come with us to the funeral parlor. It's kind of a religious thing and he's one of those guys who likes to help people with hard things."

"Perfect. Will that bother your mom?"

"I won't tell her." She paused, then went on with more energy in her voice. "This will work. Mr. Houser has never been able to say no to me."

* * *

Jake pulled to the curb in front of Cole's apartment building. He spotted Grady down the street and lifted a finger from the steering wheel in a discreet wave. Then his phone buzzed. April.

"How are you, April? And your mom?"

"We're doing okay."

She didn't sound okay. Her voice was hoarse and subdued.

"What can I do?"

"I'd like your help with something. As my—you know—my godfather?"

"Of course." If she wanted to talk about death and what came next, he'd do the best he could.

"Will you... I know this is asking a lot, but..."

"Anything."

"Will you come to the funeral home with us? Everson's? We have an appointment at five o'clock."

"Of course." Jake had to clear a sudden thick wad of emotion from his throat. "I'd be honored to help you through that."

"Thanks, Mr. Houser. Bye."

After he put his phone away Jake regretted not asking her about the big bars. He would find a way to raise the subject while they were at Everson's. If he could do it without being an ass.

He checked his watch. He had plenty of time to talk to Titus Cole before the appointment at Everson's.

The fold of carpet runner was back under the door, but now the hallway smelled of curry. Jake stopped in front of Cole's door and listened. No television. He knocked, and after a few seconds footsteps approached and the door opened.

"Detective." Cole's voice was hard and unwelcoming. He was done cooperating.

"I have a few more questions."

"I don't think I want—"

"Two different people described that blot on your face as a strawberry birthmark." Jake brushed past Cole into the apartment and sat on the couch. "But I think it's actually called a port-wine stain, right?"

"I didn't invite you in." Cole closed the door, then stood there with his hand on the knob.

"Let's say you did." Jake stretched an arm along the back of the couch. "You lied to me, Mr. Cole. A lie of omission, but still a lie. You collect silver."

Cole's brow creased. Jake gave him a minute to realize Jake knew about the coin shop and the silver bar he'd bought and that he'd gotten a copy of the receipt with Henry's name on it. If Cole kept talking, he would tell a story to cover all of that.

"I bought a silver bar from a local coin shop." His hand dropped from the doorknob and he shrugged. "Turned out Henry Fox had sold the bar to the coin shop. A coincidence."

"But you didn't know Henry then. You said you met him a month later." Jake waited for a response, but all he got was brooding silence. "Do you have an alibi for the night Henry was killed? Tuesday night."

"I was home watching the Northern Illinois football game. It was the MAC game of the week. But I live alone, so no one can vouch for me."

"I need to see the bar you bought."

"It's in a safe deposit box at Weston Community Bank." Cole lifted his hands wide. "This place isn't exactly secure."

"I'll have a patrol officer come and take you to the bank to retrieve it." Cole could make Jake get a search warrant, but if the bar wasn't the murder weapon he wouldn't bother.

"That's fine, Detective."

"Is your entire collection at the bank?"

"I'll show you the one bar."

"Who did you work for in Texas?"

Instead of answering, Cole opened the door. "Please leave, Detective."

"I don't think you moved up here for the little bars." Jake stood up, watching Cole carefully. Cole's face froze, but his eyes drilled into Jake's. "But I *can* see you moving up here for the thousand-ounce bars Mr. Fox found."

Cole worked his jaw but said nothing. Jake walked slowly, hoping Cole would spill something. Cole's hand gripped the doorknob, his knuckles splotching red and white.

Jake stepped out into the hall, then turned and gave Cole a parting shot to try and shake something loose. "You're not the only Texan up here looking for those big bars."

Cole's eyebrows rose—and he swung the door shut in Jake's face.

CHAPTER TWENTY-SEVEN

Jake walked back to his car with one arm holding his blazer shut against the cold wind, the rich aroma of dark chocolate riding it from the cookie factory to the west. Through some trick of baking science it usually smelled scorched, but today it didn't. Fresh and rich and so thick you could almost take a bite from the air. Then the wind shifted and it was gone. He turned to the west as if he could see it, but caught only the last rays of the setting sun leaking over the horizon.

He got the heater pumping in the car, called Erin, and explained the situation with Cole's silver bar. He asked her to have a patrol officer escort Cole to the bank with an evidence bag to retrieve the bar and then run it straight to the lab.

One way or another, the two Texans were at the heart of this. Even though the men weren't working together, they were chasing the same thing. How many thousand-ounce silver bars would it take to draw the men to town? A hundred? More?

Both men were solid suspects. Both had means and opportunity. Both were strong enough to deliver the blow that killed Henry. Neither had an alibi. And both had a motive: the silver.

Cole had even put out a feeler with Griffin *ten years* before the little bars turned up—which meant he'd known the silver was here for at least that long. Then when the first little bar finally turned up, he moved to town, found out who had sold the bar to Griffin—Henry—and manufactured a relationship with him. Just waiting for Henry to find the big bars. Cole had planned and acted deliberately. He took the long view and wasn't in a hurry.

Trane, on the other hand, was big and physical and quick to anger. He rushed north immediately after Griffin posted the question about the big bars. Trane was impulsive and, as a treasure hunter, used to taking big risks when the potential reward was great. Jake replayed his encounter with Trane and the fast fluidity of the man's movements. Trane could easily have struck Henry before he could react.

Grady was watching the wrong man.

Jake pulled out his phone and dialed, and watched Grady through the windshield as he answered.

"Yeah?"

"I want you to drop Cole to follow Trane—he's that big Texan the neighbor spotted near Henry's." Jake told Grady what he knew about Trane and where he was staying.

"You think he's the guy?"

"My gut says he's a possibility."

"I'm on it."

Grady pulled away, his white Jetta smooth and quiet.

* * *

Everson's was the oldest funeral home in Weston and did a lot of business. Jake had attended dozens of wakes there, and they'd done a great job when his mom passed away. He parked on the street a block away, then walked to the funeral home, joining a thin stream converging on the entrance. An after-work crowd dressed in dark business attire, some alone, but most in twos and threes. Two viewings were in process. Jake checked the lobby board and recognized the name of former city council member Drew Hampton. Jake's dad had always spoken well of Hampton, calling him the one reasonable man in a corral of ninnies.

Jake was early for the appointment and stood against the wall, scanning the crowd of politicians and businessmen coming in to be seen and pay their respects. He exchanged greetings with people he knew until the man he was looking for—Drake Lambert, the funeral home director—eased into the room. When their eyes met, Jake raised his eyebrows and snaked through the crowd to his side.

"Mr. Houser." Drake shook Jake's hand. "I'm so sorry about your friend, Mr. Fox."

"Thank you, Drake." Lambert knew everyone and how they were connected. "April Fox asked me to join them for your meeting."

"That would be very nice, Mr. Houser."

"Please call me Jake."

Lambert smiled.

"Drake... I want to pay for Henry's funeral." Saying it filled Jake with an odd swell of emotion that felt like happiness but brought a tear to his eye.

"That's very generous, Mr. Houser." Lambert paused, then lowered his voice. "As long as it's okay with his family. People often want to pay for it themselves as a kind of remembrance. A last connection."

Jake realized that was exactly why *he* wanted to pay for it. "How about I offer and we see what they want to do?"

"Very good, Mr. Houser."

They stood together in the lobby as they waited. Jake's thoughts turned back to the thousand-ounce bars; he wanted to ask both women what they knew about them, but not here. He was here as a friend and April's godfather, not as a cop.

A few minutes later the Fox women walked in. Lynn's hair was brushed and her makeup done. She wore dark slacks and a cream-colored shirt, with a wool coat cinched around her waist. April wore jeans and a sweater and a snug leather jacket.

As Lynn's gaze swung past Jake, he read a silent *shit* on her lips.

She hadn't expected to see him.

* * *

Lynn tried for a smile but knew it failed.

"Mr. Houser!" April hugged Jake. "Mom, I hope it's okay I asked Mr. Houser to come along."

"Of course, honey," Lynn lied. It wasn't at all okay. She worried Jake might question her about the affair with Bowen—and if he did, she knew she couldn't fool him for long. Everything she knew about the man came from April and gossip at the club.

She turned to Jake. "Thanks for coming."

Jake introduced them to the funeral home director, Drake Lambert, who expressed his condolences, then led them all upstairs to a small room at the front of the old house. It was dominated by a high-gloss conference table that smelled of old wood and lemony furniture polish.

Lambert stood behind the chair at the head of the table, where a portfolio and a stack of brochures were already laid out. Jake ushered April into the seat to Lambert's right and waved Lynn toward the chair next to her. But Lynn wasn't going to sit there. Jake would take the chair at the other end of the table, and she'd be stuck next to him for however long this took. She slipped behind Lambert instead, forcing him to belly up to the table, and sat across from April, as far away from Jake as she could get in the little room. Jake smiled and sat next to April.

Lambert talked them through the different parts of the process, explaining the options available. His voice was kind and comforting, but for Lynn, it was all too much. She hadn't eaten anything after throwing up the toast, and the room felt oppressively warm. She struggled out of her coat and tried to focus, with little luck.

Fortunately, April took charge. She answered all Lambert's questions and picked from long lists of options for every little detail. She was the right person to make those decisions anyway. She was Henry's only blood relation. Lynn probably shouldn't even be here. April didn't need her—and probably didn't even want her here. She'd called Jake to help with this, hadn't she?

Suddenly everyone was getting up, and Lynn followed along as Lambert led them to a huge room set up like a museum, showcasing caskets and vaults.

Lambert was saying something about... decorative medallions. For the casket's corners? She wasn't sure. But whatever they were, she was certain she'd heard him say they were three hundred dollars each. She looked at the casket April had just selected... and saw its price tag. Her empty stomach clutched and released, and she swallowed back down the sour bubble threatening to come up.

"Mr. Lambert." A tear rolled down her cheek and she rubbed it away with her hand. "I'm sorry but... the prices on these. We don't have that kind of money. Unless you have really long payment plans, we can't..."

Jake cut in. "Lynn. April. If you'll allow me to, I'd like to cover the funeral expenses. I'd be honored to do it." He spoke softly, looking back and forth between them.

"Christ, Jake." Lynn's face reddened and she shook her head. "I can't... I'm sorry, Mr. Lambert, but—"

"Mom!" April said. "Let him. Dad would be okay with his best friend helping us. Plus, Mr. Houser can afford it."

Lynn chewed her lip, embarrassed and ashamed. But what the hell was she being so proud about? She was broke, and everyone knew it.

She shrugged and nodded.

Lambert stepped forward and ushered them on to the next display.

* * *

Jake was glad Lynn had accepted his offer to pay for Henry's funeral, but had been surprised by April's comment that he could afford it. Henry must have told her that Jake owned the real estate trust that Coogan managed, and for which Henry handled the maintenance. That truth was available to anyone willing to spend some dusty hours in the probate and real estate records at the county archives, but as far as Jake knew, no one but Henry had ever bothered to look.

April looped her arms around one of his and held tight as Lynn wandered away with Drake.

"Thanks for helping with all of this, Mr. Houser."

"I'm happy to do it."

"Have you figured out who killed my dad?"

Jake frowned. "Not yet, but I will."

"Promise?"

Jake could make that promise. What he couldn't promise was a conviction. There were too many cracks in the criminal justice system where politics and influence and prejudice seeped in and corrupted the process. "I promise I will find your dad's killer."

"Do you have a suspect, at least? I mean, I know about Mom and Mr. Bowen, so…"

Jake didn't answer questions like that during an investigation. Then again, this wasn't a normal investigation. Henry had been one of his best friends, and April was his own goddaughter. And, he realized suddenly, it was an opportunity to see if April knew about the bigger silver bars. It was a definite asshole move to do that here at the funeral home—but he could do it very gently, just floating the idea of more silver to see if she questioned it.

"The silver still hidden out there has brought some bad men to town," he said. "When it's over I'll tell you the whole story."

"Thank you," she said, then hugged his arm as they continued along behind Lynn and Drake.

She hadn't even blinked at his statement that there was more silver hidden in town—which meant she already knew about the big bars. And if April knew, so did Lynn. Yet neither had shared it with him. They probably wanted to go after it themselves. Everyone who knew about the silver was hoping for a piece of it, despite what had happened to Henry.

Jake needed to hurry up and find this silver and get it the hell out of town.

After April picked a vault, they went back to the conference room and finished up. April powered through the rest of the decisions: flowers and music and newspaper notices and the guest book and on and on. Lynn kept out of it, sitting quietly, her head down. Jake caught her looking at him several times, and he smiled, but each time she turned away without acknowledging it.

When they got to the obituary he was able to flesh it out with some things Lynn had forgotten and April had never known. Like the perfect game Henry pitched when he was nine years old and how he'd held two Redhawk basketball records—season highs for assists and for steals—for over twenty years. By the time they had finished with everything it was after eight and both women looked exhausted, their faces wan and eyes bagged with dark circles. As they paused in the lobby to pull on their coats, he invited them out for dinner so they wouldn't have to cook, but Lynn declined. She said she needed to rest.

"Godfather?"

Jake smiled. It sounded corny, but he liked it.

"Thanks for helping us out with all this." April looked up at him. "Can I ask you for one more favor?"

"Of course."

"Will you do a eulogy for my dad? For the service?"

Jake felt his face light up. "I'd love to."

CHAPTER TWENTY-EIGHT

As Jake walked back to his car, the smell of fallen leaves and a faint pall of wood smoke drew him into the season and away from the case. He loved fall. He couldn't imagine living in a place that didn't experience real fall: football games and bonfires and leafy smells.

The fresh air helped release the tension that had built up during the meeting at Everson's. It was a tough way to spend three hours. April had been a trooper, and he was glad Lynn had deferred to her on the arrangements.

He fired up the car and considered his next stop. He needed to talk with the storage facility about the bill of sale Henry used to prove he owned the silver bar when he sold it to Griffin. Jake doubted Henry had actually found the silver in a storage unit, but he had to investigate the possibility.

He flipped through his notebook until he found the facility's address. It was short drive, but the office had closed for the evening. He would have to go by the next day.

As he drove home, he wondered where Henry had found the silver. The answer was important, because of the implications about ownership. If Henry had found the silver in the storage unit, then the silver belonged to the partnership—Henry and Bowen. But the unit's renter—the silver's original owner—could want it back. If Henry had found the silver in an outhouse pit, then—

Wait.

Found. The word fluttered around Jake's memory and alit on what Trane had said. *Finding and owning are two different things.* Henry had found the bars, but finding them didn't automatically make Henry the legal owner of the bars. Even in cases less complex than Trane's warship loaded with gold bullion, ownership wasn't as simple as finders-keepers. The law focused not only on who had found an item, but on who had owned it, and whether it had been lost, abandoned, or mislaid.

Of course, Jake wasn't litigating ownership; he was looking for a murderer. The murderer would likely be someone who *didn't* have legal title to the silver—but wanted it anyway.

Even if he had to kill to get it.

Jake parked and went inside his house. He needed to set the case aside, at least for a little while, to think about his eulogy for Henry. He'd been glad when April asked him to do it, but his perception of Henry had blurred—his friend was a liar and possibly a thief. And that was just with reference to the little bars. Jake still had no idea where the big bars had come from or what Henry had done to get them.

But he'd said he would prepare a eulogy, and he would. Tonight. While working on the house.

He changed into his remodeling clothes and was pulling on his steel-toed boots when his phone rattled on the worn oak floor. He scooped it up. A text from Grady: *Trane left Lanigans and wandered around the public works yard on Jackson kicking at the leaf cover then walked out through the park. He gave the Fox barn a hard look but stayed away from it. Then he went back to his room and has been inside ever since.*

The kid got long-winded with his texts. Jake responded: *Good work. Call it a night and start again in the morning.*

He'd missed an earlier text from Erin and read it now: *Patrol officer took Cole to the bank but it was closed. Will return in the morning. First thing.*

A delay, but not a serious one. The bar in the vault wasn't the murder weapon—if it were, Cole would have fought him on turning it over. Examining it was just a box to check off.

At that moment the little bubbles appeared, indicating Erin was typing out another text. It popped up: *Just heard Braff is looking for you.*

The doorbell rang. He didn't even know it worked.

* * *

Conner searched Google images for pictures of thousand-ounce silver bars, and was surprised to find they were just dull blocks of metal. He'd expected them to be shiny. Not that it mattered. All that mattered was that a single bar was worth over twenty thousand dollars. A few months ago it would have been worth sixteen thousand—and back in 2011 a thousand ounces of silver was worth nearly *fifty* thousand. He clicked around the Internet and found plenty of people arguing that the price would skyrocket in the near future—and just as many arguing it would soon crash. Nobody really knew.

But that didn't matter because he and April weren't greedy. They were going to use the money to be together and pay for college. They didn't want to buy an island or a Porsche.

His phone vibrated against his desk. April.

"What did you find out?" His words came out in a rude rush. "I'm sorry, how did it go with the funeral part of it?"

"Good. Mom kept her mouth shut for once. Mostly anyway. I think the funeral will be pretty nice. I picked out the flowers and the casket and a ton of other stuff. You'll see."

"And with your godfather? Houser showed up?"

"Yeah. I think he knows something about the big bars. He mentioned the silver still hidden here."

"Shit." Conner looked at the big bar on his laptop screen. "What about the other thing?"

"What? Oh." She lowered her voice. "I don't think he's investigating your dad anymore. He said some dangerous men have come to town looking for the silver. That's what he's been doing, I guess. Looking into them."

"Then my dad didn't do it, right? One of these men did it." Relief flooded through him and almost lifted him from the chair. But when he remembered that meant it wasn't safe for them to look for the silver, the weight came back. That money could have set them free.

He looked at the photo of the silver bar one more time, then closed his laptop. "So we're done."

"I… maybe," April said.

"You have an idea?"

"Maybe Mr. Houser investigating these men will scare them out of town. Maybe them running away convinces Mr. Houser they're guilty, so he leaves the case open like that. Never looking at your dad or my mom again. Never finding out she lied about an affair. And maybe he doesn't even believe the big bars exist. No one has seen one, right? So the silver is left waiting for us."

"Maybe," he said. "A lot of maybes."

* * *

The microwave hummed, and Lynn watched the bowl of left-over spaghetti through the window in the door. They'd had the spaghetti for dinner on Sunday night.

Before Henry's death.

Is that how she'd think of things from now on? As happening either before Henry died, or after?

The microwave dinged, and she pulled out the piping hot bowl and set it on the table, the sauce along the edge bubbling. She didn't think she could eat any of it, but hopefully April could.

She stirred the spaghetti, let it sit to warm through, then tiptoed over to April's door and listened for any sound she was awake. Softly, she heard talking. April was probably on the phone with Conner. Then silence. Then words again, but… different. It didn't sound like she was on the phone anymore.

Lynn pushed her ear to the door, and the words became clear.

"Dear God and Jesus, please welcome my dad into heaven with you. I know he doesn't need me to tell you how great he was. And not just to me but to everyone. Please help my mom do better with talking to the police and please forgive her lies. She's desperate, I guess, about money and taking care of me. But I'm an adult now and I'll take care of myself. So, please forgive me my sins and…"

A sob, then a hard string of them.

"And forgive me for… not being a better daughter. Amen."

CHAPTER TWENTY-NINE

Jake crossed the bare underlayment in the great room, his footsteps echoing hollowly in the empty space, and looked through the small window set into the front door. Callie Diggs stood on his front stoop, swaying to her own internal rhythm, backlit by a distant streetlight.

A smile broke across his face as he opened the door. "What—"

Callie held up a hand to stop him, and then Deputy Chief Braff stepped into view from beside the door.

Braff's eyes drilled into Jake's. "What the hell, Houser?"

"What—" Jake tried again.

"Save it." Braff pushed past Jake and headed for the kitchen. "You got anything to drink?"

Callie walked in behind the DC. "Nice get-up." Her eyes rode him up and down, taking in his demolition clothing, and a crooked smile spread across her face.

"I'm doing some work in the basement."

She stepped past him, one finger raking a hot line across his abdomen.

He closed the door behind her. "What's going on?" he asked, keeping his voice low.

"He found out you were with the Fox women at Everson's and why. He's not happy."

Shit. Jake followed Callie into the kitchen.

Braff pulled three bottles of Bud Light from the fridge. "Let's all have a seat," he said, pointing at the card table in the corner.

"Boss, I know the victim but it's not a problem. I've known plenty of the victims—"

"Sit!"

Braff sat, put the other two beers down, then held up one of his thick fingers. That meant to shut the hell up.

"It *is* a problem," he said. "You more than *knew* him. He was one of your best friends! Hell, I googled your names together and got hits on six different sports stories and two photos, for Christ's sake."

"Those were all from a long time ago."

"One was from the homecoming game. Two weeks ago."

Jake sat down and picked up the beer, cold in his hand.

Callie twisted the cap off her beer and took a long pull. Her gaze met Jake's then skipped away.

"I'm making Diggs primary," Braff said. "Give her—"

"There's no need for that. I'm already beyond any conflict I might have had. Henry's ex didn't—"

Braff held up his stout finger again. "Already past the ex? On day two."

"She has an alibi?" Callie asked Jake.

"Yes."

"Solid?"

"I'm telling you it's about the silver Henry found."

Braff's eyebrows shot up. "This I gotta hear. From the beginning."

"Silver bars have—"

"The beginning."

Jake started at the beginning, working his way through the storage unit business and the coin dealer and his suspicions of Bowen and how Lynn Fox provided Bowen's alibi.

"And her own," Callie said. "Did you confirm it?"

"Not yet," Jake said.

Braff shook his head, then sprang from the table and started pacing, his steps pounding out a stuttering rhythm on the bare wood floor. Callie nodded for Jake to continue, and he told them about the Texans and the thousand-ounce silver bars.

"How many of these big bars are there?" Braff asked.

"Enough to bring these Texans to town. Both of them have lied to me about why they're here. They—"

"Shit." Braff stopped pacing. "You've already talked to the Texans?"

Jake nodded, his spirits lightening. Braff wouldn't want to interfere with whatever relationship Jake had developed with the main suspects.

Callie and Jake both waited. Braff resumed his pacing, carving a lane in the underlayment, back and forth across the kitchen. Finally stopping.

"Diggs will take the ex and her lover." He pointed at Jake with his thick finger. "You stay the hell away from both of them. You only work the Texans and the silver. Got it?"

"Does the ex know about the big bars?" Callie asked.

"I think she and April both do, but I haven't confirmed it yet. Hell, I haven't even confirmed they exist."

"They exist or the Texans wouldn't be here," Braff said.

Jake nodded. "That's what I think too, Chief. And I'm sorry about—"

Braff held up his hand again. "Save it, Houser. But don't go off the reservation again or I'll suspend you. Got it?"

"I do."

Callie sprang up from the table. "I've got work to do. Tell me now if the ex is an old flame of yours."

Braff spread his arms wide. "Don't tell me—"

"She's not!" Jake said quickly.

Braff shook his head, made Jake promise that he wouldn't regret this decision, then he and Callie left.

Jake sat back down at the card table, peeling at the label on his beer. They were right: he should have nailed down that alibi, tearing down Lynn's story and examining every piece of it. It would be a shock to Lynn when Callie dug into it all. He considered calling Lynn—but that was too much like a warning. It might even be obstruction.

He finished the beer. He wasn't supposed to be thinking about the case tonight; he was supposed to be thinking about the eulogy. And that gave him an idea.

He got in the car and drove to his Spring Street property. It was originally the site of his dad's old landscaping business, but Jake had converted the offices into a half-assed bachelor pad and still had all his belongings stored there. Including his old mementos.

He shifted boxes around until he found the one he was looking for, then sat on the old leather couch in the shop area. For the next couple hours he did nothing but look through yearbooks and old photos, disappearing into the past, remembering everything about his friend that Henry's secrets and deceptions had started to push from his mind.

CHAPTER THIRTY

Jake slept until seven the next morning, waking to cloudy thoughts. He took a long hot shower, and by the time he stepped in front of the sink to shave, his dreams were coming back to him. He wiped the fog from the mirror and stared at his own reflection, trying hard to focus on what he saw, not what he remembered.

But he lost the battle. Images of his freshly murdered wife and bludgeoned friend kept flashing across his mind like slides playing on an endless loop. He gripped the counter and hung on, staring at himself and fighting the visions. The fog returned, then cleared, and finally the shuttering images faded away.

He shook himself, releasing the tension across his back and shoulders, then finished up in the bathroom and got dressed.

Today he needed to figure out both the silver and the Texans. When he had, he would have Henry's killer. He would avenge his friend.

He ate a bowl of cereal at his card table as he updated the online murder book with what he'd learned the day before. Although he was eager to get moving, he took his time, reviewed his notes, and worked to recall every word, gesture, and inflection of every conversation he'd had the day before, looking for the connections and inconsistencies and deceptions.

He added Callie Diggs to the list of people authorized to edit the murder book. He was glad she was going to take a hard look at Lynn. His failure to verify the alibi she'd given Bowen—and herself—could have been used by the real killer's criminal defense attorney to confuse a jury. But spending time verifying the alibi didn't move the investigation forward. That would come from his work on the Texans.

With Grady watching Trane, Jake decided to start his day by focusing on Cole. He called Erin.

"Did you find out anything more about Cole?"

"I was just about to call you," she said.

The excitement in Erin's voice stoked Jake's own.

"First, his silver bar will be on its way to the lab at the stroke of nine. Second, Cole worked security for one family his entire career. The Bunkers. Mostly for Huntley."

"That name's familiar." Bunker. But not Huntley. Something with an L. Maybe Leroy?

"Big Texas family. Made a gazillion dollars in oil, then got into some other areas. One brother—I think there were eight or ten of them—owns a football team. Hangs out with the Bush family. The Texas billionaire club."

Lamar Bunker—that was the name he knew. Jake had seen him on TV this past Sunday when they showed the team owner watching the game from his climate-controlled suite high above midfield. The owner always wore a suit and tie, and Jake always wondered why. After all, it was Sunday, and he was the boss.

"Hang on." Jake trapped the phone between his shoulder and his ear, then grabbed his notebook, flipped to the first blank page, and wrote down this new information. "You said Huntley Bunker, right."

"Yep."

"And that job ended, what, eleven years ago?"

"Right. That's when Cole retired as head of security for Bunker Oil. Had an army of guys working for him by then.

But still traveled with Huntley when he was on the move. Sounds like more of a companion at that point."

Jake finished writing the information down. "Thanks."

"On Bowen and his wife, I still have some feelers out, but I can tell you what I have."

"Braff put Callie on that part of it—on both Lynn and Bowen."

"What? I never heard a peep about that here or I would have tried to stop him."

"It's okay," he said. "I'm still on the Texans and the silver. She's taking Lynn and Bowen. Did I tell you she alibied him? Says they were together. Having an affair."

"That jibes with a rumor I heard that the Bowens didn't get on too well because of an affair. But it was weak, and the affair might have been hers. I found nothing else off about either of them. No criminal records. Not even a moving violation."

"Call Callie with what you have, okay?"

"Will do."

"How about forensics? Fanning report anything?"

"So far all the prints they've run have been ruled out by the comps they collected."

"Thanks, Erin."

"Sure thing, Jake."

Jake booted his laptop back up. He entered the new information into the murder book—about the Bowens, Cole's employer, and Cole's silver bar being on its way to forensics. Jake didn't think forensics would find anything on the bar. Henry had found twenty bars, Griffin would be providing proof that eighteen went to the silver exchange, and one was in Cole's lockbox. Henry kept the other one... which was now missing. That one had to be the murder weapon.

Jake realized he needed to understand the exchange well enough to write it up in the book and explain it to a jury. As he picked up his phone to call the accountant, it buzzed with a text. Grady: *Trane having breakfast at the B&B. Lanigan says he was looking through the local interest books they keep in the lobby.*

Jake was glad to have Grady's extra eyes as things heated up. He texted back for Grady to send updates whenever Trane moved.

Trane was here for the silver, so his interest in Weston history and geography had to be related to the silver.

He called the accountant. "Ryan, tell me how this silver exchange works."

"Sure. One sec." The phone muffled for a few seconds, then Beck came back on. "What do you want to know?"

"I need to understand how a coin dealer buys silver bars and sells them to the exchange."

"Okay. Silver is a commodity that is bought and sold, but not to use, like orange juice and pork bellies. Most buyers, on a volume basis anyway, never take possession of the silver they buy. It's enough for the buyer to have the contract on it. The proof of ownership he gets when he buys it and gives when he sells it. He never even *sees* the silver—probably never even thinks about it as a hunk of metal that actually exists somewhere. Though of course if it didn't, his contract would have no value."

"Okay." Jake carried his bowl and spoon over to the trash can and dumped them in. He didn't have a kitchen sink, so he used disposable everything.

"Silver is traded on the commodities options exchange, COMEX, and for silver to be traded there it has to be delivered to the exchange and stored there. Before COMEX will accept silver it has to be assayed, which means it's examined to determine if it's 99.9% pure silver. Other than that, weight, obviously, is the other important factor. The mint mark is immaterial. Some bars have a mark from the mint that created them, and some have a mark from the company that mined it, or even the company that made the bar. No uniformity, but because it isn't part of the value, that's fine. Some bars do carry a serial number, which is relatively new, and is mostly done to create the perception of security."

"So when Griffin sent the bars off to the exchange they went to COMEX?"

"They should have, yes. And he should have the paperwork accepting the bars into the exchange, as well as the assayer's certificate certifying their purity and weight."

"Well, he agreed to send that paperwork to me at the station," Jake said. He wandered over to the front window and looked out at the day. It was cloudy, the clatter of the wind-whipped tree limbs clear through the glass. A blotch of sun shone high on the high school football stadium in the near distance. "Can you keep your eye out for it and take a look?"

"Will do."

"If it isn't there by two this afternoon, rattle his cage. Erin has his info. Or call me and I'll rattle it."

"I can do my own rattling."

"Good."

Jake ended the call, satisfied that if something could be found in Griffin's paperwork, Beck would find it.

He wondered what Levi had turned up on the mint mark. It seemed trivial, but it was hard to predict which piece of information might be the key to unraveling a complex web of information. He considered calling the would-be PI, but opted for a face-to-face instead. Movement made things happen. He geared up and headed out.

CHAPTER THIRTY-ONE

Jake was pulling away from his house when his cell phone buzzed, shooting a jolt of optimism through him. Some investigatory thread was unraveling, and the end of that string was now flapping his way. He swerved to the curb and threw the car into park. Before answering, he checked the screen. Coogan.

"How about I drop by?" Jake asked his friend. "I'm headed that way and can be there in less than five."

"See you then."

Jake found a parking spot in front of the frozen yogurt shop less than a hundred feet from Coogan's building. As he climbed the rickety stairs to Coogan's office, he felt sure his friend would have something good.

Jennifer was behind her desk in the waiting area, her fingers tapping out a staccato beat on her keyboard. "He said to send you on in."

Coogan sat behind his big walnut desk, leaning back, eyes on his computer screen. He swiveled his chair toward Jake, and a big smile split his face. "That was fast."

"Tell me what you found." Jake plopped in a chair in front of the desk.

"Well…"

A good start. It meant Coogan had something so big he needed to wind himself up for the telling.

"I'm still going through it. It's a big bankruptcy, and attorney's fees are already over a million. But a couple things about it struck me, so I wanted to share them with you." Coogan flexed his jaw, veins pulsing on the side of his gaunt skull. "First, although TH filed a chapter eleven—that's the reorganization type of bankruptcy that allows a company to keep operating while it sheds debt—it shut down its treasure hunts and is already selling off its assets. When a company decides to do that—to liquidate—it usually switches to a chapter seven, a liquidation bankruptcy. But in a seven, a court-appointed trustee takes over the company. So if a company wants to maintain control over its own dismantling it stays in a chapter eleven and handles its own affairs, subject to some loose court supervision."

"Okay."

"So here's the first odd thing: Trane did not file personal bankruptcy along with his corporation."

"Why is that odd?" Jake asked. "He shouldn't have to if he did business as a corporation, right? Isn't the whole purpose of a corporation to shield the owner from personal responsibility?"

"That is a main purpose, yes. But in many large cases with a closely held ownership—here it was just Trane and a couple venture capitalists—creditors can find creative ways to get to personal assets. So the individual often files personal bankruptcy; rich businessmen typically organize their personal finances to allow them to keep as much as they can after a personal bankruptcy. For example, in Texas, even in bankruptcy a person's home is protected, no matter how lavish it is. You could invest all your money in a penthouse apartment in Dallas worth millions, file bankruptcy, and keep the penthouse."

"So Trane must be happy with how the corporation protects him and doesn't believe any creative creditors can get at him."

"Well, he *should* be worried about that. But I'll get back to that in a minute."

"What else?"

"Frequently when a company starts liquidating, its production assets—the machines and equipment that makes whatever the company sold—are bought by the individuals who ran the company into the ground. Then they open a new company and start the whole thing over."

"That sounds crooked."

Jake leaned back in the chair, his excitement leaking away under the onslaught of technical jargon and analysis. But the excitement was still rising in Coogan's voice.

"It does, but it is common and done publicly. A sale is advertised to find other buyers, and the bankruptcy judge supervises the whole thing. But often the production equipment has no value outside its industry and little value inside it because competitors already have their own equipment or are worried about the condition of the equipment for sale."

A string of school buses rumbled by outside, the kids inside so pumped up their shouts were clear through the closed windows.

"TH owned two ships outfitted for underwater exploration, each with submersibles and scuba equipment. Trane's bid to buy the smaller boat was accepted, but he still hasn't paid for it, and the judge's patience is running out."

"So Trane wants to stay in the treasure hunting business. And?"

"Trane bought something else out of the bankruptcy. This he *has* paid for."

The long-awaited point, Jake hoped. He pulled out his pen and notebook.

"He bought all right, title, and interest in TH, Inc.'s ownership of the 'missing assets of WLB Foods, Inc. as identified on the relevant bill of sale.' That's how the docket reads, and I haven't been able to find the paper on it."

"What did he pay for it?" Jake asked, as he wrote the information into his notebook.

"Ten thousand."

"What could it be?"

"The man is searching for silver here in Weston, isn't he?" Coogan said. "*Missing* silver?"

"Have you ever heard of this company, WLB Foods?"

"Nope. I searched, and as far as I can tell no such company exists."

"Let me know if you get anything more on that." Jake finished writing down Coogan's information, the notebook perched on his knee. These missing assets could be exactly what had triggered Trane. "Let's get back to your earlier point. Why shouldn't Trane be happy with how the corporation is protecting his personal assets?"

"Because more than a dozen creditors are after him. I went into the Nuesces County court database—that's where he lives in Texas—and he's in serious trouble. He personally guaranteed some loans to the business and waived his homestead. Which means they can grab his house and other assets once they get judgments against him. He's up a creek without a paddle."

"Isn't bankruptcy a paddle?"

"That's what's so interesting. He could have filed bankruptcy along with the business and delayed this whole thing, maybe even made some deals for his personal assets. Given him time. That was the obvious move."

"And he didn't take it. So… what's his plan? Is there some benefit to *not* filing personal bankruptcy?" Jake tapped his pen on his notebook.

"Well, by not filing bankruptcy, he has no one supervising him. He hasn't had to make any statements about his personal assets. And he won't have to get into it until the collection lawsuits turn into judgments. So far his attorneys are stalling those cases, along with the typical motions a lawyer files when he's either lost touch with his client or his client has lost touch with reality."

"You're saying Trane is avoiding supervision so he can keep whatever he bought that once belonged to WLB Foods."

Coogan smiled. "And maybe so he can be here, in Weston, chasing it."

CHAPTER THIRTY-TWO

Jake pulled into the parking lot at Paget County Cleaners, the sun suddenly breaking through the thick overcast grayness to bathe the day in a thin warmth. But the wind whipped that warmth away as soon as he stepped out of the car. He dashed across the asphalt and into the warm humidity of the cleaners. Maybe it was time to start wearing his winter-weight work clothes.

Levi wore the *I found something* grin Jake had hoped to see. "Check this out," he said, waving for Jake to join him behind the counter.

Jake sat on the stool and settled in. Levi liked to describe his whole hunt before revealing his results. His news was always worth the wait.

"I started with Google, searching for GWU, which gave me thousands of hits for George Washington University. I then added the word *silver*, but found people named Silver on staff at the school and references to nearby Silver Spring, Maryland. Did you know the people who live there have a Silver Spring address but it isn't a town? It's something called a census-designated place. I'd never heard of that before."

Levi delighted in digressions. He would start looking at one thing and something would catch his interest and off he went. That's why he loved the Internet—he could click from one thing to another and on and on and then hit the back button or look at his history to get back on track.

"So then I took a step back and decided maybe if I understood who buys and sells silver bars, and how and why, that might help me with this search."

Levi launched into an explanation of the silver exchange that matched what the accountant had told Jake earlier. While Levi talked, the occasional customer came in to pick up or drop off cleaning, and Levi would stop mid-sentence to take care of the customer and then start again right where he'd left off.

"So then I learned about Silver Thursday."

Levi paused to help another customer, calling her by name and commiserating with her about their inability to get a stain out of her linen jacket. But Levi was so likable and so obviously disappointed in the result, she didn't even complain.

When Levi turned back to Jake he clasped his long-fingered hands between his thighs and smiled as if he was done with his report. Maybe Jake had missed something.

"And this Silver Thursday was…"

"An attempt to corner the world-wide market on silver."

"That sounds impossible."

"It does, right? And now it *is* impossible." Levi shook his head. "The SEC wrote a bunch of rules to prevent it from ever happening again. But in the seventies a pair of oil tycoons tried it."

Oil tycoons. "The Bunkers?"

"Exactly. Do you already know the story?"

"No. Tell me." Jake's own excitement was building with Levi's. Cole worked for Bunker, and Bunker traded in silver—and Jake didn't believe in coincidences.

Levi explained how the oil-rich Texas brothers, Huntley William Bunker and Robert Henry Bunker, started buying silver as a hedge against the devaluing dollar during the oil crisis. They bought silver because at the time it was illegal for a private citizen to own gold. They paid with cash, with credit, in a consortium with some Arabs, and on margin. They started buying at $1.50 an ounce and drove the price up to $40 an ounce. Eventually, on Silver Thursday, their margin orders were called and the fragile structure they created collapsed.

"It was a Texas-sized plan and a Texas-sized failure!" Levi smiled his biggest smile. "And one of the most interesting things about the Bunkers was they took physical possession of a bunch of the silver they bought."

"Explain." Jake's phone buzzed, and he snuck a peek at a text from Callie: *Call Me!!*

Not too long ago a text like that had come after dark—meaning she wanted to get together. He put the phone away.

"Investors usually just hold the contracts. But the Bunkers wanted the actual metal because they didn't believe in the dollar. They took possession of *tons* of it." Levi's eyes were alight.

"How much are we talking about?"

"Such things are normally private, but it made the news twice. In 1973 they took possession of forty million ounces and in 1976 another twenty million ounces. They sent the forty million by plane to Switzerland for storage."

"Forty million ounces by plane? What's that in pounds, like two or three million?"

"At sixteen ounces to the pound it would be 2.5 million pounds, or 1,250 tons. But silver is traded in *troy* ounces, which are heavier: approximately 480 grains versus 437.5 grains. About ten percent heavier. So the total weight is closer to 1,400 tons."

"Sounds ridiculous." Jake shook his head. "Texas-size is right."

"And here's the part you were interested in. The name of the Bunker company that actually owned the silver was Great Western United."

The GWU mint mark belonged to the Bunkers. Jake's pulse kicked up. It was definitely the Texans. "Does this company exist anymore?"

"I don't think so." Levi gestured toward the computer. "I found nothing on it. And the brothers and all their companies filed for bankruptcy. An amazingly generous law designed to give people a fresh start. Bankruptcy law is designed to encourage risk-taking, which has led to many of the fantastic technology advancements that we'd otherwise never have seen. Did you know that—"

"So what happened to the sixty million ounces the brothers took possession of?"

"The press didn't cover that, but it was probably turned over to the silver exchange, COMEX, after Silver Thursday to cover the margin call. Or maybe given up in the bankruptcy."

"When was Silver Thursday?"

Levi clicked his mouse a few times and pulled up a Wikipedia page on the event. "March 27, 1980."

"Levi, this is great stuff."

Levi beamed, his hands caressing his keyboard.

Jake took a couple of minutes to write what Levi had told him in his notebook. As he did a question came to him, but before he could ask it his phone buzzed with another text. Grady: *Trane is now at Weston Historical Society looking through maps and plats.*

Still more research. Clearly Trane didn't know exactly where the silver was.

"Levi, what happened to the silver bars when COMEX got them?"

"They would have gone back to the exchange warehouse where they would sit as people bought and sold the contracts representing them, until somebody else took possession of them. Big investors don't take possession."

"Who does?"

"Small investors, sometimes. More often people who actually use the silver—silversmiths, jewelers, electronics companies, medical device companies. But only the investor leaves them as bars."

"Did a company called WLB come up in your research?

"Sure. GWU was a division of a Bunker company called WLB Foods, Inc."

"Did any of Bunker's silver go missing?"

"Missing?" Levi lit up at the idea. "Not that I saw."

Jake was sure it had. The so-called "missing assets" of WLB Foods. Trane's purchase of those missing assets connected the man to the Bunkers, and through them to the silver.

And through the silver, to Henry.

Jake clapped Levi on his knobby shoulder. "Thank you very much, my friend."

As Jake headed out to the car, he was wearing his own broad smile. Just like that, he'd connected both Cole and Trane to Henry's silver.

He got the car's heater pumping and texted Coogan the news about WLB Foods and GWU. He was about to call Callie when a thought about Cole stopped him. Cole was here chasing the silver. He had put out his feeler years ago, because he knew—for a fact—the silver was here. Or at least, he knew it *had* been here. Then Henry sold the little bar to Griffin, and Cole knew the silver was *still* here. That's when he moved to town. He wanted the big bars and thought he might be able to get them. Then Griffin told Cole a thousand-ounce bar had turned up. Even if Griffin hadn't said who found it, Cole would have suspected Henry, and he would have sensed that his window for getting the silver before Henry went public with his discovery was closing. The clock ticking. He had to act fast, and he was prepared to do so; he had moved here expecting that he would have to.

Cole was definitely a suspect. Cole and Trane. It was one of the two.

The heater was making the car steamy. He turned it back down and returned Callie's call.

"That alibi is complete bullshit, Jake. I'm about to surprise the ex Mrs. Fox here at her house with what I know so far."

"What did you find out?" Jake rubbed an ear that was suddenly burning with shame. He'd know Lynn for forty years; he should have been able to detect that she was lying. And why had she lied to him? One of these Texans had killed Henry for the silver, not Lynn, or even Bowen.

"First, I interviewed her co-workers at the country club, and there was nothing between her and Bowen. Lynn has been banging some banker from Wheaton. Second, I talked to Bowen's neighbors. I figured with his boy away at college and his wife traveling for work he might have a lady friend over to the house. But nothing. Nada. Occasionally has a buddy over to watch the game or something, but that's it. And third, none of Lynn Fox's neighbors have ever seen a man over here other than Henry and then you, yesterday."

"So why did Lynn lie about the alibi? She didn't kill Henry—it was one of these Texans. I'm closing in on the complete backstory on the silver right now."

"Her lie was probably about the silver, too," Callie said. "I'll break her and let you know what she's after."

Jake didn't tell Callie to go easy; Lynn had earned what she had coming. "Thanks for the update."

"After that I have a meeting with The Great Hallagan and his client."

"Good luck."

"You too, partner."

Partner. The word strummed a longing in Jake for what they'd had between them until he got greedy and asked for more than Callie had been willing to give him. Maybe he should let it go. Maybe, in time…

He gritted his teeth and pushed the thought away. He had a murder to avenge.

He decided to visit the storage facility. Jake doubted the silver had ever been there, or that the facility would know even if it had, but they could tell him who had rented the unit. That name might open things up, unless Henry had grabbed a random file for proof he owned the bars.

But random was not how Henry did things.

CHAPTER THIRTY-THREE

Jake cut through the Brookdale neighborhood, caught Ogden Avenue near the entrance to Weston Self Storage, and arrived there within five minutes. Weston had annexed so much land over the years that addresses within town could be as much as ten miles apart, but every place and person he'd visited in his search for Henry's killer fit within a three-mile circle. The anomaly saved a lot of time.

Weston Self Storage's main building was a blocky three-story structure—brick, stucco, and glass with an odd minty green highlight—with an awning built of steel girders, painted in the same funny green, over the entrance. Long single-story concrete block buildings guarded the outer perimeter with roll-up steel doors facing inward, and a gate on rollers and controlled by a keypad barred entry to the yard.

Jake pulled his copy of the bill of sale from his blazer pocket and headed inside.

The door opened into a linoleum-floored room with a row of plastic chairs against the far wall and a pyramid of cardboard boxes in one corner. A window cut into the back wall held a counter with a coffee mug full of pens, and on the glass hung a plastic-coated chart showing the storage unit sizes and rental prices.

Jake pushed the doorbell screwed to the counter, and a muffled buzz sounded somewhere deep in the building. The space behind the counter held a pair of desks butted together, each with its own computer and clusters of photos and knick-knacks. A printer sat on a file cabinet against the wall.

He pushed the button again, and this time someone shouted, "Coming!"

A minute later a young woman popped through the doorway in the back. "Hey, Jake." She smiled.

Jake smiled back while he scoured his memory for the name to go with the familiar face. "Wendy!" She cut his hair. Seeing her out of context had stumped him for a second. "I forgot you work here too. Your parents own it, right?"

"I help out when I can. I get a lot of homework done when things are slow." She pointed at a textbook open on one of the desks, and he remembered she was also working on her bachelor's degree in nutrition. "Today is not one of those days."

She came to the counter, curly red hair bouncing with her walk. "Do you need to rent a unit?" She stretched an arm to the chart. "Here are the sizes and the costs. The small ones are inside this building and climate-controlled between fifty and eighty degrees. The big ones are outside and are not."

"Actually, I'm here on police business." He laid the bill of sale from Henry's file on the counter and slid it across to her. "I need to know who rented this unit and what was in it when it was auctioned off."

She scooped up the paper and looked it over. "Auctioned it off back in May. Oh, Henry. He's a good guy. Some of them are jerks."

"You knew Henry Fox?"

"Sure. He's in and out of here all the time. And he's bought a bunch of units."

"He ever have another guy with him? Big guy. About the same age."

"Not that I remember."

"Mr. Fox was murdered Tuesday night."

Her face paled. "That was Henry?" She looked down at Henry's name on the paper, and her hands started shaking. "You think it had something to do with this?"

"Right now I'm just gathering information to understand what Mr. Fox was working on."

"I remember this unit, actually. I watch the auctions. I'd like to bid, but can't because I work here. He got it cheap because most guys won't take a flyer on unlabeled boxes. Worried they might contain medical records or old tax returns. Or books, like these did."

Jake pulled out his notebook. "How do you know these boxes were full of books?"

"I went out there when Henry loaded his truck, and he opened a couple. There were also eight or ten black garbage bags stuffed with soft stuff. He tore one open. Flannel shirts and like that."

"How heavy were the boxes? Twenty pounds? Fifty pounds?"

"Henry didn't have any trouble with them and he's an older guy, you know. And not very big. Doubt they'd have been even thirty pounds." She pointed at the box pyramid behind Jake. "They were like those medium-size boxes there. In the middle. Not that big and not heavy-duty enough for real weight."

"Can you tell me who rented the unit?"

"That's private. I mean... I'm not supposed to." She crossed her arms, then uncrossed them and clenched her hands into fists. "This is for Henry, right?"

"It is. But I can ask a judge to issue a search warrant if you prefer." It would take an hour, but giving him the information in response to a court order would protect her from any customer complaints.

"Well, let me take a look." She took the paper over to a computer and clicked away for a few seconds. "Here it is." She clicked the mouse a couple more times, and the printer issued a high-pitched whine and spit two sheets into her waiting hand. She brought them to the counter and laid them out side by side.

"I think I can tell you without getting in trouble. This page here shows the original rental." She tapped the page on Jake's left. "This one shows who'd been paying the bill at the end." She tapped the other page.

"Two different people?"

"Yep." She slid the left page forward. It was an imaged copy of a form agreement with the renter's information written in by hand, but everything was clear and legible. A two-hundred-square-foot exterior unit was rented by Lucy Bristol and Lawrence Bristol of 1112 West Jackson, Weston. The original "Rent Paid" was $4,000.

"Is that a mistake?" Jake put his finger on the dollar entry. Four thousand dollars to store old books?

"Some people pay a long-term in advance. Like if they're going to be out of town or whatever. That was the only payment we ever got from the original renter. When the rent ran out, we sent out our standard notices, but all the mail came back. Then the public guardian picked up the payments."

The public guardian handled the affairs of wards of the state, mostly special-needs adults who either didn't have family or whose family couldn't, or wouldn't, take care of them anymore.

"When was that?" Jake asked.

"Ten or twelve years ago." She slid the other sheet forward. "This page shows a copy of the most recent check from the PG. For the last year of storage, which expired at the end of April."

The check was drawn on the public guardian's checking account, made out to Weston Self Storage, and had "Bristol Storage Fee" printed on the memo line.

The sound of someone whistling came from behind the back wall. The *Sunday Night Football* theme song.

"That's my dad," Wendy said just before the door into the back opened. "Dad? This is Detective Houser. He's investigating a murder. Mr. Fox. I'm showing him about a unit Henry bought."

Wendy's dad was short like his daughter, but wiry. He stepped to the counter with a frown and rubbed at his bushy gray mustache. "Anything we can do." He reached over and shook Jake's hand. His hand was rough, but his grip wasn't. "I'm Bill. Henry was a good man."

"Wendy showed me—"

"I know I shouldn't have, Dad, but—"

"It's okay, honey." Bill smiled. "It's the right thing."

"Wendy walked me through these already." Jake gestured to the pages on the counter. "Anything else you can tell me?"

Bill picked up the pages and looked them over. His face flushed red and his eyes shot to his daughter, then back to Jake. He rubbed his mustache again, like something in it bothered him. "I remember this unit." He tapped the page. "Guardian paid rent through April, then came and moved the personal stuff—family records and photographs and the like—to his big unit, then signed the waiver and we auctioned the rest off."

Jake considered going to have a look at the personal stuff. But the guardian would demand a warrant, which would take time, and Henry hadn't needed to see the personal stuff to find the silver. Jake decided to leave it for now. If he got stuck, he'd rethink it. "Guardian look through all of it?" he asked.

"Yep. In fact, Cubs were rained out so I helped him." More mustache scratching. A glance at his daughter. His eyes staying away from Jake's. "He's a good customer. It was just books and clothes."

"Henry ever have another guy along to help him with other units? Big guy?"

"Back in the beginning, yeah. Prissy kind of guy. The stuff in the units always has a layer of dust on it, you know. The big priss didn't like getting dirty."

"Anything else?" There was something else. Something bothering Bill.

"That was it."

Jake waited.

Bill finally met Jake's eyes. "Wendy," Bill said. "Can you go make us a fresh pot of coffee?"

"Sure, Dad."

Wendy gave Jake a quick wave as the door closed behind her. When it clicked shut, her dad leaned over the counter and spoke in a lower voice.

"Another guy came by. Tall guy with a long coat. He asked about this same unit. I told him I couldn't tell him anything. He offered me fifty bucks, but I'd seen what was in those boxes and knew there wasn't anything in there worth fifty dollars. I did tell him that."

"He wear a hat with a red and white logo on it?"

"Sure did."

Trane.

"I did end up taking the fifty."

"In exchange for what?"

"For the name and address of the original renter."

"The Bristols on Jackson?"

"I figured that couldn't hurt anybody. That family is long gone."

"Thanks for telling me, Bill."

Jake folded the new pages around the receipt and slid them all into an inside pocket of his blazer.

Back in the car he took a few minutes to enter the new information in his notebook. The name "Bristol" set off a familiar tingle in the base of his brain, and he finally placed it. When he was a kid, the big house on the bluff at the end of Jackson had been owned by a woman the kids had sometimes called a witch, especially around Halloween. The rest of the year she was just Old Lady Bristol. He pulled out his smart-phone and zoomed in on the area using Google Maps. Jackson ended at the driveway to the public works facility. The map said it was called "The Bristol Yard."

Jake re-checked his text threads with Grady. Trane had been poking around in the "public works yard" last night. The Bristol Yard.

Nothing random about Henry using this bill of sale at all.

And Jake saw he'd missed another text from Grady while he was in the storage facility: *Trane poked around the yard again but a city employee ran him off.*

The Yard; the Bristol Yard.

Henry had bought the contents of this storage unit full of things owned by Larry Bristol. He used the storage unit bill of sale to prove he owned the silver. Trane was now snooping around the Bristol Yard. The Bunker silver—Jake had no doubt it was their silver, or had been— must be connected to the Bristol family.

It was only a mile away, so Jake fired up the cruiser and headed for west Jackson. Maybe something there would answer all his questions.

You never knew.

CHAPTER THIRTY-FOUR

Lynn felt better this morning. No tears, and she'd eaten a whole piece of toast and kept it down. She'd been unable to eat any of the spaghetti the night before, so this was her first real food since Henry died.

There it was again. Thinking of something as coming either before, or after, Henry's death.

She sipped her coffee, thinking about Henry. Thinking about how they would never be together. Thinking about the hole his death had created in April's world.

Thinking about the silver.

She squeezed her eyes shut and tried not to think about the silver, but it was useless. *And natural*, she told herself. When you need money, you think about money.

Even without the silver, April was going to inherit Henry's house—that was good. The house itself wasn't any better than Lynn's, but the land it was on was worth real money. Rich people were building mansions all up and down that street. Huge things with layers of decks and turreted corners and three-car garages. And Henry's lot was big. It stretched all the way down to the park. It might be big enough to split it in half and put up two of those giant houses. Those people didn't care about having yards. One of the guys at the club said a developer was paying four hundred thousand for dumps all through downtown just to tear them down. She'd called the developer about her own house—four hundred would clear all her debts and set her up in a nice townhouse on the south end of town—but he told her every lot on her block was too narrow by five feet. Some dumbass law.

Figures.

But Henry's land was wide and deep. Splitting it in half would make it worth eight hundred thousand. Maybe more because it was so close to the river. The money would be April's, not hers, but they were a team, right? So April would—

A knock on the back door.

Lynn pushed her fingers through her hair and puffed her cheeks to try to smooth the lines out of her face, then went to the door and stretched up on her toes to look through the window. A black woman with short knotty hair and no eye makeup.

Lynn opened the door. "Yes?"

"Lynn Fox?" The woman pulled the storm door open.

"Yes?" Lynn took a step back, crossing her arms.

"I'm Detective Callie Diggs." She stepped into the house as if Lynn's retreat was an invitation, pulling back her little man-jacket to show a badge on her belt. "I'm working with Detective Houser on your ex-husband's murder. You and I have a few things to discuss."

"We do?" Lynn backed into the kitchen, fighting an urge to run for the front door. Why was this woman here instead of Jake? She searched her brain for an answer, but found nothing but her own fear. Her bowels twisted and sweat broke out in her armpits and across her forehead.

She needed time. She lied best when she could plan it out. "Please have a seat and I'll get you a cup of coffee."

The woman sighed. "Okay, then."

Lynn took her time, hands shaking, the coffee pot clattering against the mug and again when she stuck it back in the drip machine. She used two hands to bring the mug to the table, setting it on a newspaper so it wouldn't rattle. Then she sat down and tried for a smile. Her mind was still nearly empty, except for two simple thoughts: *Run!* and *Help me, April!*

The detective looked at Lynn with a blank face. Her skin was very dark and she was so still and her cheekbones so sharp, her face looked like an African mask. *Is that racist?* The woman didn't touch the coffee, just sat with her hands together in front of her.

"Detective Houser is handling a few other issues today, so I was assigned to confirm your alibi."

A bead of sweat ran down from Lynn's temple. Then another. She wiped them away and tried to smile.

April burst through the hallway door. "Mom?"

"Come here, baby." Lynn sprang from the table and hugged her, long and tight. "What is it?"

April whispered in her ear. "Read this." She held her phone down low, blocked from the detective's view by their bodies. A text message from Conner: *Black woman cop has been talking to our neighbors. One of them told me she's asking if a certain woman ever visits my dad at our house. Had a picture. Probably of your mom because of the alibi!*

Lynn pushed the phone down, and April slipped it into the pocket of her hoodie.

"April," Lynn said, "this detective works with Jake." She tried again for a smile, but it froze half-formed on her face then crumbled away.

"Good morning, April." The detective smiled gently. "My name is Detective Diggs. First, I'm so sorry about your dad. Detective Houser said he was a good man."

"Thank you."

"Please sit, ladies," Diggs said.

They sat, Lynn pulling April's chair closer.

"As I explained to your mom, Detective Houser is looking into some other leads so I'm doing his follow-up."

"Following up what?" April put her hand over Lynn's twiddling thumbs. A nervous tic April called a "tell" when they played Scrabble. Said she always knew when her mom held the Q and the Z and had no place to put them as the game wound down.

Lynn put her hands on her lap under the table.

Diggs smiled. "Following up on ground Detective Houser already covered. It's how we do it." She turned to Lynn. "Would you prefer we speak alone, Mrs. Fox?"

Absolutely not. "I want April with me. She knows about… what I said."

Diggs nodded. "Okay." She waited a beat then dropped her smile. "I looked into the affair you claimed to be having with Jim Bowen, and it's complete bullshit."

Lynn's stomach clenched. "Uh… what do you mean?"

"I *mean* I talked to your co-workers, who all told me you're seeing some other married man and they've never seen you near Bowen. I *mean* I talked to Bowen's neighbors and they've never seen you at his house. I *mean* I talked to your neighbors and Bowen has never been here. I *mean* you lied to Detective Houser. That's what I mean."

Lynn fought to hold back a sob—and failed. April put an arm around her shoulder. Lynn leaned into her.

"Your story about Bowen being here that night was total bullshit, right?" Diggs said.

Lynn nodded, unable to speak.

"Giving Bowen a fake alibi makes me think you were involved with him in killing your ex-husband. Convince me you weren't."

Lynn grabbed a napkin from the holder in the center of the table. She wiped her eyes and then clutched the napkin in her hands. Finally she looked at Diggs. The detective's eyes traveled smoothly from April to Lynn, back and forth, reading them.

"Did Detective Houser tell you to talk to all those people?" April asked.

Diggs ignored the question. "I need the truth right now."

Lynn twisted the napkin, the fragile paper tearing. "I… I didn't have anything to do with killing Henry." April snatched another napkin from the dispenser and pressed it into Lynn's hand. Lynn grabbed her daughter's hand; she needed the hand more than the napkin. "I still loved him."

"Why did you give Bowen an alibi?"

"Why don't you go talk to Mr. Bowen?" April said. "He's the one who hated my dad."

Diggs didn't even glance her way.

Lynn fought down a sob. "I'm broke!"

"And?"

"I… I thought maybe he'd give me some of it if I helped him." Lynn choked back a sob and looked to April for help. April smiled and squeezed her shoulders.

"Some of what?" Diggs asked.

"The silver," April said and squeezed again.

Diggs shot daggers at her.

April didn't flinch. "Didn't Detective Houser tell you about the silver, Detective Diggs?"

Diggs didn't answer, her black eyes drilling right into Lynn's brain.

"She's right," Lynn said. "I wanted some of the silver." She didn't want to talk about the silver, but April wouldn't have brought it up without a plan.

"You were trading the alibi for a cut?"

April squeezed, and Lynn nodded.

"Did Bowen agree to the deal beforehand, or were you going to blackmail him into it?"

"I—he didn't—"

"Tell me the story."

Lynn paused, hoping April would jump in, but she stayed silent. "Henry found some silver bars and because of this stupid business they were in together buying the storage unit junk, Bowen thought he owned half of them. Henry didn't agree and I… I think Bowen killed Henry over it. I thought if I gave him an alibi he'd share them. They aren't his anyway. They were Henry's, which means they're really April's now."

"To be clear, what you wanted from Bowen was a cut of the mysterious *big* bars. The smaller ones were all accounted for."

Squeeze. Lynn nodded, afraid she'd give something away if she opened her mouth.

"How do you know Bowen knew about the big bars?"

Lynn didn't have an answer, but April jumped in.

"Conner told me."

"Conner Bowen?"

"Yes, ma'am."

The detective's mouth puckered like she'd tasted something sour.

"He overheard his parents talking about it," April said, her face red. She lowered her voice to almost a whisper. "Dad was scared of him. Mr. Bowen is so big and Dad was... He was strong from all his work but he was small, really."

Lynn was proud of April for getting that in.

Diggs frowned. "Frankly, we doubt the big bars exist. We think it more likely the little bars got your dad playing the wouldn't-it-have-been-cool-if game."

"My dad didn't lie to me."

"He told you he found them?"

"He showed me one."

The big bars are *real.* Lynn's pulse kicked up. Maybe... just maybe.

Diggs froze. Then: "I thought you were leaving something out." She turned to Lynn. "Did you see it?"

"April isn't a liar."

Diggs turned back to April. "Where was the bar?"

"On the table in his writing room."

"When was this?"

April looked at Lynn, then licked her lips and shifted in her chair. "A week ago."

"It isn't there now."

"Is it important for you to see it?" April asked.

Lynn's head snapped around.

Diggs leaned forward. "Do you know where it is?"

"Dad gave it to me." April's hands shook and she clamped them between her thighs. "For my college expenses."

Diggs scooted to the edge of her chair. "Do you still have it?"

Lynn had been about to ask the same question. She realized she was holding her breath, and let it go.

"In my room."

April got up and led them into her room. She knelt on the floor and reached under the bed.

"Stop!" Diggs's sharp voice bit the air. "Is it under there?"

April nodded. "Yes."

Diggs dropped to her knees. "I see it. I'll call our forensics team to recover it, and it will be evidence. When did your dad give it to you?"

"The day he showed it to me."

"He showed you one, but there were more, right?" Diggs asked.

"He... he said there were five hundred of them."

"Did you see the rest of them?"

April shook her head.

"Where are they?"

"He never told me."

Lynn knelt and looked under the bed. She could see a dark square shape like a narrow shoebox. That was a lot of silver. "April will get it back, right?"

"If she owns it, she'll get it back."

"Do you think Mr. Bowen killed my dad?" April asked the detective.

"I don't know."

But Lynn was sure the detective thought exactly that.

CHAPTER THIRTY-FIVE

Jake slowed as he passed the VFW, then started checking addresses. There were three mini-mansions on the north side and a well-kept brick ranch on the south side. The highest address number fell short of the address on the storage facility contract. As he'd thought: Lucy Bristol was the Old Lady Bristol who once lived in the big house up on the bluff. The land now occupied by the Bristol Yard.

Jake did a three-point turn in front of the pole gate blocking the driveway into the Bristol Yard. The sheds and garages where the city stored some of its out-of-season vehicles were visible through the bare trees. He cruised slowly back the way he'd come and eyed the ranch. It was a wide building with a two-car garage on the east end. The front door was set in the middle of the house and reached by a long curve of concrete sidewalk. A flagpole shot into the gray sky from a white gravel circle in the front yard, the Stars and Stripes snapping in the breeze. Old-timers and veterans flew flags. Jake hoped for an old-timer who had known the Bristols.

He pulled into the driveway, stopped his car just off the street, and got out.

A horn honked, the long deep sound of a semi, tires scuffing asphalt. Jake jumped away from it, turning to see a giant white pickup swerve off the street and onto the driveway, braking to a halt with stuttering chirps from its tires.

Trane's truck.

The driver's door flew open and the big man was yelling before his feet hit the concrete. "Are you following me now, *Jake?*"

Trane came at Jake, his long coat flowing behind him in the breeze, hat pulled low.

Jake stood his ground, his pulse rushing to ready him for action. He shot a glance down the road but didn't see Grady's car behind Trane. He took a short step forward with his left foot to change his profile, pushed back the flap of his blazer, and gripped his gun. His fingers tingled.

Trane stopped and swept back his own coat to put his hands on his hips. He wasn't armed. Jake released his gun and covered it with his blazer.

"Who needs to follow you?" Jake said. "Driving *that* thing, you stand out wherever you go." He gestured at the pickup, its diesel engine still clattering. "And it looks more like *you're* following *me.*"

"You trying to tell me you didn't see me as you were coming down this street?" Trane leaned in close, his coffee breath washing over Jake. "You looked right at me."

"I was looking for Larry Bristol's address," Jake said, watching Trane closely for a tell. He wasn't disappointed. Trane's eyes bugged and his mouth clapped shut, hands squeezing into fists. "The same address you bought from Bill at the storage facility."

"You're trying to pin your murder on the guy from out of town. I fucking knew it. God *damn* it."

"He used to live over there." Jake pointed over his shoulder with his thumb. "Where you were just poking around."

"You leave me the hell alone. I…" Trane snatched off his hat and slapped it against his leg.

Jake resisted the urge to step back. The man towered. "Is that where the thousand-ounce bars are?"

"You don't know what you're talking about."

"When that question about them popped up on the forum, you came running."

Trane's jaw worked and his hands flexed open and closed. He took another step forward.

Jake stood his ground. "If you own them, why all this sneaking around? Why didn't you just tell Henry they were yours? Show him your paperwork."

Trane's face was red now, his eyes squinting.

"You didn't have to kill him," Jake said.

"You are *not* pinning that on me!" Trane's voice dropped. "And I already told you about ownership."

He slapped the hat again, then put it on and got back in his truck. He revved the engine, a cloud of thick black smoke pumping from the exhaust, and backed away with a roar, spinning the steering wheel and slashing the front tires over the edge of the lawn. After revving the engine again—and giving Jake a dark look—he roared away. All four tires bounced and grabbed at the pavement, and diesel exhaust almost obscured the truck from view.

When the truck disappeared over the hill by Centennial Beach, Grady's white Jetta nosed out of the VFW driveway and followed.

Jake's phone vibrated. Grady: *Sorry about that. Didn't see he was coming at you till it was too late to warn you.*

Jake shot back his own warning: *Trane thought I was tailing him so might be looking at his mirrors.*

His phone vibrated as he was slipping it back in his pocket. He paused to look at it, the wind flapping his pant legs. Callie—calling this time. He turned his back to the wind.

"Houser."

"The ex didn't last ten seconds. She thinks Bowen killed Fox and got the silver, and she hoped he'd pay her for the alibi with some of it. The money is more important to her than catching the man who killed her daughter's father."

Jake appreciated that Callie didn't gloat or celebrate. She expected people to lie, and catching them at it was just what she did. "What do you think?"

"I don't think she was involved. Too dumb. Too… ruined."

"That's good." He shook his head at himself. He shouldn't have a stake in who did it.

"What did you say? I lost some of that."

Jake cupped his free hand around the phone. "Sorry, I'm outside."

"I'm liking Bowen. He argued with Fox about the little bars, and if he owned half of those why wouldn't he own half the big ones? We can't have two silver hoards in Weston. All the same stuff, right? One treasure."

"That makes sense," Jake said. But Callie's theory ignored the Texans.

"And you're going to love this. The kid had one of the big bars under her bed. Forensics just picked it up."

"A thousand-ounce bar?" Jake's chest ached. Another lie from the Fox women. Another lie he'd fail to spot.

"Yep. Fox gave it to her for college expenses. The mom didn't even know it was there. When she saw it I swear she had dollar signs flashing in her pupils like a cartoon. The girl probably kept it secret so Mom wouldn't steal it from her. I've seen desperation before."

"Did April know anything more about it? Where he found it? How many there were?"

"Five hundred is what her dad told her. She says she never saw the rest or knew where he found them."

Five hundred! At twenty thousand each. That's… ten million dollars. Talk about motive.

"I'm headed to Bowen's house," Callie said. "Told his lawyer it was there or the station."

"You get the deal papered up? Is it tight?"

"The state's attorney sent it over. I'm good to go."

They talked it through. Callie would start by telling Bowen he was off the hook because of the alibi Lynn had given him. If he confirmed the alibi, she'd bite him in the ass with it and take it from there.

CHAPTER THIRTY-SIX

Jake stuck the phone back in his pocket and continued up the driveway. The wind snapped the flag and tugged at his blazer but wasn't strong enough to cool the heat of failure from his face. He should have verified that alibi, and he should have seen that April was hiding something. Those screw-ups could have left the case against the real killer ripe for attack by a defense attorney.

He shook himself out of it. He needed to focus on his job. Dwelling on his mistake instead of focusing on his case could lead to him making more.

As Jake approached the front door, his view through the picture window opened up into the living room. An old man sat in a recliner, a lamp over his shoulder and a book on his lap. His head came up, and he met Jake's gaze. He closed his book and started to pull himself to the edge of his chair.

Jake mounted the stoop and waited, the heat generated by his encounter with Trane bleeding slowly away. Eventually the door pulled back and the old man appeared on the other side of the glass storm door, hunched over but otherwise well put together in chinos and a blue button-down. His full head of silver hair had been swept back from his forehead with the help of some shiny hair product.

"Yes?" The storm door barely muffled his strong voice. His eyes were bright and interested, his eyebrows raised. Age spots blotted his cheeks.

"Sir, I'm Detective Jake Houser with the Weston PD. Do you have time for a few questions?"

"Whoa! I'm not deaf."

"Sorry, sir."

"Come in."

Jake pulled the door open and stepped up into the house. It was warm inside. Very warm. He closed the doors behind him.

"I did answer questions for a young officer the other day." The old man shook his head. "Mr. Fox was a fine man."

"We appreciate your cooperation. My questions are about something else."

"Another mystery here on our little dead end?" The man stepped aside and motioned with his hand. "I'm going to sit down. Not so steady on my feet."

The old man turned and headed back to his chair, and Jake followed him into the living room. The house had a cozy feel. Hand-crocheted pieces draped across the arms of chairs and the back of the couch. Needlepoint here and there. A rich meaty smell wafting in from the kitchen, a little spice with it—a stew, or maybe chili.

The old man dropped into his chair with a sigh. "Grab that chair and bring it over here, Detective." He pointed to a delicate-looking spindle-back on one side of a wide opening that led to the dining room. Across the dining room table a big window framed a view of the back yard, a green expanse that dropped gently away from the house to the line of trees atop the bluff.

Jake grabbed the chair and brought it over to within a few feet of the old man. "What's your name, sir?" He took off his blazer and draped it over the back of the chair, then pulled his notebook out of his blazer and his pen from his shirt pocket.

"Joe Martin."

"I'm pleased to meet you, Mr. Martin. I—"

"Call me Joe. Now what do you want to know about? I am something of an expert on Weston. I've lived in this house since I got back from the war."

Excellent. "Did you know the Bristol family? Used to live next door?"

"Well, of course! From Camden all the way through Jonathan and down to Lawrence." He smiled. "Even knew Lucy pretty well—Jonathan's wife—which is more than most can say."

"How so?"

Martin eyed Jake wisely. "You look like you're of that age. Did you grow up here in Weston, Detective?"

"I did."

"Well then you surely knew of Old Lady Bristol and her salt pellet gun."

Jake laughed. "As a matter of fact…"

A memory wormed into his head, and he shared it with Martin. Back in those days the estate was fenced in and heavily wooded and had its own pond—and on a dare, Jake climbed the fence and fished the pond. He'd had his line in the water just long enough to start thinking about fishing instead of getting shot, when she appeared on the opposite shore. He was alone… and then he wasn't. She stood watching him, wearing bib overalls and holding a rifle. He reeled in his line slowly, keeping his eyes on her, then grabbed the ammo pouch he used to hold his tackle and ran. She never made a sound and never raised the gun.

Martin chuckled. "That sounds like Lucy. She loved surprises and secrets. But she was as shy as could be. Always carried that varmint rifle. Plucked away at anything that moved. Heard it pop a couple times a day until a year or so before she died. She never shot a kid with a salt pellet, but that story kept 'em off her property, I'm proud to say."

"It wasn't true?"

"Nope! Just a rumor I started. Fed it to the neighborhood kids and they spread it through town, and it lasted for generations. Otherwise that fenced-in woods was too tempting. Amazing it worked so well."

"When did she pass away?"

"Oh, let's see. Eighty-nine, I think. Yeah, that sounds right." Martin pulled a handkerchief out of the pocket of his sweater and coughed into it. "Maybe ninety."

"And you knew Lawrence?"

"Of course I knew him." Martin looked inside the handkerchief, then folded it over and pushed it back in his pocket. When he looked up, his eyebrows were furrowed and his face had drooped. "You can't think Lawrence killed Henry?"

"Why would he?"

"He wouldn't—and couldn't. He's a simple and gentle soul. Shy like his momma, but something happened during birth and he isn't exactly right."

"Where is he now?"

"Been over in the home—Weston Oaks—since just before his momma passed. Going on thirty years. Used to visit him regularly back when I got around on my own. Now Ursulina takes me a couple times a year. I'll be seeing him again in a couple weeks for Thanksgiving."

That explained the public guardian paying the storage fee; Lawrence Bristol must be a special-needs adult. "I see the old Bristol place is now owned by the city."

"Yep. Lucy left it to the city in exchange for taking care of Lawrence. She was going to leave him with us, but we were already getting old and my wife wasn't well. So…" Martin shrugged, and his voice drifted off softly. "She signed Lawrence into Weston Oaks right there at the end. With Lucy gone, Lawrence was the last Bunker in Weston."

"Bunker?" Jake sat up straighter.

"Yep." Martin smiled. "A bit of almost-lost Weston trivia for you, young man. Werner Lafayette Bunker Senior raised eight kids on that land. Ran a junk business out on Plank Road. The youngest two were twins, Werner Junior and Brumhilde. Junior moved to Texas and made it big in oil. Had his own passel of kids. Broomie stayed right there and married Camden Bristol. Their son Jonathan brought his wife Lucy home to live on the property, and she helped Broomie look after Senior until the day he died. Junior came back for his dad's funeral, took his chunk of the inheritance, and left again. Broomie took the land on the bluff as her share and left it to Jonathan when she died a few years later. Lawrence lived right there with his mom until just before she died."

Jake wrote all this into his notebook, his excitement making his scribbles almost illegible. But he would remember this without the notes, he was sure.

"Do any of the Bunkers ever come back for a visit?"

"Not that I recall. Jonathan got along real good with his Uncle Junior. Went down there every summer, high school through college, to work the oil fields. Made great money and more than paid his own way through undergrad and medical school." Martin shook his head. "Broomie's other siblings all moved away after grabbing their share and never came back. Lawrence is the last of them here. Jonathan told me the whole family history. We used to play chess together on my back porch."

Jake finished his notes and looked back up at Martin. The man had his head cocked to the side, looking off into the past.

"I seem to recall telling this story to someone else not long ago," Martin said. He looked at Jake. "Sitting right here in these same chairs."

"Someone you know?" Jake asked gently. "Or an out-of-towner?" It had to have been either Henry or one of the Texans.

A door opened and then banged closed in the back of the house, shaking the windows with the pressure change.

CHAPTER THIRTY-SEVEN

"Mr. Joe?" A woman's voice, followed by footsteps and the rustle of nylon clothing. "We have a visitor?"

"That's Ursulina," Martin said. "She's gonna want you to skedaddle. But it's my house."

A petite Hispanic woman bustled across the dining room. She was bundled up like it was twenty below outside instead of fifty above.

"Mr. Joe, who is this?"

"He's my visitor and I'm fine."

"I heard you with the coughing from outside." She unwrapped her scarf and pulled back her hood. Her black hair shone against the dull green of her Michelin Man–style coat. "Who are you?"

Jake stood to introduce himself. She grabbed his offered hand and pulled him into the dining room, nearly yanking him off his feet.

"Please don't stay long. Mr. Fox being murdered just down the river has tired him enough."

"What is she telling you?" said Martin. "I can help, Ursulina. Mr. Fox deserves what help we can give him."

Ursulina let go of Jake's hand and peered around him. "Yes of course, Mr. Joe." She looked back at Jake. "Please."

"Okay," Jake said.

She stepped into the kitchen, a well-lighted open space with a huge picture window above a wide counter, and Jake went back to finish his conversation with Martin.

"So Lawrence was Jonathan and Lucy's son?" As Jake sat down he took a close look and decided Ursulina was right. Martin was tired. He needed to cut this short.

"One and only, pride and joy." Martin coughed into his handkerchief again. "And ours too, to an extent. My wife and I—Ruth was her name, God rest her soul, she's been gone for over twenty years now—didn't have children of our own. Jonathan worked a lot of hours and Lucy was too shy to leave her property, so Lawrence spent time with us. Took him to fireworks and parades and such. Used to follow me around in the yard. He went to school for a couple years, but he couldn't keep up. Lucy taught him at home. In his teens he became more like his momma. Stayed on the bluff, in the woods, and along the river. He'd come by from time to time to help with the yard work or to show me something he'd found from time to time."

"Do you know what happened to Lucy's personal belongings?"

"She sold it all off before the end, everything but her books and photos I recall her saying. She caught the cancer, and it took its time killing her. Got everything straightened away before the end."

"Did Lawrence, or Lucy, ever talk about getting silver bars from their Texas relatives?"

"Silver bars?" Martin shook his head, then his eyes widened with a memory. "I do remember Lawrence telling me a story about a silver treasure one time. I... all I remember of it is the, watchamacallit... punch line. He said, 'Silver is heavier than gold because a hundred dollars of silver weighs more than a hundred dollars of gold.' He surprised us sometimes with clever catchy phrases and such. He liked words."

Lawrence Bristol talking about the weight of silver. The man had touched the bars. "Was he talking about a real treasure?"

"Of course not." Martin laughed. "Boy had a great imagination from playing by himself his whole darn life."

"Mr. Martin," Jake said. "I really app—"

"It *was* Mr. Fox," Martin said. "Henry. He's the one asked me about the Bristols and the Bunkers."

"Henry." Jake couldn't help repeating it, excitement coursing through him at the idea of following in Henry's footsteps.

Henry would lead him where he needed to go.

* * *

Lynn's stomach twisted. She didn't know if it was from the coffee she'd been drinking all day or April's betrayal. Just thinking the word made her stomach heave, but what else should she call it? April had had that big silver bar under her bed all this time and never said a word about it.

She jumped up from the kitchen table so quickly the chair chirped against the floor.

"April?" Lynn heard the accusation in her own voice and brought it down. "Honey?"

She pressed her cheek to her daughter's bedroom door. "April?"

"What, Mom?"

"I want to understand about the big silver bars."

The door swept open. April wore gray sweatpants and the purple Northwestern hoodie. "What about them?"

Angry heat came to Lynn's face, but she pushed it down. "Why you didn't tell me you'd seen one? Or that you had one right here in our house? Everything." *And where are the rest of them?*

"Dad didn't…" April shook her head and pulled her mom into her room. They sat on the bed, holding hands. "Conner found out about them, like I told that cop. I figured Dad was waiting to surprise me. You know how he liked to do that. And that's what happened. Last Saturday. He told me about them, but he didn't want me to tell anyone else because he found them on city land, so he wasn't sure if there was a way he could keep them. Which isn't even a fair question, because no one else even knows the silver exists, so what's it to them?"

"Of course he should have gotten the silver," Lynn said. "He found it. Without him—like you said—no one would even know it was there."

"Right."

"But he told you *where* he found them? On the city land?" Lynn licked her lips, her heart fluttering with excitement.

April looked away, then back. "Dad said he found them buried behind the Bristol Yard."

"Where's that?"

"That place at the end of Jackson—the street Dad lives off of? Where it dead ends? That's the Bristol Yard."

"Five hundred big silver bars. Right there?"

"I'm sorry I didn't tell you, Mom, but… well, Dad told me not to, and you're really bad at keeping secrets and really bad at lying, so…"

"I understand," Lynn said. She *was* bad at keeping secrets—but she was a better liar than most. "But why did you tell that detective about it?"

"To get her off you and your lie about the alibi. She'll go after Mr. Bowen now. The little bars weren't enough… what's it called. Motive."

That was for sure. "If she arrests him we may never get a chance at the silver."

"I had to tell her, Mom. She wanted to pin it on you. Maybe just to prove that Mr. Houser had made a mistake. Cops are crooked, Mom. We see it on TV all the time."

"I didn't…" Lynn couldn't finish the sentence. She'd been too embarrassed at getting caught in the lie about the affair to see it. Too embarrassed to admit she cared more about the money than catching Henry's killer.

Thank God April had been there to save her.

CHAPTER THIRTY-EIGHT

Jake sat in Martin's driveway, piecing what the old man had told him together with what he'd already learned. Trane was interested in the Bristol Yard, where Lawrence Bristol had lived, who was related to the Bunkers, who took possession of thousands of tons of silver back in the seventies.

The picture was coming together.

Jake drove to the end of the street and parked in front of the pole gate spanning the driveway into the yard, then stepped over the gate and walked down the gravel drive. A dozen yards in the drive opened into a wide gravel expanse fronting a pair of dilapidated garages. The faint odor of motor oil rode along the cold breeze, and the branches of the bare trees circling the area clattered together in the wind.

"Hey! You can't be back here!" A heavyset man in brown overalls appeared in the open garage door, his arms raised. "No trespassing. It's posted." He pointed back at the gate and started toward Jake.

Jake flashed his badge. "Police business. What's your name?"

The man stopped a few steps away. "George. I work here."

"George, tell me about the guy you ran off the property."

George wiped his hands on a rag he pulled from his back pocket. "I didn't call you."

"What was he doing here?"

"I keep telling them we need a proper fence around here. Anyone can step over that gate. And people keep stealing the no trespassing sign."

"The man."

"He was poking around the place. Looking for who knows what. Maybe the owls."

"What owls?"

"Some bird watcher told me there's a rare kind of owl in here that lives underground. Burrowing owl, he called it." George's hand went to his jaw line.

"Guy with a birthmark on his face?"

"That's right."

Cole and Trane had both been snooping through here. "When did you last see the birder?"

"It's been a while. Last week or the week before."

"And the guy today?"

"He was looking around mostly over where the house used to be."

"Take me there."

George led the way behind the garages and through the thick underbrush. Branches and thistles snagged Jake's pant legs. George stopped in a wide space about fifty feet from the edge of the bluff, lumpy with settling ground.

"It was here," he said.

Light filtered through the bare trees to the thick layers of fallen leaves. Jake kicked his way across the space, back and forth, the smells of decay and mold filling the air. The ground was spongy in the dips where it had settled, squelching under his feet, but he didn't find any fresh digging.

"Did you talk to the guy this morning?"

"Just told him to get out."

"Has anyone been digging in here?"

George's face turned red and his eyes slipped away.

"Where?"

"You gonna jam me up here?"

"I'm investigating a murder." Jake waited until George's eyes came back to his. "That's all I'm interested in."

"I let a guy dig out a pair of outhouse pits. He gave me a couple old glass bottles he found in them. They're pretty cool."

"And?"

"A hundred bucks."

"Show me."

George led Jake to a smaller clearing a bit farther back from the bluff. "The holes are right here." He pointed at an area of undisturbed leaf clutter. "The guy put all the dirt back when he was done. Packed it down and everything."

"When was this?"

"Months ago. May, maybe early June."

Which was exactly when Henry had found the little bars. And Henry was famous for his clean-up. He wanted to be sure the owner at each potential new location only heard good things about how he treated the property at previous projects.

"So the digger and the birder and the guy today have all been poking around the Yard?"

"I guess." George shrugged.

"Anyone else?"

George shook his head.

"Where were the owls burrowing?"

"The bird guy never found their burrows. He walked through the whole place." George waved his hands. "No burrows and no owls."

Jake's phone buzzed with a message. Callie: *Bowen bit on the alibi!* She would tear him apart, and Hallagan couldn't save him.

"George, did anyone else do any digging here after the outhouse pits?"

"Well…" George's face reddened again.

"Spill it, George."

"A couple weeks ago the digger came back. Said he did some research and there should be another outhouse hole." George pointed northwest. "Over closer to the church. Gave me another hundred."

"Did he find it?"

"Must have. He was back and forth on his little machine."

"I'm going to look."

"Suit yourself."

George headed back toward the garage, and Jake cut through the trees in the direction George had pointed. It was cold here, damp, and dense with underbrush and fallen logs. Jake ran into a chain-link fence suddenly, the metal covered by vines and weeds growing up through it. Beyond, Jake could see a black asphalt expanse holding a scatter of cars and then a brick building. The church on Jefferson.

He turned away from the river and cut back and forth across the property. Finally he found a trail of flattened weeds that were already springing back up. He followed it to a small clearing back from the bluff and kicked through the leaf cover until he found some dead vegetation. He bent and looked closer. The surface vegetation had been removed in squares and then replaced, the plants now struggling to recover.

Henry had dug here.

* * *

Back in the car Jake warmed his hands over the vents. The story Henry had told April was the truth. He'd found the twenty smaller silver bars in an outhouse pit. But in order to sell them, he needed proof of ownership—which was why he claimed they came from the storage unit. Unfortunately for Henry, that story caused Bowen to believe he was entitled to half of the income. Henry was stuck with the story at that point, and had to split the profits.

Then somehow, Henry found his way to another hole—with the big bars. At least one, and maybe five hundred of them. He definitely wouldn't have wanted to give Bowen half of those. But when Bowen found out about them he might have had the same thought that Callie had: that the big bars had to be part of the same find. Because there was no way there were two hidden silver hoards in Weston. Bowen would have thought Henry had held out on him a second time—that Henry's reveal about the twenty little bars had been a smoke screen to hide that he'd also found five hundred big ones.

And Bowen didn't have an alibi.

Maybe it hadn't been one of the Texans after all.

CHAPTER THIRTY-NINE

Jake's enthusiasm for talking to Lawrence Bristol rose as he drove east along Jackson. Lawrence Bristol had told Martin a story about a silver treasure... and then silver was found on the old Bunker property—where Lawrence had lived. That wasn't a coincidence.

Jake pulled to the curb by Centennial Beach and called Levi to see if he'd come across a connection between the Bunkers and Weston in his research.

"No, but their silver came close."

"Explain."

"I told you that they took physical possession of a bunch of silver. Well half of the 1973 load—twenty million ounces—came from the COMEX's Midwest region storehouse in Kirwin. They picked it up in a convoy of armored cars and transported it to O'Hare, where a fleet of chartered jets took it to Switzerland. And get this. To pick the men who would escort it, the brothers had shooting contests on the Fourth of July among their security guards in Texas. The winners got to ride along to Switzerland the following week."

And Weston is directly between Kirwin and the airport. "Can you look for a Bunker connection to Weston? And to the Bristol family?"

"Will do!" Levi said. "But why do I have the feeling you already know what I'm going to find?"

"You never know."

Jake was about to put his phone in his pocket when he stopped to check his text messages. He wanted to know where Trane had gone after their confrontation. The man had been pumped up. Energy led to action. Action revealed truth.

He scrolled through his text history and found the thread with Grady. Nothing new. He dialed Grady's number, but he didn't answer. So he sent him a text asking for a phone call. He considered swinging by the B&B to see if Grady was there, but the officer could handle himself, and the case was accelerating too fast for a detour. Jake needed to stay on task—and that meant talking to Lawrence Bristol.

The phone buzzed with a text alert while it was still in Jake's hand. He hoped it was Grady, but it was Beck. He'd received Griffin's documentation on sending the other bars to COMEX. It was consistent with Griffin's story.

Jake got moving.

* * *

Conner backed into the corner of the dining room as far away from the cops as he could get. There were at least six of them, all answering to the black lady cop who'd been talking to the neighbors. Two were in his bedroom right now.

He hugged himself to fight the tremble running through him. His stash was in a pocket of his backpack—and if he got busted for the weed he'd probably lose his scholarship. There was no way his parents could afford to send him to Northwestern without it. His student loans only covered room and board.

But the silver would solve that problem. It would solve all their problems.

If he and April got to it first.

As soon as the cop in the dining room finished pawing through the china cabinet and left, Conner pulled out his phone and called April. "Come on," he whispered. He needed to hear her voice.

"Hey, baby," she answered.

"That lady cop's back here with like ten cops. They're tearing the house apart. They're going to find my stash."

"Does she have a search warrant?"

"No! My dad told them they could search. His lawyer's here and he said not to let them, but Dad always thinks he knows better than everybody. Why'd he even hire a lawyer if he's not going to listen to the guy?"

"She was already over here when you texted me about her," April said. "I should have called you, but Mom's been a wreck."

"What did she want?"

"She had figured out the affair with your dad was a lie and made Mom admit it."

A sudden flurry of voices from Conner's room. He stepped over until he could see up the stairs. A cop leaned out of his room, looked up and down the hallway, then yelled, "Detective?"

The black lady cop ran up the stairs from the lower level. "What do you got?"

"There's something you need to see in the kid's bedroom."

Conner started to shake again. "I'm screwed. I gotta go."

CHAPTER FORTY

Jake crossed over the Paget River at Mill Street then circled around the Weston Settlement outdoor history museum and south to Osler Drive. Weston Oaks was a mental health facility on the Edgar Hospital campus. It occupied a rambling building close to the Little League fields. Jake was familiar with the facility; it wasn't the first time he'd been there to interview someone.

He headed up the front walk, pulling his blazer around him against the stiff wind blowing from the west. He'd always tried to deny the start of winter by using mind over body, but maybe he should follow Ursulina's lead, break out the heavy coat first thing, and never feel the cold at all.

He spun through the revolving door and into the lobby. It was a large space with a high ceiling and a glass wall looking out over the grounds. The expanse was peppered with low tables circled by club chairs. Several seating clusters held small groups that looked to be families visiting a loved one. Piped-in classical music provided a peaceful background for their quiet conversations.

He followed the tile path winding through the carpeted room to the counter guarding the entrance into the facility itself. He flapped his blazer as if he could shake the cold out of it. It didn't work.

The woman behind the counter greeted him with a smile. "Getting chilly out there?"

"Starting to." He smiled back. "I'm here to see Lawrence Bristol."

"Friend or family?"

If Jake announced himself as a police officer, the facility would probably contact the public guardian and ask for permission to allow the visit. The PG would draft a long-winded motion and put the question in front of a judge, thereby avoiding any blowback for an unpopular decision. All of which would take at least a week.

"I'm a friend of Mr. Martin's—Larry's old neighbor—and he told me Larry could help me with a bit of Weston history." Jake held up his notebook to show her he was a serious scholar.

"How's Mr. Martin doing?" She handed Jake a clipboard with a sign-in sheet.

"He's doing well. I just came from his house. Ursulina will be bringing him for a visit over Thanksgiving." He took the clipboard and filled in his name and the time and checked the box for friend.

"I'm sure Lawrence will be happy to see him." She looked at what he'd written. "Please have a seat and I'll have a nurse ask Larry if he'll accept your visit."

He thanked her, then walked over to a table near the windows and stood gazing out at the meticulously maintained plantings now going dormant for the winter. It was a pleasant view, but it couldn't hold his attention. Something in the Bristols' storage unit had led Henry to the silver. First the little bars, then the big ones. And with the elder Bristols having passed away, if anyone alive knew the truth about what Henry had found, it was Lawrence Bristol.

But what if Lawrence wouldn't see him? Jake pushed that worry aside because he could do nothing about it. Besides, why wouldn't Lawrence be happy for any break in routine after nearly thirty years here?

Jake sat in a chair facing away from the glass and flipped through his notebook, reviewing what he knew and what he wanted to know that Bristol could help him with. But it wasn't complicated; it was all about the silver. He put the notebook back in his pocket.

Footsteps across tile. A nurse approached with a wiry man walking beside her. He was a slender five-six with the shoulder slope of a manual laborer. He wore khaki pants and a blue button-down shirt like his friend Mr. Martin, and his eyes were bright and intent. He clutched a black marble composition book. Jake had used one like it for his in-class writing assignments in Mrs. Swanson's seventh-grade English class.

"Here we are, Mr. Bristol." The nurse had long straight hair running to gray, but a smooth unlined face. She guided Bristol into the chair next to Jake. "I'll be back for Mr. Bristol in about fifteen minutes for afternoon group exercise. He leads it, so he can't be late."

Jake thanked her, and she left without a glance back.

"Mr. Martin-next-door sent you to see me?" Lawrence clasped his hands between his thighs, the book trapped with them, his eyes piercing. "That's what Nurse Linda said."

"Yes he did, Lawrence." Jake scooted to the edge of his chair and leaned over so he could keep the conversation as private as the big public room allowed. "He thought you could help me with something."

"Call me Larry." Larry smiled. "That's what Mr.-Martin-next-door calls me and you're his friend, so you're my friend too."

"Larry, I'd like to talk with you about your family."

"Lucy was my mom. My dad died but his name was Jonathan." Larry sat the book on his lap and opened it to a page marked with a paper clip. He pulled a pen from his pants pocket. "What's your name? You didn't say it."

"Jake Houser." Jake spelled it for him.

Larry bent over his lap and started writing.

Jake asked Larry a couple soft questions to get him comfortable: about how he liked living at Weston Oaks and how he liked to spend his time. Larry was open and honest and appeared comfortable with Jake and his questions.

"Larry, I am curious about the silver bars."

"Secret, secret." Larry wrote some more.

"What's a secret?"

"I didn't say that." Larry closed the book.

Jake didn't challenge him. His eyes were locked on the cover of Larry's diary. He'd seen a notebook just like it recently. More recently than seventh grade.

"What do you have there?"

Larry held up the book and showed Jake the front cover. A white card taped there said, *The Life of Larry Bristol: June 1, 2016 – _____* with no end date written.

"May I look at it?"

"Do you want to read it?" Larry's voice rose. "Momma said probably no one would ever want to read my books but it was still worth writing them. Momma was smart like that. She's dead, God rest her soul."

"I do want to read your book. What do you write in it?"

"It's my about-o-pography."

"How long have you been writing about your life?"

Larry closed the book and hugged it against his chest. "Since Mrs. King's class."

"I had her as my teacher too," Jake said. "I saw her yesterday."

"Say hi for me," Larry said.

"I will." Jake reached out, and Larry poked the book into his hand. Jake smiled and opened the book to the clipped page:

*Jake Houser came to ask me about my family and
the secret, secret.*

Jake smiled up at Larry, who gave him a tentative smile back.

"Do you like it?" Larry asked.

"I do." Jake flipped back through the pages to get a sense of what Larry wrote about. He mainly narrated the high points of his day—meals and story time and routines for group exercise —and occasional observations like "Mr. Hemmings has big nostrils." Jake flipped forward to the previous few weeks and read through a long string of entries describing a routine existence. Until the previous Friday.

I have a new friend! His name is Henry.

He is a friend of Mr. Martin next door. Henry came to see me about momma and Uncle Werner's boys. He knew all about the loafs and I told him they were a gift to Momma for taking care of my daddy's daddy until he died. I got the buns just for being me!

Jake's pulse sped up as he read the entry. Henry had found the silver and was trying to figure out its story. Exactly as he'd done when writing the book about his outhouse finds, he was pulling together a narrative of the artifact and the people who'd once owned it.

Jake read on.

Lawrence had had another visitor just this morning:

The man with the angel's kiss on his face came to see me about the heavy loafs. He looked a lot older but I still knew it was him! He should have worn a better disguise. I kept the secret, secret.

Cole.

Jake wanted to ask Lawrence about the silver, but a direct question about his "secret, secret" might shut him down.

"Do you ever see your relatives from Texas? Werner Bunker and his family."

Larry smiled. "Great Uncle Werner gave me the buns. Just for helping Momma with her big loaves. I got one each for my fingers and toes." Larry held up his hands and splayed his fingers wide, then lifted his feet off the floor and laughed.

"Twenty buns?"

"Yep. Twenty." Larry nodded.

"That's a generous gift." Twenty buns, and Henry had found twenty little silver bars. So the big loaves had to be the thousand-ounce bars. "What did your mom do with the big loaves?"

"I put them away for her."

"Did you write about them in your book?" Jake held it up. "One like this?"

"Yep." Lawrence took the journal back from Jake and placed it on his lap.

The rush of discovery pumped through Jake. He now remembered where he'd seen notebooks just like Larry's: in the stacks of books on the floor by Henry's reading chair. Henry must have found them in one of the boxes from the Bristols' storage unit. Henry would have loved reading the old journals for the historical perspective on Weston. All Jake had to do was find the right journal and he'd know exactly where the silver was.

He spotted the nurse coming back for Larry. He was out of time.

"I know the man with the angel's kiss on his face," Jake said. He watched Larry closely.

Larry looked down and away, then back at Jake from the corner of his eye. "He didn't watch me empty the truck. He drank coffee with Momma."

"That was a big job. He told me there were five hundred of them in the truck."

"Yep."

"He said you did a good job emptying the truck, and he was glad to see you again this morning." Jake didn't like lying to this gentle man, but he needed everything Larry could tell him.

"I didn't tell him anything about the secret."

"Larry?" The nurse was back, her return silent on her soft-soled shoes. "Are you ready for exercise time?"

"You betcha." Larry bounced out of his chair and stuck his hand out for Jake. Jake stood up, and Larry grabbed his hand and pumped.

Jake thanked the nurse, said goodbye to Larry, and headed for Henry's house—and the stack of black-marbled notebooks.

CHAPTER FORTY-ONE

Lynn stood in the doorway watching April put together the photo boards for Henry's wake. She had boards propped up against the couch and photos strewn across the living room. Lynn had tried to help, but April said she had it handled and to go take a nap.

A nap was out of the question. April's betrayal still had Lynn's brain buzzing. How could April keep that from her own mother? Especially after they'd talked about whether the big bars even existed.

A thousand ounces of pure silver. The police officer who carried it away was grunting like he was moving a piano. If April hadn't been a high school gymnast, she probably wouldn't have been able to bring it home.

"What do you think of the boards, Mom?"

Lynn pulled on a smile. "Very nice." And they were. April had sorted through every photo they had, plus a box full of them the police let her get from Henry's house, and had broken them up into four piles: Henry pre-high school, Henry in high school, Henry with Lynn, and Henry with April. She'd included pictures with as many other people as she could find. Which was smart. People loved to see themselves in pictures.

"I'm sorry about keeping the big bars secret, Mom." April sat on the couch and pulled Lynn down next to her.

"I understand, honey. But did you have to tell that detective about the silver? She'll—"

"You're more important to me than the silver."

Lynn's heart swelled. She reached up and stroked April's face.

"And it worked, too. That detective's got a bunch of cops searching Mr. Bowen's house right now."

"Conner called?"

"His dad's lawyer is there, but Mr. Bowen said they could search."

"If he didn't do it then they won't find anything, right?"

April looked down. "They already found Conner's stash."

"Of pot?" Lynn knew April smoked marijuana. She'd never seen her do it but they had talked about it. April made her read a bunch of articles that said it was safer than alcohol. Lynn still didn't like it. It was illegal, and getting arrested would cloud April's future.

"He could lose his scholarship."

"Consequences," Lynn said.

"Geez, Mom, I know. But saying so now doesn't help."

Not with this, but teaching April that actions and decisions have consequences—consequences that could sometimes stretch on forever—was the one thing Lynn had gotten right as a parent. She'd certainly had no shortage of examples to show April from her own life. Divorcing Henry was just one of them.

April shot a hand into the pocket on her hoodie and came out with her phone. "It's Conner." She looked at her phone and her face went slack. "It says, 'The cops just went crazy about something.'"

"What is—"

"He's typing." April stared hard at her phone. "They found something in his dad's office."

"That doesn't sound good." Lynn reached out to touch April's hand but her daughter pulled away, holding one hand up in a "wait" gesture.

"The murder weapon. They found the murder weapon in Mr. Bowen's office."

"Jesus," Lynn said. Bowen really did do it. "Did they find the silver? No—never mind. It doesn't matter. We'll be fine without that damn silver. It will be hard, but we'll do it."

"We won't even be able to pay my tuition to community college, Mom."

"Of course we will." Lynn reached for her, but April leaned away, shaking her head. "Why would you think that?"

"Because without the silver we have nothing."

"No, honey. You'll have your dad's money, eventually."

April's head snapped up. "What?"

"After all the legal mumbo-jumbo. You get his house and all his stuff. That's why I wanted you to call your dad's lawyer, Mr. Coogan. Remember?"

"I thought Dad gave his money to some charity? A trust, or something."

"He put it all into a trust, but it's for you, not for a charity."

Tears welled in April's eyes.

Lynn grabbed her and pulled her into a hug. "Oh, honey. Of course your dad provided for you. He loved you more than anything."

She meant the words to comfort her daughter, but they just made her cry harder.

* * *

Jake was sure one of the journals stacked next to Henry's chair would lead him right to the big bars, just as they had done for Henry. Even if Larry had described the silver bars as buns and loaves, it would have caught Henry's interest: he loved Weston history and the thrill of discovery, and he lived only a few houses from the Bristols' old estate. And if Larry used the same "secret, secret" phrasing back then… well, that would have *really* grabbed Henry's attention.

Then when Henry discovered the "buns" were hundred-ounce silver bars, he would naturally have concluded that the "loafs" were even bigger silver bars. If money fever had hit him—like it had Cole and Trane—that's when it happened.

Jake checked his phone for a message from Grady. It had been almost two hours without a report, and Grady still hadn't responded to Jake's earlier text. He called again but it went to voicemail after a couple rings.

He called Erin. "I have Grady tailing Trane and haven't heard from him in a couple hours." Worry made his voice rise, and he tried to bring it back down. "Have you heard from him?"

"No." Erin's voice echoed his worry. "You want me to put a BOLO out on him?"

"On his Jetta and on Trane's truck. And talk to the downtown zone patrol officer personally, okay? Have him check the B&B and up and down the Riverwalk by Centennial Beach."

"Right away."

"What's the status on Henry's house?" His phone buzzed with a message and he hoped it was Grady. He pulled it away from his face to check the screen. Another *Call me!* text from Callie.

"All dusted and forensics collected. The house and the barn both. Locked up tight and sealed with tape."

"Guarded?"

"Let me look." Papers rustled and computer keys clacked. "No guard as of about one this afternoon. Two hours ago. You think this silver is real and it's hidden there somewhere?"

"If it was at Henry's, it's gone by now."

"If you're going over there, I can have an officer bring the keys."

"Please do."

It would take the officer a few minutes to get to Henry's with the keys, so Jake called Callie. She answered immediately.

"We found the murder weapon here."

"What?" He was so surprised his voice squeaked.

"A hundred-ounce silver bar stuffed in the back of the credenza in Bowen's office. Field test for blood came back positive."

"He let you search his house?"

"He consented in writing. Trying to save himself after I trapped him with the alibi from Fox's ex-wife. Guess he thought we wouldn't find it."

"Hallagan was there?"

"Yep. He tried to talk Bowen out of letting us search."

Callie had been working the case for less than twenty-four hours and might have already solved it. Motive, means, opportunity, and the murder weapon. Jake was so surprised one of the Texans hadn't killed Henry that he was speechless.

"Jake?"

"I'm here. Sorry. Anything else?"

"He revoked consent and clammed up. Insists he's being framed. We have a search warrant on the way so we can keep going."

"You want me to come out there?"

"No. I got this. Anything going on at your end?"

"I've about got the silver part of it nailed down."

"Good. I'll call you later."

The call ended. Then Jake said, "Bowen did it," just to hear the words out loud. They sounded wrong, but if they were right, then his screw-up with Lynn's phony alibi had almost let the man get away with it. His entire body flushed with a hot shame, and he apologized to his dead friend for failing to avenge him. Thank god for Callie.

He put the Crown Vic in gear and headed back to Redhawk Court, his spirits lifting as he realized that if Bowen killed Henry then maybe Trane wasn't dangerous and Grady was fine. Maybe his cell phone battery had died.

Halfway to Henry's house, his phone buzzed again, this time with a call. He pulled over to the curb across the street from Centennial Beach and answered. It was Levi.

"You find a connection between the Bunkers and Weston?" Jake asked.

"Yep. The head of that Texas family came from right here in Weston."

"Werner Lafayette Bunker," Jake said.

"Must be why they called their sugar trading business WLB Foods."

"WLB Foods," Jake repeated, thinking. "And Great Western United—GWU—was a division of the food company, right?"

"Yep."

"Thanks, Levi."

Jake hung up and got back on the road to Henry's house. Since Great Western United, GWU, was a part of WLB Foods, it would have been included in WLB's bankruptcy. And if the lost assets of WLB Foods and the silver were one and the same thing, as Coogan had speculated, that explained why Trane was in town. He thought he owned the silver.

So why was he keeping his purpose secret?

* * *

Conner sat on the living room couch, shoulders curled forward, head down. The room was full of cops, but they were all joking about something that happened at a bowling league and had forgotten about him. His parents had gone out on the back deck with the lawyer, where they huddled together arguing about what had just happened. His dad was insisting he'd been framed. Conner wasn't sure anyone believed him.

Conner sure didn't.

He pulled out his phone and looked around the room, but no one was paying him any attention. Not even the detective. She'd been on the phone since they found the silver bar, making call after call.

She looked up suddenly, her eyes locking on his. She gave him a sad smile, then looked away.

His dad had killed Mr. Fox.

His dad was a killer.

Because of the silver. If Mr. Fox had never found it, his dad would still just be an asshole. Now he was a killer.

Not worth it, he thought to himself. *We don't need the silver because we have each other.*

He texted April those exact words.

She texted him back immediately: *We are enough.*

He smiled and put his phone away.

CHAPTER FORTY-TWO

Jake sped down Jackson toward Henry's place, eager to get his hands on the black-marbled composition books. One of those books had led Henry to the silver bars. If Jake found the right book, and the right entry, he'd find the silver hoard. Even with Henry's murder solved, Jake still needed to find the silver. A lost hoard worth ten million dollars would only bring more men like Cole and Trane to town. That would mean trouble.

He turned into Redhawk Court, driving too fast, the big car slewing in the ruts. He parked in Henry's front yard, but left the engine running as he waited for the officer Erin sent with the keys. Brueder's house to the west now blocked the setting sun, and the deep shadow in Henry's yard felt heavy and cold.

Jake flipped through his notebook absently, coming across the page where he'd listed his suspects: Griffin, Cole, and Trane, with Bowen penciled in at the bottom after Callie destroyed his alibi. Bowen had seemed the least likely killer among them. Jake had been so sure it was one of the Texans.

He closed the notebook, thinking about Henry. He shouldn't have doubted that Henry had found a hoard of five hundred giant silver bars. Henry got pumped up from finding a glass medicine bottle; a single thousand-ounce bar would have been enough for him without feeling the need to invent hundreds more. And he never lied to April, about anything. Not even Santa Claus. If Henry told April there were five hundred big bars, then there were five hundred big bars.

Millions of dollars in silver hidden right here in Weston.

His cell phone vibrated and he checked the screen. Coogan.

"What do you have?"

"The missing assets of WLB Foods." Coogan was excited. "I don't know how this never hit the news."

"Tell me."

Coogan had spent the day combing through bankruptcy records. With Levi's information that WLB Foods was part of the Bunker empire, he'd finally figured out the reference to its "missing assets." It went back to the Bunkers' attempt to corner the silver market. The Bunkers traded silver using the GWU name—a division of WLB Foods, Inc. And when their attempt to control the silver market failed and their loans were called, the Bunkers put WLB Foods into bankruptcy. As a result, the exchange seized the silver—the brothers had given COMEX a lien on the silver in their possession—but when they did, they found the brothers a million ounces short. COMEX then tried to get the brothers indicted for criminal fraud. The FBI took a look before deciding it was a business dispute, not a criminal matter.

"Remember Mike Johnson?" Coogan asked. "From our law school class?"

"Sure." Johnson had gone into the FBI.

"I reached out to him, and he called around and found a retired agent who remembered the case. That agent told him they figured out the missing million ounces was from the silver the brothers shipped to Switzerland in 1973. Only thirty-nine million ounces made it into inventory there. They dug into the flight records and learned the cargo weight for both shipments—New York and Chicago—was light by a half million ounces each.

"Anyway, the judge wanted to close the bankruptcy case, so he listed the missing silver as an asset in the bankruptcy, and that's what TH Inc. bought: legal title to the missing million ounces. For one hundred thousand dollars."

A half million ounces was five hundred of the thousand-ounce bars. The "missing assets" were indeed the silver bars, just as they had suspected.

Jake told Coogan about April's bar and that Henry had told her how many he'd found. "Are the bars all subject to COMEX's lien?" he asked.

"Nope," said Coog. "That was wiped off in the bankruptcy. Trane himself then bought clean title from TH Inc. for ten thousand."

"The Chicago half of those assets is worth over ten million dollars. That has to be enough to save Trane's business, or he wouldn't be here chasing it."

"It doesn't look like the judge overseeing the TH bankruptcy case looked into what the asset was before selling it to Trane. Probably figured it was so old it couldn't be worth anything."

The crunch and pop of tires on gravel sounded in the driveway. The officer had arrived with the keys.

"You know, I've studied Weston history my entire life," Coogan said. That was true—Coogan had spent countless hours in area archives piecing together Weston history, especially the founding families like the Bunkers and Jake's mom's family, the Warrens. "It's strange that there's not even a hint of this."

"I guess there's been ten million reasons to keep it a secret," Jake said. "Hey, I have to go—but thanks for the info."

"Any time."

The patrol car's spotlight popped bright, shining on Henry's front door. Jake was stepping out of his car to tell the officer to shut it down when the officer—it was Bantam—shouted. "Front door is cracked open."

Jake sidestepped around the back of Bantam's car until he had a clear view of the door. The yellow tape used to seal the door was split vertically.

"Shut down that spotlight." Jake didn't want to be backlit when he opened the door. "Cover the back of the house while I go in the front."

The spotlight winked off, dusk filling back in around them. Bantam got out of his car. "Should I call for backup first?"

"Do it. Then go around."

Bantam grabbed his shoulder mic, made the request, then darted across the yard in a half crouch, his gun drawn and his feet kicking through the thick leaf cover with a loud rustle.

Jake drew his gun and held it down along his leg. He stepped up on the concrete stoop and flattened against the wall on the knob side of the door. He leaned his head around the jamb. A crescent-shaped dent next to the doorknob showed where a heel had struck the door and driven it inward. Massive splinters from the shattered wood around the lock prevented the door from closing all the way.

He put his left palm on the door and pushed. The wood shards groaned and squeaked against each other before the door released with a sudden rip. Someone had worked hard to close the door. No burglar would do that while he was still inside. Which meant Jake wouldn't need the gun. But he kept in in his hand.

Just in case.

He stepped inside, gun leading the way. The fading afternoon sun did a poor job lighting the room, but it was enough to see the place was a disaster. Every stick of furniture had been moved, every knick-knack and souvenir thrown to the floor.

Jake cleared the house room by room. Henry's office in particular was a paper tornado, files pulled and flung across the space. But there was no one here.

He took the basement steps slowly and found the lights on. Cabinets had been flung open and even the detergent boxes emptied. But behind the canvas curtain, everything looked untouched. The search must have ended before it got here. Which meant either the searcher found what he was looking for… or he was interrupted.

Jake climbed the stairs two at a time, ducking his head to avoid getting brained by the low ceiling, then bee-lined to the front room and the stack of journals by Henry's reading chair.

A pair of feet protruded from behind an avalanche of books.

Grady!

CHAPTER FORTY-THREE

Jake scrambled to the body, pawing away books and magazines.

It wasn't Grady.

It was Titus Cole.

"Thank God," Jake said. He pushed back on his heels and wiped sweat from his face. Grady was still missing, but at least this wasn't him.

Jake pulled a pair of latex gloves from his jacket pocket and struggled into them. He scooted forward and knelt next to the body. Cole lay on his back with his arms flung out. Jake checked for a pulse on Cole's neck, then at his wrist: nothing. He pulled his flashlight out of the inner pocket of his jacket and shined it on Cole. His face was swollen and red from a beating, one eyebrow split. His corduroy coat gaped open and his shirt reflected a dark, shiny red in the light's beam.

Jake stood and straddled the body, lifting the coat aside to get a better look. Four—no, five slits stabbed through Cole's denim shirt, blood pooled in each. He put his palm on Cole's face; his flesh was still warm. According to the algor mortis tables—on body cooling—a dead body held its temperature for up to five hours.

He pushed back one of Cole's eyelids with a knuckle. It resisted—rigor mortis had set in. Although rigor develops in all muscles simultaneously, the smaller muscles are fully involved much more quickly. He next tried the progressively larger muscles, working Cole's jaw and his neck. Both were already stiff. But his limbs were still pliable, only the smallest finger joints stiffening. Cole hadn't been dead long; maybe an hour. The coroner's interior temperature would give a more accurate estimate. But the hour made sense—the house had been guarded by a patrol cop until a little over two hours before.

He scanned the scene. When Cole visited Lawrence Bristol this morning, he must have seen Bristol's current journal and made the same leap Jake had: that Henry had found one that showed the way to the silver. So Cole came here—but the killer got here before him.

Cole would likely have ignored the busted door and ransacked house—he was a tough guy and had spent a career handling people. And maybe he thought the burglar was gone. But by the way the search had been interrupted in the basement, Jake knew the killer had been here when Cole entered. The killer would have heard the footsteps overhead just like Jake had when the forensic team came in while he'd been in the basement. So the killer came upstairs, overwhelmed Cole, and beat him for the secret of the journal.

Then killed him.

Jake used his flashlight to probe the mess for the journals, shuffling the spread of books with his free hand. He found eleven journals, each with a date range on the front. But the journal covering July of 1973, when the silver was moved, was missing.

He called Callie Diggs.

"You find the silver?" she asked before he got a word out.

"I found Titus Cole beaten and stabbed to death in Henry's front room. How long has Bowen been with you?"

"Three hours, going on four. How long your guy been dead?"

"No more than two hours. An officer was guarding the door until then."

"So it wasn't Bowen."

"I doubt we have two killers," Jake said. Both victims were chasing the silver hoard and were killed in the same place, both violently, within a few days of each other.

"Which would mean Bowen *was* framed?" Her voice held a cop's skepticism. "I think you're taking that too far. At most you can say there's only one motive."

"I have to go," Jake said. He ended the call, then dialed Erin. "I need you to switch the BOLO on Trane to an APB."

"You want him picked up?"

"Immediately!" He rubbed his face. "I've got Titus Cole dead over here at Henry's and Trane in the wind. And I can't get ahold of Grady. Bowen's been with Callie Diggs all afternoon, so this wasn't him. And tell Deputy Chief Braff I want more uniforms on this search. Call in the next shift early. Call in everybody." He'd put Grady in harm's way; he was responsible for him.

"As soon as backup's here I'm going to—"

Erin cut in. "Bantam can hold the scene, Jake. I'll call forensics and the coroner's office. You go find Grady."

Erin was right. He ended the call and called Bantam inside. Bantam's face drained white when Jake told him about the body, but the man would do his job. Jake got in his car and got moving.

As he cleared the driveway the first screaming siren turned onto Jackson.

* * *

Jake sped down the short stretch of Jackson to the Bristol Yard. The gate was open, and he rolled down the rutted gravel drive and into the open space in front of the garages. It was nearly full dark, and the gravel expanse was a ghostly white in the gloom. No Jetta. No pickup.

George came out of the garage, and Jake spun his car in a tight circle to bring his window to the man, lowering it as he went.

"Did that big man come back here this afternoon?"

"No." The yard light went on over George's head. and he flinched. "What's going on?"

"How about a thirtyish guy in a white Jetta?"

George started shaking his head before Jake finished his question. "I haven't seen anyone since the gravel guy dumped a load an hour ago." He pointed to a load of crushed stone at the far end of the lot.

"The gate's open."

"I guess I didn't close it after."

Jake pulled a card from his shirt pocket. "My cell number's on the back of this. Call me if the big man or the Jetta come in here."

"I was just about to leave."

"Now you're staying. Think about the overtime." Jake gassed it and spun gravel as he fishtailed his way back onto Jackson.

He cut through the VFW parking lot to the long narrow curve of parking lot stretching along the river from the Bristol Yard to the big lot at Centennial Beach, the swimming facility built into an old limestone quarry. With the pool closed and the baseball season long over there were only a few cars clustered near the skateboard park.

No Jetta. No truck.

Jake gripped the wheel tight. *Where are you, Grady?* He wove through downtown toward Lanigan House. Traffic was building into the after-work rush hour, and he had to wait five cars deep at most stop signs. Neither vehicle was at the B&B.

He swung his car around and started a concentric sweep, edging a block out on each pass. He saw multiple Jettas, but no white ones. Multiple trucks, but not Trane's.

He pulled into the library parking lot and called Erin.

"Have the communications division look at the downtown video for the last two hours." There were cameras all through downtown. If they caught Trane driving through it might give him a clue where to look.

"DC Braff put them on it a few minutes ago. He also called Sheriff Warren, and she put it out as high priority to her patrols and sent three cars to cruise our streets."

An excited commotion broke out on Erin's end of the line.

"What's going on?" Jake asked.

"Hang on. They might have something."

Jake couldn't make out the words, but the tone was frantic.

Erin came back on the line. "A patrol unit found Grady's car where Webster dead ends at the tracks."

"And Grady?"

"Just his car."

CHAPTER FORTY-FOUR

"What about Trane? Or his truck?" Jake asked.

"Neither. And Jake? There's blood."

Shit!

Jake ended the call and got moving. He pulled out of the library parking lot and shot east on Jefferson to Webster, then fought traffic for two blocks. It thinned out as he left the shopping district. Ahead, the red and blue of squad car lights strobed down the tunnel of trees hanging over the road.

His phone vibrated with another call. He answered without looking.

"Have we found him?"

"Mr. Houser?"

Shit—it was April. He should have checked the screen. He pulled to the curb and tried to focus. "Hello, April."

"I just saw a tweet that said you found a body at Dad's house. I was there yesterday!"

"It happened today," he said quickly. How the hell did this information get out so fast? "Just a few hours ago."

"Who is it? Do you know who did it? I know Mr. Bowen didn't do it."

"How do you know that?"

"He's been with that other detective all afternoon."

"Who told you that?"

"His son. Conner. We're, uh, friends."

More than friends, by the hesitation. He thought back. He was sure the boy she'd been caught with hadn't been Conner Bowen. That kid had been thick and hard like a linebacker. Bowen was a whip-thin artsy type. "You never mentioned that."

"I guess it never came up, but we're together. He came home from Northwestern to be with me because of... what happened."

"April, I'm sorry, but I need—"

"If there's a killer still out there, are my mom and—"

"We'll talk later, okay? I'll come over."

"Tonight?"

"Yes." He needed to get off the phone. "I promise."

"Okay."

Jake looked at his phone for several hard seconds. Conner and April. He'd missed it. But did it matter? All signs pointed at Trane, and that needed to be his focus. He'd stop by to talk to April later tonight as he'd promised. Then he could drill her about Conner *and* about the big silver bar under her bed.

He pushed the phone into his pocket and got the cruiser moving again.

* * *

Webster ran straight into the circular driveway of a townhouse development that spread along the railroad tracks. The patrol unit with the flashing cherries sat in the right hand of the circle with its headlights blazing on Grady's Jetta. Jake circled around to the left and added his lights to the brilliance, then levered himself out of the car.

A uniformed officer scanning the pavement around the Jetta swung his flashlight beam up into Jake's eyes.

Jake held up his badge. "Lower the light, officer."

"Sorry, Detective."

The light pulled away, and Jake joined the officer in the wash of headlight glare, blinking away the afterimages from the flashlight. "Wallace, right?" he asked the officer.

"Yes. I—"

The rest of his words were lost in the rattling roar of a passing commuter train, the ground trembling slightly, the flash of the train's lit windows a blur through the brush and trees choking the embankment. They both waited it out.

When it had passed, Jake said, "Show me the blood."

Wallace pointed out a dark splatter on the Jetta's roof by the driver's door and a puddle on the pavement below it. The splatter was dry, and the pool had a thick skin on its surface. One edge of the pool was pulled into a long tail.

Jake walked around the car, using his own flashlight to examine the scene. As he finished circling the Jetta the shift sergeant's squad car pulled up and added its headlights to the flood illuminating the scene. Beyond it, at the intersection of Webster and Spring a cluster of emergency vehicles was assembling, lights flashing, doors slamming, excited voices breaking out.

Jake turned away from the noise and focused. He didn't like the story the blood told him. As Grady got out of the car, he was hit hard enough for his scalp to split; that explained the blood splashed onto the roof. He fell, lay there long enough for his blood to pool, and then someone moved him, his head dragging away from the puddle and the car.

Trane must have spotted Grady tailing him and led Grady here. It was as secluded a place as you could find this close to downtown: row houses on two sides, the train embankment to the north, and the thick wad of plantings in the middle of the circle.

So Trane had lured Grady here and surprised him, but then what?

Trane would have either left Grady where he landed, or he would have moved him immediately. The pool of blood meant

Grady had lain there for some period of time before his body was moved. That didn't make sense. Why would Trane wait? Unless...

Unless Trane left Grady where he landed and *Grady moved himself.*

He was alive!

Jake dropped into a crouch, sweeping the flashlight low over the pavement.

There—a dark smudge, glistening with wetness. Jake scrambled over to it, holding the light a few inches above the pavement, sweeping a narrow arc, continuing in the direction the first smudge established. Nothing.

Wallace stepped into Jake's line of sight, pointing at the ground. "There!"

Jake speared the spot with the light.

Blood.

Working together, the two traced a path north across the parking lot and over the curb. From there the trail became obvious in the flattened grass and disturbed leaves, heading straight for the tracks.

Jake ran his light up the trail and smiled. Grady was a Weston native and had found himself a hidey-hole Trane could never find. The old cow tunnel under the railroad tracks. The city had filled it in for the first time back in the seventies, but from time to time a new generation of boys discovered it and dug it out.

"Follow me." Jake sprang up from his crouch and shoul-dered his way through the thick stand of bushes separating the street from the Burlington Northern tracks. He scrambled up the base of the embankment, his light leading the way, his feet slipping on the loose stone. Grabbing a sapling with his free hand, he fought his way up the hill to a mound of stone and dirt, then he was over it and stabbed his flashlight beam into the arched opening in the hill.

The waffled bottom of a pair of boots protruded from the narrow hole.

"Here he is!" He turned to find Wallace right beside him. "Get those paramedics up here."

While he waited, Jake dropped to his knees and probed the tunnel with the light. Grady's ankles were wrapped with duct tape halfway to his knees.

"Grady! Can you hear me? We got you."

No response. Jake grabbed Grady's foot and shook it, but still nothing.

He reached deeper into the tunnel and felt his way past the duct tape. Grady's skin was warm through the polyester pants. A muscle bunched under Jake's hand, and both feet moved.

Then a paramedic pulled Jake away. "We got this, Detective."

Jake stepped back. Shaking with relief that Grady was alive, he skated back down the embankment on the loose scree.

The paramedics rolled a stretcher to the edge of the parking area, and a team of first responders carried Grady gently to it. He was strapped in, rolled to the ambulance, and taken away.

The cold wormed its way into Jake and he shivered. He pulled his blazer together and buttoned it. The shift sergeant reassigned the gathered patrol cars to search for Trane, keeping back one unit to guard the scene. The rest of the emergency vehicles dispersed, leaving behind a forensic van. Jake now noticed civilians gathered in clusters behind long threads of yellow crime scene tape tied from tree to bush to street sign.

Grady was safe, but Trane was still in the wind. And Trane wouldn't stop moving until he had the silver—not after all he'd done to get his hands on it. He'd spotted the tail and stopped it. Where would he go from there?

Jake didn't know enough about Trane to anticipate his moves. Understanding people was what solved cases: their motivations and connections and relationships. Trane was connected, through the silver, to three other men: Henry and Cole and Bowen. Two were dead, and the third was with Callie.

No, not three. Four.

Griffin.

Griffin bought Henry's silver, sold the first bar to Cole, posted the forum question that brought Trane to town, and bought Bowen's silver. Griffin kept portraying himself as a simple businessman trying to make a slim profit off some metal ingots.

Jake didn't buy it anymore.

He got in his car and headed west. It was time for Griffin to talk.

CHAPTER FORTY-FIVE

Jake parked in a dark spot under a burned-out overhead light in front of Paget County Coins. Through the big windows he spotted Griffin holding up a tray of coins to a father and son who both nodded and smiled at what they saw. Jake locked the car and headed inside.

As he pushed through the door his eyes were on Griffin. The man looked up and met his gaze, then frowned and shook his head before getting back to his sale.

"Can I help you, sir?"

A twenty-something man in jeans and a yellow button-down stood to the right of the door wearing a weak smile. Jake remembered him from his earlier visit.

"Yes, you can, Jason." Jake turned his back on Griffin and showed his badge.

Jason licked his lips. "Mr. Griffin talks to the police. Not me." He craned his neck to look at his boss.

Jake didn't have time to massage this kid; he needed to cut through the bullshit and get the truth. He stepped into his sight line. "How long have you been here?"

"I've worked here for—"

"Today. How long have you been here today?"

"Since noon."

"Did you leave for lunch or dinner or to go to the dentist?"

"No, sir."

"How about Griffin?"

"He's been here all day. At least since I got here. We had a pizza delivered for dinner."

"Let's be clear on this, Jason. You will take the stand in court and tell a judge and jury Griffin has been here since you got here at noon. He didn't leave for a half hour to go to the bank or to get his nails done."

"Yes." The kid stood up straighter. "I will."

Griffin's customer left, and the big man made his way over, heavy footsteps slapping the concrete floor. "What are you doing here again, Houser?" His voice vibrated with anger. "You're getting to be a pain in the—"

Jake stepped into Griffin's space, his chest bumping against the soft mound of the man. "Shut up, asshole."

Griffin didn't back away, but he kept his mouth closed, chewing his bottom lip.

"I have more questions, and you're going to answer them or I'll shut this place down and make you jump through every hoop available in our great American bureaucracy."

Griffin's face flushed red, and his eyes shot to his employee. "I'll handle this, Jason. You take over at the counter."

Jason scurried away without a word.

"Let's go to your office."

Griffin led the way through the curtain into the back room. The tables that had been spread with inventory on Jake's last visit were empty now, the women gone. In the office, Griffin took his fancy chair and Jake stood over him at the end of the desk. The man's neck and face were red, and sweat stained the collar of his blue shirt.

"Spill it," Jake said, leaving Griffin to interpret the generic *it* as the one thing he was worried about. The thing making him sweat.

"James didn't kill Henry."

James. Not "Bowen" or "Mr. Bowen." Jake wanted to talk about Trane, but he would start with Bowen if that's where the leverage was. "Convince me."

"He was with me that night but he didn't want to tell you because of his wife."

"Bullshit," Jake said, though something about the words *with me* strummed a suspicion in his mind. "I'm going to need more than your say-so."

Griffin shot a red-faced glance at Jake then turned away and started banging away on his keyboard and clicking with his mouse. A black-and-white video appeared on the left monitor. It was cut into quadrants, each showing a different view of the store. Then one of the sections swelled to fill the screen. Griffin and Bowen sitting on the leather couch right here in this office. A bottle of wine and two glasses on the desk.

"Freeze that."

Griffin clicked the mouse, and the screen froze on an image of Griffin leaning in for what could only be a kiss. Jake stepped around the desk and behind Griffin to take a closer look at the time stamp in the corner of the screen: 10:07:29 on the night of Henry's murder. "How late was he here?"

"Until after two."

That covered the time of Henry's murder. Bowen was innocent. Which meant Trane had planted the murder weapon in his house. "Run it on fast forward."

The camera only took a few images a second, so the video was quick. It wasn't pretty, but two bloated, hairy, pasty-skinned men engaging in consensual sex was tame compared to what Jake had seen while working a child porn case the year before.

"Bowen's alibi for Henry's murder." Jake worked to keep his voice even. "And yours."

Griffin nodded.

"I'll have to get our techs out here to verify your system integrity and date stamp."

Griffin looked away. "Okay."

"You told Bowen about the silver bars Henry sold you because he was your lover."

"He wasn't then, but I… felt it. I wanted him to know Henry wasn't being straight with him. How could Henry be right for him if…?"

"If what?" Jake asked. Griffin's words—*right for him*—echoed in his mind. Another damn secret.

"If he was lying to him about their business."

"To be clear, Griffin. Are you telling me—"

"James and Henry were… together. But when Henry tried to steal James's share of the silver, that ended it."

No deception. Jake absorbed the news and let it settle in. It changed nothing but his perception of his friendship with Henry.

"Tell me about Trane."

Griffin's eyes shifted away and his shoulders slumped. "He came in here right at closing last Saturday. Said he had a big transaction to discuss with me and wanted to talk in private. After my employees left I locked up and brought him back here." He shrugged. "I thought he had something to sell. Some collectors are secretive and don't want anyone to know what they have."

"And?" Jake asked. Griffin was having trouble getting to the point. Whatever happened with Trane couldn't be as embarrassing as the sex tape.

Jake's phone buzzed. "Hang on a second."

A text from Erin: *Trane's truck found parked on Liberty west of the mall. No sign of Trane. Still searching for him.*

Jake put the phone away. "Spill the rest, Griffin."

"He'd seen my post about the thousand-ounce bars and wanted to know all about it. I told him our privacy policy didn't allow me to talk about it. He offered me money and then threatened me and slapped me around." He swallowed and turned away.

"And you gave him Henry's name and address."

Griffin nodded. "And a copy of the proof of ownership."

The storage facility receipt with Henry's address. "And Bowen's info?"

Griffin shook his head.

Of course not. "Do you have all this on video?"

"Like with the… uh… first video there's no sound, but I have it."

Jake chewed his lip. He wanted to join the search for Trane, but even a silent stop-action video might tell him something worth knowing. "Queue it up for me so I can see what we're talking about."

Griffin turned back to the computer and clicked through a few menus.

"Here it is."

A video filled the monitor: Griffin talking animatedly as he escorted Trane into the office. Selling him. The men sat and talked for a few minutes, and then Griffin was shaking his head.

"That's when I told him I couldn't reveal who had the thousand-ounce bars."

A few seconds later Trane held a fan of bills and waved it around before throwing it on the desk. Griffin left it there and crossed his arms. Suddenly Trane sprang up and slapped Griffin across the face, his head snapping one way then the other. Griffin tried to get up but Trane pushed him back down and another series of slaps left Griffin huddled in his chair. Trane picked up the money and put it in his pocket, then stood waiting. Griffin did something at the computer and gave Trane a document that shot from the printer. Then Trane was gone.

"That it?" Jake asked.

Griffin nodded, looking so beaten that Jake was sure he now had the man's full cooperation. Jake told Griffin to wait for the forensic team to come copy the videos and verify the system, then left.

Back in the car he called Callie and gave her the news about Bowen's alibi for Henry's murder. "A real alibi, this time," he said. "Bowen was framed just like he claimed." And Jake had made it possible. Griffin hadn't told the big Texan about Bowen. It must have been Jake who had led Trane there.

Then he told her about Griffin's claim that Henry had been in a romantic relationship with Bowen that ended when they argued about the silver.

"Which gives his wife a motive," Callie said.

"Whose wife? You mean Lynn?"

"No—Bowen's wife. I busted *her* alibi, too. When we searched the house we found receipts for a hotel stay at the Starlight the night Henry was murdered."

"She wasn't in Cincinnati like she told me?"

"Nope."

"What did she say about it?"

"I haven't confronted her with it. Yet."

"There's only one killer."

"That's an assumption," Callie said.

Maybe, but it wasn't a stretch.

They talked it through and decided Callie would work the Bowens together, covering both Griffin's alibi sex tape and the wife's busted alibi, and see what shook out of it.

"I'll set up the tech guys to get Griffin's video and confirm the time stamp," Callie said. "How is Grady?"

"Trane hit him hard. I… don't know." Jake's stomach roiled as he thought about the blood splatter on Grady's car.

"He's young and tough, Jake."

"I know." Jake squeezed his phone hard, the edge biting into his hand. "I've got my fingers crossed."

CHAPTER FORTY-SIX

Conner heard cops out on the driveway laughing about something. He cracked his bedroom window to listen in, but they were just talking about the errors they spotted on some cop show on TV. He stepped into the hallway and heard voices coming from downstairs. Pressing up against the wall, he edged toward the top of the stairs until he could peer into the living room. His parents were on the couch, their lawyer on the chair next to it. The black lady cop stood in front of them.

"Who do you represent here, Mr. Hallagan?"

"What do you mean?"

"Do you represent Mr. Bowen or Mrs. Bowen?"

"Jim retained me, but why—"

The cop angled her back to Hallagan and looked directly at Conner's mom. "Mrs. Bowen. We have learned that you lied about being in Cincinnati the night Mr. Fox was killed. You never left town, but were checked into the Starlight Motel the whole time you pretended to be gone."

What the fuck?

Conner's mom looked down, and his dad looked back and forth between the lawyer and the cop.

"Susan?" The lawyer. "You don't have to say anything. I can represent you—"

"Can you, Mr. Hallagan?" The cop glared down at the pompous lawyer. "What if her best defense is to blame her husband?"

The lawyer's mouth snapped shut.

Defense? Did the cop think Conner's *mom* had killed Mr. Fox?

"Why did you lie to Detective Houser?" the detective asked.

Conner's mom said nothing.

"Susan?" Conner's dad twisted in the couch to face her. "Why—"

"As if you care," she snapped.

"I do care—"

"You want to know why I was at a hotel instead of at home, Detective? The conference was canceled, but I'd been so... happy at the thought of getting away for a couple days that I checked into the Starlight."

Conner's dad shook his head. "I leave you alone all day long. You're—"

"But you're *here*, aren't you?" she yelled back. "Always locked in your office doing... whatever the hell it is you do."

"I'm writing."

"Writing." She said it like it was a curse. "Bullshit."

The black lady cop again. "You admit you were here in Weston the day Henry Fox was murdered."

"Yes."

"And you hated Mr. Fox for coming between you and your husband."

What the hell is she talking about? Conner wondered.

"Detective Diggs," said the lawyer. "Is my client, Mr. Bowen, no longer a suspect in Mr. Fox's murder?"

"That's correct, counselor."

Conner's dad crossed his arms and looked at the lawyer. "I told you I didn't do it."

"Are you sure?" Conner's mom asked.

"We found his real alibi."

"What alibi?" Conner's mom scooted to the front of the couch.

Conner's dad swept a big hand around and put it on her knee. "That doesn't matter, Susan. What matters is I'm totally innocent, just like I've been saying."

She flinched and pushed his hand away.

"We have a video of your husband—"

"It doesn't matter!" Conner's dad shouted. He poked the lawyer in the shoulder. "Tell them, Don."

"I agree—"

The black lady cop continued. "—with Mark Griffin, the owner of Paget County Coins, at the time the murder occurred."

"*With* him?" Conner's mom asked, her eyes narrowed at her husband. "Were they 'writing'?"

"We have also learned that before your husband's current romantic relationship with Mark Griffin at the coin shop, he was in a romantic relationship with Mr. Fox."

Conner's stomach flipped and folded around itself. Mr. Fox was gay too? Did April know that?

"That gives you a motive," the cop said. "So, again, why did you tell Detective Houser you were in Cincinnati?"

"Because… it's hard to admit to myself, much less to a stranger, that my marriage is over. And how it ended," she waved the back of her hand toward her husband, "makes the whole marriage a lie. Twenty-one *years* of lies." Conner's mom pushed back into the couch, shot an ugly look at her husband, and said, "Look what you've done to us."

The cop nodded and started pacing. As she turned she spotted Conner and froze, their eyes locked. She grimaced, shook her head as if in apology, and turned back to Conner's mom.

* * *

As Jake drove, he sent his mind back through how he'd handled the case. Thanks to Lynn's phony alibi he hadn't wasted a lot of time on her or on Bowen, but the lie still pissed him off. So did April's omission about the big bar Henry had given her.

He shook his head, his anger with the Fox women flaring. Hell, knowing about the big bars earlier might have made *the* difference. Might have saved Cole's life.

Shit!

The Fox women were as connected to the silver as Cole and Trane and the rest.

And Trane had to know the women existed: he'd mentioned the media coverage himself, and the media always talked about surviving family members. And he'd talked to Griffin, so he probably knew April had been along when Henry sold the first bar.

A possibility.

More than that.

A probability.

Trane was desperate and had nowhere else to go.

CHAPTER FORTY-SEVEN

Lynn put the pot of tomato soup on a metal trivet shaped like a pumpkin. The frying pan sizzled and she darted to the stove and flipped the grilled-cheese sandwiches, the smell of the melting cheddar so sharp her mouth watered. Maybe her appetite was back. Maybe things were getting better. Her heart didn't feel like a giant hollow space anymore, and her eyes were dry. Maybe she and April would be okay. Even without the silver.

She pressed the sandwiches down with the spatula, a glob of cheese escaping the bread and sizzling on the pan. She flipped them again. Both sides were perfectly brown and crispy. She turned off the stove, plated the sandwiches, and put them on the table. Grilled cheese and tomato soup. Their favorite meal this time of year.

Wind rattled the window over the sink. The glass was dark and her hair looked crazy in the reflection. She smoothed it down, then checked the table again. Everything was ready.

"April!"

Nothing.

She pushed through the swinging door to the dining room and clicked it into the open position. April had tidied up—all the loose photos were back in boxes and the photo boards were now leaning against the wall. Lynn turned the stereo on and started a country CD, then reversed course through the kitchen and through the swinging door into the hallway. "April?"

"A minute." The closed bathroom door muffled her voice; water ran and splashed.

Lynn went back into the kitchen, folded paper napkins at each place, and sat down to wait.

April came in wearing the green hoodie Lynn had bought her with the Paget Community College logo on it. It looked good on her; just tight enough people could tell she was a woman.

"What's that bird on the logo called again?" Lynn asked.

"I looked it up on Wikipedia. It's a roadrunner."

"But that's not—"

"The school calls it a chaparral. I guess it sounds fancier."

"I like it. You hungry, honey?"

"I am, actually."

They started eating, silence between them, but that was okay. Everything was going to be okay. Lynn dipped a corner of her sandwich into the soup, then blew on it. Now she understood what they meant by comfort food.

"Jake said he was coming by tonight?" Lynn asked. "To tell us more about the body at the house?"

"That's what he said."

"Had to be another guy who got between Mr. Bowen and the silver, right?"

"Not Mr. Bowen," April said. "He was with that lady cop when this happened."

Lynn put her sandwich down, her appetite suddenly gone. She'd been so focused on April that she hadn't thought of there being another killer.

The back door made its familiar *squelch* as it opened. Jake must be here.

"Hello?" Lynn called out. When he didn't reply she got up and headed for the door. "Are you letting yourself in now?"

The laundry room doorway filled with a big man in a long brown coat, his eyes wild and his face red from the cold. His eyes bored into hers then slid to April, and his mouth pulled into a hard smile.

Lynn jumped in front of him and pushed against his chest with both hands. "Get out!"

The man punched her between her breasts and she flew back, hit the wall, and sprawled on the floor.

"Hey!" April screamed and sprang from her chair, circling the table to keep it between her and the man. "Get out or I'll call 911."

"Shut up." The land line phone hung on the wall by the doorway, and he ripped it down and pulled the cord until it snapped. "The coin shop guy says you know about my silver."

Lynn couldn't breathe. She flopped onto her stomach and rose to her hands and knees, mouth working to pump air in. Her chest was paralyzed. She fought against a rising panic. *You're not dying. You've just had the wind knocked out of you.*

April appeared next to her, kneeling. "Mom! Are you okay?"

Lynn nodded and a squeaking ribbon of air snaked down her windpipe. *Relax.* She let her shoulders slump, then her abdomen. Another tendril of air, and her windpipe opened and she was breathing again.

"Help me up," she said.

As soon as she was back on her feet she pushed April behind her and faced the man. "Get out!"

He came across the room so fast he was a blur, and his backhanded slap snapped her head back. She stumbled and her face burned and her right eye watered.

"Get out of here!" April yelled.

The man grabbed Lynn's shoulders and pushed her down into a chair. He jabbed a finger at April. "Sit your ass down."

April sat.

Lynn grabbed April's hand and held it tight. When this nut realized they didn't have the silver, he would leave. Wouldn't he? Her cheek stung, but if that was as bad as it got she'd be fine. They'd both be fine. Everything would be fine.

The man paced back and forth on the other side of the table, his coat flaring around him at each turn. His eyes darted around the kitchen, scraped over them, and moved on. His lips moved constantly, a harsh mumble too low to hear. Finally he stopped and faced them.

"It's my silver."

"We don't have it," Lynn said. *It's my silver.* That's what he'd been mumbling. Over and over.

"Well it ain't in your garage," he said. He spun around and slipped away so smoothly the only sound was his coat flapping. He went to the front window, stuck his head between the sheers, and looked up and down the street.

April yanked her hand out of Lynn's and pulled her cell phone out of her hoodie pocket. She held it under the table, stabbing at the screen.

"Quickly," Lynn whispered. She kept her eyes on the man.

The man closed the drapes, yanking the edges together until they overlapped. Then he stepped toward the front door and out of her sight. Sounds came from her bedroom. The closet door. Something hitting the floor.

"Come on," Lynn urged.

The phone clattered onto the floor, and April whimpered. "Shoot!" She bent and scooped it up.

The swinging door from the hallway burst open. The man's wild eyes landed on April. "Give me your damn cell phone."

"I don't have one."

He came around the table and grabbed a handful of Lynn's hair, twisting it and wrenching her head sideways. The pain forced tears from her eyes but she kept her mouth shut.

April threw her phone on the table. The man snatched it up and dropped it in the pot of soup.

"Yours too, Momma."

Lynn lifted her hip, pulled her phone out of her back pocket, and flung it on the table. He dropped it into the soup with April's.

"You're going to tell—" The man twitched, darted into the living room, and pulled aside the curtain to look out the window. He disappeared into the front hall and she heard him moving through the rest of the house, and then he was back. Breathing hard.

"You killed that man in Henry's house," Lynn blurted. She knew it was true. She also knew she shouldn't have said it.

His eyes fixed on her. He nodded, then pulled a knife out from under his coat. It had a long blade that curved up in a wicked tip. He moved it back and forth in front of them like he was carving the air; the flat side of the blade caught the light and flashed it in Lynn's eyes.

The terror surging through Lynn was overwhelming, paralyzing. *Oh, God no. Please don't hurt us. Please… not April.*

He stepped behind Lynn, reached around, and grabbed her chin. His hand was cold from being outside and rough with callouses. He brought the knife in front of her face so close that her breath fogged on the blade.

"You're going to tell me what I need to know," he growled, "or you'll end up like him." He released her and resumed his pacing.

Lynn grabbed April's hand. It was cold and damp and her face was pale. April's gaze jerked toward the small window over the sink, then dropped back to the table. She'd seen something. Maybe it was Jake! Lynn fought the urge to look for herself, hope swelling inside her, mixing with the terror. Adrenaline was coursing through her, but she had to stay calm. She had to buy some time until Jake rescued them.

"W-we didn't have anything to do with the silver," she said. She fought to control the tremor in her voice. "Neither of us. That was Henry's silver. We don't know anything about it."

The man darted into the living room and again looked out at the street. Why didn't Jake come in and rescue them? Maybe he wouldn't. Maybe it was up to her. She'd push April ahead of her out the back door then stand guard while she got away. It was now or never.

Lynn pulled her feet under and started to rise, but her legs shook so badly she collapsed back to the chair.

It would be up to Jake.

The man's boots pounded down the hallway, and she heard a clatter from the mini-blinds on her bedroom window.

Then he was back again.

He pointed at April with the knife. "I know your dad took you to that coin shop with him, so you know about the silver."

"She doesn't know any—"

The big man hit Lynn again, his giant knuckles like hammers against her cheekbone. Her vision blurred.

"Stop it!" April yelled, coming off her seat.

"Sit the fuck down."

Lynn squeezed April's hand as her daughter's face began to fade behind the blackness.

"*Mom!*"

CHAPTER FORTY-EIGHT

Outside, Jake ducked down beneath Lynn's kitchen window. Trane was losing it, waving a big knife and hitting Lynn and darting around the house in a fast circle to check the windows every couple minutes. Maybe he was on something.

Jake snuck around to the front of the house and stood behind the big tree so Trane wouldn't see him when he made his next circuit through the house. Trane had no reason to kill the Fox women while he was in control, but if he saw a squad car or any officers… things would escalate very quickly. Jake could not let that happen. Not while Lynn and April were still trapped inside.

Which meant Jake couldn't risk calling in backup. He had to handle this alone. He had the gun and surprise on his side.

Jake could sneak inside and wait for Trane's next mad dash to separate him—and his knife—from the Fox women. Jake could hide in the hallway and confront Trane there. That way he would be between Trane and the women, and Trane would have the front door at his back if he decided to make a run for it.

A squad car rounded the corner, tires scuffing on the asphalt, lights flashing, but siren quiet. Jake pulled his badge off his belt and held it up as he ran into the street, heading off the squad before it got to Lynn's house. He slashed his free hand across his throat and the lights winked off.

He ran to the driver's window and started talking while he was still moving.

"Lights off. Lights off. Hostage situation."

"Emergency services got a 911 call. A hang-up."

"Park your squad behind that truck." Jake's gaze stopped on the truck. It was a large box truck with a double axle in the back and a power lift gate. Heavy-duty. Perfect for loading and hauling a silver hoard. And Trane's pickup was found less than a block from a company that ran a fleet of these trucks. Trane was making a last run for the silver, just as Jake had guessed.

He followed the squad and explained his plan to the patrol cop.

"I'm going in," he said. "Tell your sergeant I want you all to be invisible until I give a signal."

"Is the perp armed?"

"With a knife. Do you understand my instructions?"

"Out of sight. Come in on your signal."

"Exactly."

"What's your signal?"

"You'll know it when you hear it."

Jake left the patrolman and went back behind the tree. He squatted, then darted to the front stoop and waited, crouched well below the window. Less than a minute later a rustle at the front curtain, then a scrape on the floor a few inches away behind the door. Then silence. Trane was headed back to the kitchen.

Jake eased open the storm door, its piano hinge squeaking long and tight. He waited, listening, until he was sure Trane wasn't rushing back to the front door, then turned the knob. It twisted smoothly and he pushed gently, increasing pressure until the weather-tight seal gave and the door opened into the house with a slight puff of suction. He paused again. Still nothing. Just Garth Brooks warbling from the stereo.

He pulled his Glock from its holster and held it low in his right hand. He carried it with a round chambered so the pistol was ready. But was *he* ready?

The answer to that question had to be yes.

He stepped through the front door and pushed it closed behind him. The hallway went past three open doors on the right before ending at a closed door that led into the kitchen. The left side of the house held a living room that flowed through a wide arched opening into the dining room, with the kitchen behind it through another swinging door.

A shadow moved through his line of sight, and he realized the door between the dining room and the kitchen was open and Trane was pacing again. He heard voices, excited and quick, but the country music drowned out the words.

He stepped carefully toward the hallway. The hardwood floor was solid and didn't creak as he crept along, his gun in front of him. He closed the bedroom doors and the bathroom door and left the ceiling light off. When Trane rushed off on his next circuit to look out the windows Jake would get between Trane and the Fox women and flush the killer out the front door.

Or shoot him, if that's what it took.

* * *

The darkness ebbed. Lynn felt April's arm wrapped around her shoulder, holding her up in a chair. At their kitchen table.

Then she heard voices. April's and… the madman's.

"I'm not helping you until I know my mom's okay," April was saying.

"You'll look at this now or you'll both—she's awake."

Lynn gripped the table and breathed deeply, her vision clearing.

"Mom? Are you okay?"

"I'm fine," Lynn said. Her face throbbed. She touched it; the skin was sore and blood seeped from an open gash. But she could cry later. Right now she was the only thing between this madman and her baby girl. She grabbed a handful of napkins and pressed them to her face. "Tell him what you know about the silver."

"It's *my* silver." The madman stabbed his knife into a notebook splayed open on the table. "This book that your dad used to steal it proves it." He flicked the knife, and the book slid across the table and hit April in the chest.

April released Lynn and picked up the book, angling it so Lynn could see it too. "Dad told me about the journals he found." It was a diary, the handwriting loose, almost childlike. "This is Dad's handwriting, in pencil here in the margin." She pointed, her finger shaking. But her voice was strong. "It says silver, with a question mark."

The madman came behind them and stuck his head between theirs, his breath hot on Lynn's neck. The knife came around April's shoulder and the point scraped the page. April flinched away from it. A dark red sludge circled the blade where it met the handle. Lynn's stomach heaved, and she fought the urge to puke.

"Read that," he said, pointing with the knife. "That's the first time the book mentions my silver."

April's index finger swept back and forth over the paragraph as she scanned it. Lynn read along.

> Today was one of the most interesting days ever. A man came to the house in a neat truck. I got to unload what was in it. It was full of secret things that looked like buns for meat sandwiches and loafs of bread. Gifts for Momma and me from my Great Uncle Werner. The loafs were for Momma. The twenty buns were for me. Do you know why silver is heavier than gold? Because a hundred

*dollars of silver is a lot heavier than a hundred
dollars of gold. That's why!"*

"Twenty *buns*?" April said, her voice questioning. "Those
must be the little bars Dad found. Dad would have figured the
loaves were big bars. And he was right. They look just like a
loaf of bread."

"You've seen my silver! I knew it!"

The madman spun away, the point of his knife dragging
across April's shoulder.

She yelped and turned away. A thin line of blood stained
her sweatshirt, then spread wider. Tears squeezed from Lynn's
eyes at her daughter's pain. She dropped the napkins pressed to
her cheek, wrapped her arm around April, and held her tight.

The man stepped toward the living room, then turned
around, his face splotchy red. He held the big knife under
April's chin. "Tell me the truth, God damn it! I looked through
your daddy's entire house and barn. There was nothing there
worth two squirts. Where's my silver?"

"I just saw the one bar!" April's voice shook. "I swear.
That's the truth."

"Where is it?"

"The detective—the woman—took it from me today."

"Damn it!" He pulled the knife from under her chin and
went back to his pacing, mumbling over and over that the silver
was his, then growling: "You're no god damn help to me at all."

"Wait!" April said. "Here's something about hiding the
buns... the little bars."

"I don't give two shits about where the little bars were! I
want to know where the big bars are and I want to know *now*!"

"Caves!" April shouted.

CHAPTER FORTY-NINE

Jake pushed the swinging door open a few inches. April sat at the far side of the table facing his way. Blood soaked her right shoulder through a tear in her sweatshirt, and damp strands of hair framed her pale face. Lynn sat with her back to the sink giving him a three-quarter view of her face. Her right eye was swollen nearly shut, the skin over her cheekbone split, and blood ran down to her neck.

Jake pulled his gun from his holster and held it along his leg, squeezing the grip. Trane would pay for every drop of that blood.

Trane stood behind the women, his wrist resting on April's bloodied shoulder with the knife next to her face. "I didn't see anything about caves."

"Listen," April said. She read out loud.

> "I put Momma's loaves where I found the beer bottles. It took me almost four full days going up and down that long ladder and lowering them in a bucket one by each one. But they're hid good."

"The beer companies a hundred years ago or whatever all had tunnels under their breweries where they stored the beer to keep it cold," April explained. "Some were dug up when the library was built." She pointed at the journal. "But the Spiner Brewery—like it says on this beer bottle my dad drew in the margin—cooled its beer in caves. Dad told me all about it."

"Where are these caves?" Trane stepped out from behind the women.

This could be my opportunity, Jake thought. He brought the gun up into a two-handed grip.

"The Spiner Brewery was up on the bluff back before the Bristol mansion was built there," April said. "I know this cave. I can take you there."

"How can I trust you when you think I killed your daddy?"

"Because we want the silver too," Lynn said. "At least a piece of it."

Trane laughed. "You are a cold one, even for an ex-wife."

April's gaze flicked Jake's way. She squinted, and her face went still. She'd seen him.

Trane stepped toward the living room. When he entered the hallway on this loop through the house, Jake would flip on the light and have Trane in his sights.

He would not let Trane get past him.

* * *

Lynn followed April's gaze and saw the door into the hallway cracked open, a dark shadow covering most of the gap.

Jake! What is he waiting for?

The big man's crazy eyes jiggered away, then he darted off to make another loop through the house.

"Now!" Lynn yelled, jumping to her feet.

The big man was back quicker than he'd left, the big knife out in front of him, coming for her. "*Now* what?"

Lynn looked for Jake, but the door was still closed. Her knees shook. "Get out of here!" she yelled.

He lunged, the knife's wicked tip punching into her shoulder.

Lynn screeched, then bit off the sound as he raised the knife to stab her again.

April sprang up from her chair as Jake burst through the door, gun in front of him.

"Freeze!"

The big man spun, his left arm encircling April and pulling her to his chest. "Well, if it isn't *Jake*. Looks like I brought a knife to a gun fight."

"Drop the knife and let go of April," Jake said.

The man pulled April tighter against him, then put the knife against her throat.

"Drop your gun or I slit this pretty throat."

April fought against him. The blade caught the soft flesh on her neck and a line of blood began to run along the blade.

"For God's sake shoot him!" Lynn shrieked. "Shoot him!"

April tilted her head back and off the blade, panting through clenched teeth. "Shoot him!"

CHAPTER FIFTY

Jake didn't shoot. His plan had failed when Lynn's yell brought Trane back into the kitchen. But no one had to die. He'd find another opportunity.

"I said drop the knife, Trane. Let April go and I'll let you leave."

Trane hunched down behind April, nothing visible but the side of his head, his encircling arm, and a sliver of his body as his weight shifted from foot to foot. He kept the knife on April's neck, and her blood ran down over his knuckles.

"It's my silver," he said. "I paid for it." He re-gripped the knife, and the motion gouged another slit in April's neck, blood running faster, dripping off the hilt and splattering on the linoleum. She whimpered, then squeezed her lips tight. "Drop the gun or I'll slit her stem to stern right fucking now."

"Do *something*, Jake!" Lynn yelled.

Dropping the gun was a bad idea, but Jake had to get the knife off April's throat. And there were distractions here: greed and anger and Lynn and April. One of those could help separate April from Trane. When that happened, Jake would make his move.

Jake put the gun back in its holster, then raised his hands. "It's going to be okay," he said, looking from April to Lynn.

"We *will* work this out." April's eyes were wild, her breath coming in snorts, tears and snot running down her face.

"Will we? What do you propose?" Trane scoffed, but the knife came an inch off April's throat.

"It's not too late, Trane. I'm sure what happened with Cole was self-defense. And Officer Grady is going to be fine." Jake edged around the table. Trane was directly in front of him now. Nothing between them except April.

"That cop is on *you*." Trane gestured toward Jake with the knife, the motion flinging April's blood in his face. But the blade was back at April's throat before the saltiness registered on Jake's lips. "I only figured out he was trailing me when you said you knew I'd been searching the Bristol Yard," Trane said.

Jake had given Grady away. He'd think about that failure later. Now, he needed to focus.

"Why are you sneaking around?" Jake asked. He had to keep talking, waiting for his opportunity. Weight on the balls of his feet. "Like you said. You own the silver, so why not be up front about it?"

Trane laughed, the knife bouncing near April's throat. The blood was shiny on her soft white flesh and on the glinting blade. "Oh, I own it all right. I even have proof. But when lawyers get involved the truth gets slippery. Plus my creditors will snatch it before I can use it if I get too public about it. I got plans for that money. A wreck off Florida that'll make my last discovery look like chump change."

"The one you lost to Spain."

"That was bullshit." Trane took a step toward Jake, pointing the knife, but he moved April with him, held tight against his chest. "Lawyer bullshit."

Jake took a short step back and Trane bit, buying it as a retreat and taking another step forward, shaking the knife, his body emerging from behind April.

Jake went for his gun.

Trane's eyes bugged out and he raised his knife.

April spun out of Trane's grip and dropped to the floor.

Jake sighted and fired, the report a cannon shot in the small space. Trane lurched backwards, blood splotching his chest. He yelled—an unintelligible bellow of rage—then stepped forward, leading with the knife. As Jake brought the gun back to acquire another sight picture, Lynn kicked the side of Trane's knee. It buckled. He slashed at her as he went down.

A red splash against the cabinets.

Trane on his knees now. The red stain growing on his chest. He planted a foot and started to rise.

Jake shot him again, the bullet punching a hole in his forehead, the back of his head blowing out in a pink and gray mist. Trane toppled back against the cabinets, then slid sideways until his slack face hit the floor, a red smear against the cabinet.

"Call an ambulance!" Lynn yelled.

Jake found his holster and put the gun away, then dropped to his knees next to April. Trane's desperate lunge with the knife had missed Lynn and hit April across the side of her neck. Blood pumped from a sharp-edged furrow.

"April!" Lynn pressed her hands over the wound. "Help me, Jake!"

He pulled out his phone and dialed 911. A beam of light stabbed through the window in the back door, and another lit the curtain on the window above the sink.

Jake told the emergency dispatcher to send an ambulance to the address, and when she repeated it back to him he hung up.

The back door burst open.

"Police!"

"Stand down!" Jake yelled. "Detective Houser here. The suspect is down."

A patrol officer stepped through the door with his gun drawn and his eyes wide. He blanched when he saw Trane.

But when he saw Jake, recognition passed over his face and he lowered his gun.

Jake knelt beside Lynn. She had both hands pressed to her daughter's neck. He put an arm around her. "An ambulance is on its way," he said.

April's face was turned to the side, eyes open. Her eyelids fluttered, her face speckled with blood, her mouth opening and closing. Weak, airy gasps.

"Hang on, April. Help's coming," Lynn said, tears dropping onto her daughter's face.

April's eyes went wide and a faint sound came from her lips. Lynn bent low, bringing her ear to her daughter's mouth.

"I'm sorry, Mom. I'm the—"

The front door burst open. Shouting and confusion.

"Back here!" yelled the officer who'd entered through the back door.

A pair of uniformed officers came in from the dining room, guns leading the way.

"Detective Houser here." Jake waved his arms to get their attention. "Look at me."

The officers pulled their eyes off the blood.

"Lower your guns."

They did.

"Clear the house and secure the scene."

As they left the room, Jake took over applying pressure to the wound on April's neck. The blood pumped weakly against his palm.

"I do forgive you, honey." Lynn pressed her forehead to her daughter's. "I know you didn't mean it."

The rhythmic pressure against Jake's hand slowed and weakened. April's face went slack and her eyes were suddenly dull.

"*My baby!*" Lynn's wail rattled the back window. She turned to Jake and pummeled him with her fists. "Why didn't you *shoot* him? She'd be alive if you had just shot him!"

"No. I—" Jake started to defend himself, then shut up. He kept his hands in place on April's neck until the paramedics pulled him away. An officer took Lynn's arm and walked her into the living room. Jake stood in the corner and watched the paramedics bustle around until he admitted the obvious and called the coroner. Then he leaned back against the wall and slid down to a squat. His vision faded and blurred.

Time passed.

Then Callie came.

"You got him, Jake. You got Henry's killer."

Jake said nothing, because now he wasn't sure.

He let Callie take him home.

CHAPTER FIFTY-ONE

Jake rose early the morning of the funerals, his head thick from its nighttime churnings. He was on modified duty while the department investigated his officer-involved shooting, and he'd spent most of his time split between rehashing the events in the kitchen and chasing down a few last details to complete the book on Henry's murder. When he received the forensics reports and the transcripts of Callie's interviews, he was sure he'd then know the truth.

He stepped out onto his screened-in porch and pulled in a lungful of the clean cold air.

Thank God Grady had pulled through. It had been touch-and-go for the first forty-eight hours, his brain swelling, the doctors' efforts to relieve the pressure failing. Jake had been there often, talking with Grady's family and watching football news with the unconscious man. He was there when Grady suddenly woke at three thirty in the morning. Grady's first words were, "Did you get him?" Jake explained how it shook out, then called Grady's family with the good news. The doctors now expected Grady to recover fully.

Jake decided to go for a run while he waited for the reports. He dressed in his running gear and got moving, starting slowly to get his blood pumping and warm his leg muscles. Only Weston's earliest risers were out: deliverymen and dog walkers and a few other runners. When he hit the brick path along the river, he lengthened his stride and his mind began to clear. The air was thick and heavy with humidity and the rich organic smells coming off the rain-swelled waters of the Paget River. The path was dry and clear on the high ground by Centennial Beach, but when it dropped down near the river along the base of the bluff, wet leaves and rain-washed mud made the trail treacherous. Jake slowed and ran with short flat steps until the trail was clear.

He crossed the river on the Jefferson Avenue Bridge, then cut north on the asphalt bike trail.

His plan for handling Trane had been solid. Trane kept making that fast circuit through the house every few minutes. Waiting until Trane's next circuit separated him from the women had been Jake's best chance to end the situation with the least risk to Lynn and April. With the gun in his hand and the women behind him, he could have forced Trane to surrender. Or scared him out the front door where uniformed officers waited.

Without firing a shot.

But Lynn's scream for Jake to enter the kitchen "Now!" had stopped Trane's circuit and forced a situation that led to... everything else that happened.

Lynn had told the investigators working the shooting that April died because Jake waited too long to shoot. Jake worried that she was right. He'd been quick with the gun the afternoon he shot Royce Fletcher and had been haunted by it ever since. Had that experience and its long aftermath slowed him down in Lynn's kitchen?

He'd had a chance to shoot Trane when he first burst through the door into the kitchen. Instead he'd yelled, "Freeze." If he hadn't given Trane that chance to surrender—and instead shot the man immediately—Jake would have always wondered if a warning would have worked. He would have always wondered if he'd had to shoot. If Trane had to die.

Like with Royce Fletcher.

He pushed himself harder, focusing on his form and his breathing. He passed a dog walker and two women speed-walking, and then was under the Burlington Northern tracks, his foot strikes echoing off the concrete.

Once Trane was using April as a shield, Jake's best play had been to put his gun in its holster and draw Trane out. And that play had worked. April had seen the opening and spun out of Trane's grip. And Jake had acted immediately. At the earliest safe moment. He'd had to shoot; that was clear without a doubt. And his shot had struck true. Center mass. But that first shot hadn't taken Trane out. And before Jake could reacquire his target…

It was a fluke, his knife catching April like that.

Jake's legs burned as he pushed up the hill leading away from the railroad bridge, leaning forward and lifting his feet to maintain his pace, his calves tightening into twin knots of pain.

It had been his call to go into the house alone. With his gun and surprise on his side, that had been the best option. He still believed that. If he had called in backup, or even SWAT, things would have likely ended even worse.

But at least then, the disaster wouldn't have been Jake's fault.

Not directly, anyway. Like it was now.

The double wake for Henry and April had been a tough six hours. April's friends had kept to themselves, but he'd been approached by a steady stream of old friends and townies of every type. Many of them talked like Jake was a hero for taking Trane out. But nothing about it felt heroic. Not with April dead.

He crested the rise and powered down the steeper side of the hill, picking up speed as gravity helped him along, close to losing control. He lifted his gaze into the darkness under the Ogden Avenue overpass and clomped to an awkward stop.

The rain-swelled river had flooded the path. He bent over, hands on his knees, breathing in big slugs of air. He could climb the concrete-block retaining wall to road level and wait for a break in traffic to get across Ogden, but he'd only have to do it again on the way back. He did a couple leg lifts to keep his hamstrings stretched, then decided to go back to the house.

On the run back he fought to keep his head clear of the kitchen and Henry's killer and the day ahead of him. But it was a struggle, and resulted in ragged breathing and a stuttering pace.

As he skirted the base of the bluff he spotted a pair of uniformed officers yelling at a treasure hunter wedged in a crevice halfway up the bluff. An investigative reporter had found her way to the story of the silver hoard hidden on the old Bristol land. From her article the story had spread with amazing ferocity, luring in every kind of fortune hunter, from the weekend hobbyist with a discount-store metal detector to the full-time professional. Fortunately the cold rain had kept most of them inside scouring the Weston Historical Society archives for clues. A few—like this guy—skipped the research and hoped dumb luck would lead him to the treasure.

Jake didn't need dumb luck. He had Henry's laptop, which held his friend's draft manuscript for his next outhouse excavation book. Henry had written down every detail about the silver.

How and where he'd found it.

Where he'd re-hidden it.

And that he'd planned to turn it over to its rightful owner.

Jake cut away from the river and down the narrow parking lot along the Riverwalk west of Centennial Beach.

Larry's journal had described hiding the big bars in a beer-cooling cave under the Bristol property. A vertical fissure in the limestone bluff led to the cave system, where an early Weston brewery had once cooled its beer. The fissure had been filled in, but a hundred years of weather had washed enough of the fill away that Larry found it. And Henry knew where to find the fissure because he'd read a historical novel for children on Weston settlers that pinpointed it on a map. That's where he'd dug that second time, over near the church.

That's where he'd found the silver that would lead to his death.

* * *

Showered and dressed in his black suit, Jack sat down at the card table. The service at the funeral home was starting in an hour, but he wouldn't be attending. Lynn had passed word through Coogan that she didn't want him there.

Still, he would go to the graveside service.

He flipped open his laptop and signed into the department's system. All the investigative reports he'd been waiting for were there; everyone was scrambling to get the case closed. He started with Duke Fanning's five forensic reports: Henry's house after his murder, the murder weapon found at Bowen's house, Henry's house after Cole's murder, Lynn's kitchen, and a brief report on the big bar April had under her bed.

Then Jake read the transcripts of Callie's interviews with Jim Bowen, Conner Bowen, and Lynn.

When he finished, he leaned back in the hard little folding chair, closed his eyes, and worked through the new information and what it meant.

Means. Motive. Opportunity.

Check, check, and check.

The truth was easy. Justice—and his duty to Henry—demanded more.

Time passed, and the square of sunlight from the kitchen window edged across the plywood floor as he worked through it all. It was simple, really. He bent the facts—old and new—into a story he was willing to tell, then revised his narrative summary and hit "publish."

The case was closed.

But he'd kept the truth for himself.

CHAPTER FIFTY-TWO

Jake dodged a minivan as he ran across Hillside. The sun was higher now and the clear sky and still air let the fall sun generate some real warmth. It felt good after the long days of cold rain. He entered the cemetery grounds at the side gate across the street from his house.

In this old section of the cemetery, the trees were tall and the deep shade still held the early morning chill. Henry and April were to be buried in a new section to the west.

He broke out from under the trees and spotted the white tent, the folding chairs, and the expanse of Astro Turf pegged to the ground around the graves.

He was the first one there.

He'd planned to stand in a back corner of the tent out of Lynn's sight, but found the shade under the tent too cold. So he stepped back into the sun and circled the large hole. He had to bite back an involuntary laugh at an unexpected moment of humor. Henry—the outhouse king—might call this double burial a two-holer.

He found a place to stand: fifty feet east on the brick patio surrounding the veterans' memorial. The sun was so bright he regretted not wearing sunglasses.

His phone vibrated in his pocket. Coogan. He'd been tied up negotiating with the city for a finder's fee for the silver.

"How's it going? Jake asked.

"Once the city attorney got in his usual thousand words of bluster, we were able to cut a deal. It was inevitable. We have the silver and proof of who owns it."

Lawrence Bristol's journal proved that the silver had been a gift to Lucy Bristol *before* the Bunker brothers gave anyone a lien—which meant she owned it free and clear. And Lucy's contract with the city for Lawrence's care had transferred the silver to the city, along with the property where the Bristol Yard now stood. It had been right there all along, in a clause everyone had misunderstood.

> *My estate, including my real property at the west end of Jackson Street, including but not limited to everything found on or under the surface, whether in a man-made or natural structure or cavity, and of any kind whether natural or man-made or elemental (Ag) including buildings and timber and other natural resources.*

Until now, everyone who had read the paragraph had interpreted the "Ag" to be a typo for "e.g."—which meant "for example." But it was no typo. "Ag" was the chemical symbol for silver.

"What's the deal?" Jake asked.

"They've agreed to pay Henry's estate five percent."

"Once it's all papered up, tell them which storage unit it's in and we're done," Jake said.

Wendy at the storage facility had told him that Henry was in and out of there all the time *and* that he bought the contents of abandoned storage units. Two different things. One call to her dad, and Jake had learned that Henry had rented a unit right at the time when he started digging that second hole on the bluff. He must have spent days sneaking those bars away, a few at a time, from the Yard to the storage facility.

"Will do," Coogan said.

"Thanks, Coog."

They hung up, and Jake closed his eyes and tilted his head back to catch the sun. A peaceful calm descended over him, his muscles relaxing. With the silver hoard accounted for, the nutcases and treasure seekers would leave, and life could go back to normal. Except for those people suffering the losses of Henry and April. Their new normal, and Jake's, would be a long time coming.

A sudden flapping of fabric. A hearse emerged from the trees, yellow funeral flags attached to the hoods flailing. Then a second hearse, and a long line of cars snaking behind it, the sun reflecting off their windows.

* * *

Lynn peered through the front windshield at the back of April's hearse. Henry's hearse had led the way. That one decision—which car should go first—had about killed her. Thank God for Judy.

"Are you ready?" Judy asked.

"No," Lynn said. She heard the anger in her own voice and wanted to apologize, but Judy didn't need it. She'd turned out to be a better friend than Lynn remembered. Her only real friend. She couldn't quite figure out when that happened, or why. She was even staying in the Coogans' guest bedroom. The house where April was taken from her could burn to the ground for all Lynn cared. She would never step inside it again.

A stream of people started to walk past the car. The back of April's hearse opened and a cluster of men gathered behind it to remove the coffin. Judy had arranged the pallbearers. All men from their high school class. And every one of them had asked where Jake was when he didn't show at the funeral home.

"We need to go," Judy said, her voice soft.

Lynn pushed open the door with her good shoulder. The doctor said that with all the tendons, nerves, and arteries in a shoulder, she'd been lucky the knife had only damaged muscle. She didn't *feel* lucky. Two weeks ago she'd had a daughter and the world's best ex-husband. Now she had nothing. Except his money.

She'd always told herself that money would solve all her problems.

It didn't.

As she stepped out of the car, she spotted Jake standing off by himself, looking over the crowd. She tensed.

Judy put a hand on her arm. "They were friends their whole lives. And he was April's godfather."

"I know," Lynn said. Detective Diggs had told her of Jake's plan to wait in the hall for Trane to run another loop around the house so he could put himself between the nut and the women. When she screamed, she had foiled that plan. But weren't cops trained for exactly that? To think on their feet as situations changed? Shouldn't he have had a back-up plan? What if Trane had never gone on another loop around the house? What was Jake's plan for that?

"Let's go," Judy said. She hooked her arm through Lynn's and started them toward the tent.

Lynn shot a glance at Jake and found him watching her. He gave one of his little nods.

She didn't return it.

* * *

"Conner! Wait up!"

Conner looked back and saw Detective Diggs getting out of a big car parked along the curb. She wore Aviator sunglasses and a black suit like the one she'd worn to search his house. Conner didn't want to talk to her, but figured he didn't have a choice.

She jogged over and they walked together.

"I wanted you to know Detective Houser closed the case this morning and both your parents are now officially in the clear."

"It wasn't closed when the guy from Texas killed April?"

"Now it's official," she said. "And I left what we found in your backpack out of the reports."

"Really? Thanks." He wouldn't lose his scholarship after all. He could go back to school, and away from here.

Alone.

"I'm sorry you overheard the conversation I had with your parents about their false alibis. Especially your dad's."

Conner's stomach churned and his mouth went dry. "My parents are splitting up. Finally. I think... I think that will be better for everyone."

"I'm sure it will."

They stepped through the gate onto the cemetery grounds. A large white tent stood in the sun, a long chain of cars strung along the road beside it. A tight cluster of men walked awkwardly together between the two. Conner realized they were carrying a coffin.

He squeezed his hands into fists.

He wasn't going to cry.

The cop patted him on the back, then cut away as he approached the tent. He ducked under the low edge of it and found a chair in the back row. He didn't need people staring at him the whole time. The coffins were on either side of the grave, but with the lids closed he couldn't tell which one was April's.

His chest ached with longing for her. Their old high school friends had crowded around him at the wake and flooded him with idiotic advice that time heals all wounds and to get back on the horse. Bullshit. Time wasn't going to change anything. They had been perfect together. They had told each other everything.

At least that's what he'd thought until Detective Diggs told him about the giant silver bar April had under her bed. He wished he could ask her why she'd kept it a secret. Maybe she'd wanted to surprise him when she finally transferred to Northwestern.

He pulled his eyes off the coffins to look for April's mom. He spotted her walking toward the tent, arms linked with another woman. Mrs. Fox wore all black and giant sunglasses and had her right arm in a sling.

He fought down a sudden wish that she'd died instead of April.

Mrs. Fox sat down in the front row, but the other lady went to talk to the guy from the funeral home who was standing next to the coffins. Conner stood, threaded his way through the chairs, and slipped into the empty one next to Mrs. Fox.

"Mrs. Fox?"

She turned his way, then reached across with her free hand and squeezed his arm. "How are *you*, Conner?"

"I'm… I wanted to tell you how sorry I am about April."

"Thank you, Conner. You and I… Well. Only the two of us know how special she was."

"I know." He suddenly lost his words and fought to find them. "And I wanted to apologize about my dad. Maybe if he had told the complete truth right away the cops would have figured it all out sooner."

She pulled off her sunglasses and stared hard at him. "That silver twisted up more than just your dad."

Conner met her gaze but didn't understand what she wanted him to see there. "Well, that's all I wanted to say."

"Thank you." She patted his arm.

He took a last look at the coffins, then left the tent and cemetery. He didn't know if there was a heaven, or if April was in it, but she wasn't in that box.

CHAPTER FIFTY-THREE

Jake was surprised to see Callie. It wasn't uncommon for a detective to go to a victim's funeral, but she wasn't the sentimental type. He realized the skinny man walking next to her was the Bowen kid. She patted him on the back, then split off from him and joined Jake on the bricks.

"Jake," she said.

He nodded, hoping his silence would keep her quiet. But Callie wasn't the silent type. She also didn't do small talk.

"Saw you closed the case."

"You read my interview with the Bowen boy? She never told him she had the big bar. I guess their so-called 'perfect love' turned out to be one-sided. The girl took after her momma and wanted that silver for herself, to hell with the boy."

"Looks that way," he said, agreeing with her to avoid any back-and-forth.

The graveside service started, Drake Lambert's voice smooth and even, and they fell silent. Jake relaxed, his mind floating.

"So that's that," Callie said.

Her words pulled Jake out of his stupor. The crowd clustered around the graves was breaking apart, people heading for their cars.

"You want some company? Talk about what… happened?"

Jake smiled. "I'm going to stay here for a bit."

She frowned, the dark circles of her sunglasses staring at him. "Call me if you change your mind." She spun on a heel and left.

Jake pulled his eyes off her departing form and waited for an opportunity to talk to Lynn. Cars started and the hearses rolled away. Lynn's limo pulled off the pavement and onto the grass to let the string of cars behind it go by, the flags now gone. Life back to normal. A few last lingerers talked to Lynn, then left.

Judy hugged Lynn, then walked to the limo and stood beside it in the sun. Now was his chance.

Jake crossed the sunlit grass and passed into the cold shadow under the tent.

"Lynn," he said.

She pulled off her sunglasses and twisted in her seat—looking for help, maybe. Judy waved to her from where she stood next to the limo. Lynn turned back, scowling. The bruising and sutures from Trane's attacks were hidden under makeup. Her right arm was in a sling.

"I don't want to talk to you," she said.

Her anger shook his prepared words out of his mind. He blurted, "I wanted to tell you I closed the case with Trane as Henry's killer."

"That's what the papers and the TV have been saying."

"But you and I know it's not true."

Her eyes bored into his, but she said nothing.

"You told Detective Diggs that Trane admitted to killing Henry," Jake said. "That he said, 'I killed him, so what.'"

"That's right. He killed Henry, and the other Texan, and then my April."

"But I was there, remember?"

"I'll never forget you were *there*, Jake. April died *because* you were there."

The words cut, but she'd said them for effect. He could read it in the jitter of her eyes. She wanted to shut him down and get rid of him. That wouldn't work.

Jake held her gaze. "I heard what Trane actually said."

"He must have confessed before you came inside." She shifted in her seat and rubbed her jaw, her tongue flicking out to wet her lips. Deception.

"He said to April, 'How can I trust you when you think I killed your daddy?' If he had already admitted to killing Henry, he would have just said he couldn't trust her because he killed Henry."

She chewed her lip, her eyes darkening.

"The lab found Henry's blood on the big silver bar under April's bed, even though it wasn't the murder weapon."

He paused, waiting. But she stayed silent. April had been a gymnast all the way through high school. She was strong enough to carry that bar home from Henry's, and plenty strong enough to swing the much smaller bar over her head. Means.

"April wasn't at her friend Lucia's that night. I checked," Jake said. "And you already said she wasn't home with you." Opportunity.

Still nothing.

"The murder weapon was found in Bowen's office. When April visited Conner he fell asleep, and he woke to find her in his dad's office standing in front of the credenza where the weapon was found."

Lynn shook her head, twin streams of tears now running down her face.

"Conner and April told each other everything," Jake continued.

Lynn shook her head again, then fought back a sob.

"But April never told Conner how many big silver bars there were or that she had one under her bed. She *couldn't* tell him—because she got that bar, and learned about the others, on that last night she was at Henry's. The night when he told her he was going to turn the bars over to the city." A decision Henry had worked through by writing about it in a draft of his book in progress. Motive.

Lynn pulled a handkerchief from inside the sling and dabbed at her tears. "So you got her killed and now you want to destroy her memory? Tell everyone she killed her own father so you look a little less bad for getting her killed."

"Of course not."

"So it's about me then. You don't want me to get Henry's money." Lynn's voice was harsh with accusation.

"What are you talking about?"

"I know that rule. If you say April killed her dad then she can't inherit from him and all his money goes to some stupid charity like it says in his will."

The Slayer Rule: a person can't inherit from a person they killed.

"Lynn." Jake's voice rose to penetrate her self-pity. "Like I said. I closed the case as Trane killing Henry. She inherits, then you inherit from her. April's memory is preserved and you get Henry's money."

She looked at him, her eyes still streaming tears. She wiped her face with the handkerchief, makeup coming away to reveal the bruising and sutures around her eye.

"She couldn't have planned it," he said.

"She didn't."

There it was.

"Henry started the whole thing," Lynn said. "Telling April he'd pay for her to go to Northwestern. She *deserved* to go. She got a thirty-five on her ACT, you know. She was brilliant."

"What happened?"

"After promising to send her to Northwestern he told her he changed his mind and couldn't keep the silver. Said he figured out whose it was and he couldn't keep it. She... I... she cracked. It was an accident."

"Thank you for telling me," Jake said. "I won't be sharing it with anyone, so you don't need to leave town."

"You think *that's* why I'm leaving town?" Her eyes, still filled with tears, went cold. "I'm leaving town to avoid *you*! My daughter is dead because of *you*! You don't have any children so you don't know what it feels like for your only child to be murdered in front of you. To see the man responsible for her death—and yes, *you* are responsible—walking around town with everyone looking at him like he's a goddamn hero."

Jake didn't say another word as Lynn stood and strode to the limo. He just stepped out into the sun and watched her go. Judy opened the door and helped her inside, then climbed in after her. The limo pulled away, the sound of its engine fading.

An empty silence descended.

Jake turned back to face the two coffins. One held his goddaughter, the other, one of his oldest friends. Both died because of the silver, but April...

You are responsible. Lynn's accusation rang in his mind. And he couldn't deny it. He'd said the same thing to himself. Though not out loud. And not with a mother's voice squeezed with the pain of her ultimate loss.

A cold gust of wind blew through the cemetery, cutting through Jake's thin jacket.

He turned away and walked home.

Alone.

THE END

**If you enjoyed this Jake Houser mystery,
please consider posting a review on amazon.com.**

COMING SOON

in the Jake Houser Mystery Series

As It Never Was
A Jake Houser Mystery (Book #3)
Years ago, young Mark Siebert was snatched off his paper route. His confessed killer has been rotting in prison ever since. When a man claiming to be Mark shows up at his parents' house—only to disappear again—Mark's parents come to Detective Jake Houser for help. They have one condition: that he keep the cops out of it.

Jake owes the Sieberts, so he accepts their terms.

He will wish he hadn't.

Jake's off-the-books investigation digs up the depraved and twisted secrets of powerful men with unlimited resources. Will these dangerous forces erase every link to the past before Jake can find the truth?

That Was Then
A Jake Houser Mystery (Book #4)
When Detective Jake Houser agrees to take on a cold case, he is stunned by the police department infighting it generates and by how deep his investigation reaches into the city's political underbelly—and into his own family's past.

Before he's done, Jake will not only have to confront the city's power elite, past and present, but also his own father.

Can his department, his city, and his family survive the truth?

To learn more about Bo Thunboe
and the Jake Houser Mystery series
please visit www.thunboe.com

ACKNOWLEDGMENTS AND A HISTORICAL NOTE

This novel started as a NaNoWriMo (National Novel Writing Month) project in 2013. It took five years and dozens of drafts to turn that rough beginning into this final product.

I would not have been able to do it without the support of my wife, Diane, and our children, Meghan and Jack. Diane also read an early draft of this book and provided me with valuable insights. Peter Thompson, Irene Reed, Tim Chapman, and Adam Henkels were my test readers and gave me great ideas for fine-tuning the story.

I also had help from the following professionals, without whom this book would not look as good, or read as well, as it does. Thank you!

Ron Edison, Developmental Editor.
David Gatewood, Line Editor. Website: lonetrout.com
Kevin Summers, Book Formatting and Design.
Jeroen Ten Berge, Cover Design.

Historical Note: Silver Thursday was an actual event. I fictionalized it and attributed it to my characters, the Bunker brothers. The eccentric Texans involved in the real-world Silver Thursday were the Hunt brothers. Google it!

ABOUT THE AUTHOR

Bo Thunboe is a suburbanite—born and raised—and still lives in Chicago's western suburbs. When bad eyesight killed his dream to fly helicopters for the Marines, he went to college. It didn't go well, and a few lost years later Bo was out in the world laying bricks and repossessing cars. Then he met his wife, Diane, got his head on straight, and went back to college, where he earned a BA in Economics and a JD from Northern Illinois University. (Go Huskies!) After a couple decades spent lawyering he is now a full-time writer.

Please visit www.thunboe.com to sign up for news and to learn more about Bo and the Jake Houser Mystery Series.

41381520R00187

Made in the USA
Lexington, KY
06 June 2019